Meriel Fuller lives in a quiet corner of rural Devon with her husband and two children. Her early career was in advertising, with a bit of creative writing on the side. Now, with a family to look after, writing has become her passion… A keen interest in literature, the arts and history—particularly the early medieval period—makes writing historical novels a pleasure.

Also by Meriel Fuller

Conquest Bride
The Damsel's Defiance
The Warrior's Princess Bride
Captured by the Warrior
Her Battle-Scarred Knight
The Knight's Fugitive Lady
Innocent's Champion
Commanded by the French Duke
The Warrior's Damsel in Distress
Rescued by the Viking

Discover more at millsandboon.co.uk.

PROTECTED BY THE KNIGHT'S PROPOSAL

Meriel Fuller

MILLS & BOON

First published in Great Britain 2020
by Mills & Boon, an imprint of HarperCollins*Publishers*
1 London Bridge Street, London, SE1 9GF

Large Print edition 2021

© 2020 Meriel Fuller

ISBN: 978-0-263-28923-7

MIX
Paper from
responsible sources
FSC C007454

This book is produced from independently certified FSC™ paper to ensure responsible forest management. For more information visit www.harpercollins.co.uk/green.

Printed and bound in Great Britain
by CPI Group (UK) Ltd, Croydon, CR0 4YY

3478626 0

Chapter One

Devon—December 1234

Rain swept in a misty sheet across the wooded valley. The veil of moisture darkened the spreading branches of the bare oaks, then dropped to the dead, crinkled leaves, yellow and russet, cast upon the soaked grass like tiny sparkling diamonds. And in the distance were the muffled sounds of horses, their pace deliberate and determined, advancing.

Lady Cecily of Okeforde jerked back from the window, heart thumping heavily. Panic slithered through her slender frame, an uncomfortable, rippling sensation. Nausea rose in her gullet. Not again. She had hoped the dreadful weather, this hard, icy rain, would have deterred Simon of Doccombe today, but, nay, he had come again. The man's persistence was on the verge of defeating her. If only he would stay away from the castle until the baby was born! She wondered if he knew the truth, if someone, a servant or a household knight, had whispered something. What if she and her mother and sister were found out and hanged for their deception?

Her slim hand fluttered up, drifting across her forehead, the rosy blush of her cheek, an unconscious, hesitant gesture. A tendril of ash-brown hair, smooth and curling, had escaped the confines of her white linen wimple; she tucked it back beneath the cloth. Turning from the window, Cecily jammed the slender curve of her hip against the low stone ledge, as if for support.

'He's back.' Her light green eyes dulled, glassy with trepidation. She glanced at her mother, perched on the wooden stool by the four-poster bed.

Marion glared coolly at her daughter; her pinched features shimmered with loathing. 'The guards will deal with them if they come to the gate again,' she said harshly. Disapproval crinkled the vertical lines around her mouth. 'They've managed to keep them away up to now.' Her eyes jerked away, her narrow shoulder hunched towards Cecily, a barrier.

In the bed lay her younger daughter, Isabella. Marion leaned across the bedcovers, fussing over her, sponging her forehead with a wrung-out cloth. Droplets of water rolled from Isabella's fevered skin, wetting the linen pillowcase, but she slept on, her breathing harsh and laboured. Marion stroked her daughter's hot cheek, squeezing her upper arm in a gesture of courage, of support. Her fingertips rustled against Isabella's linen nightgown, damp with sweat. 'This babe will come today, or this night, at least. And then our future will be secure. This child, my grandson, will inherit this castle, the whole estate. And there's not a damn thing that man can do about it.'

'Are you sure about that?' Anxiety edged Cecily's tone. 'Do you not think that Lord Simon has his suspicions? Why else would he return to this castle, day after day, if not to try and catch us out?' She stepped over to the bed, the train of her over-gown slipping behind her, emerald silk velvet against the polished elm floorboards. Sitting back on the fur coverlet, she hugged the carved wooden bedpost, facing her mother.

Marion shrugged. Her golden circlet, jammed tightly down over her wimple, winked in the light of the single candle by the bed. 'If he does, then you've only yourself to blame, Cecily.' Her eyes fell pointedly to Cecily's rounded stomach, the feather pillow beneath her gown falsely swelling out the voluminous woollen folds. 'You'll have made a mistake somewhere along the way, or spoken out of turn to someone.' Marion jerked her chin in the air, her green eyes, identical to Cecily's, blazing up at her.

'I have been careful, Mother.' Cecily acknowledged the glittering hatred in her mother's expression. How could she hold on to so much resentment for so long? Her brother, Raymond, had been dead nigh on ten years now and yet…her mother refused to let her forget what she had done. The damage she had wrought on the family. For when her father had died, there had been no son to inherit and their home had passed to her father's brother. He and his new French wife had thrown her mother and sister out, and with Cecily newly married to Peter of Okeforde, they had come west to live with her. Was she to spend her whole life making amends?

'I sincerely hope that you have.' A hollow anger coloured her mother's voice.

Cecily pushed down at the lump of fabric pushing out the green silk velvet. 'I hate all this lying.' Her dark eyelashes flicked upwards, regarding her mother closely. 'It's not right.'

'It's not right that you didn't produce an heir with your dear departed husband,' her mother snapped back. 'God in Heaven, what your father and I had to do to persuade that man to even marry you! Life isn't fair, Cecily. This is the least you can do after...'

Cecily raised her hand, guilt flooding over her, a widening sorrow that lodged beneath her ribs. She shook her head sharply, chewing on her bottom lip. 'Nay, Mother, please don't say it. I know what I did.'

'And remember, Cecily, I will tell you where William is after you have done this.'

A scathing look crossed Marion's face, her lips curling superciliously. 'We will both have what we want in the end.'

William. The familiar name fell from Marion's lips as if it were dirt. The boy who had been her friend. She might even have married him if her mother had not spirited him away and ordered her to marry Peter of Okeforde instead. One day he had been there, at her family home, his quick smile lighting up her dreary days, and the next, he had been gone. And her mother would not tell her where.

'Keep up the charade, Cecily, for a few more days yet. And make no mistakes.'

'What do you think?' Simon, Lord of Doccombe, nudged his horse beneath a denser copse of trees seeking shelter from the relentless needling rain. He hunched down into his thick cloak. Bringing their own horses beneath the trees, his household knights gathered in a circle around him. The horses' hot breath emerged from their nostrils as clouds of steam, hazing the damp, chill air.

Squeezing his knees against his horse's

flank, Lachlan of Drummuir steered the animal round the leafless birch saplings. The trunks gleamed bright white, shining out from the gloom. Twiggy branches waved up into the iron-grey skies, a dark latticed fretwork. He grinned at his friend, a wide smile softening the rugged set of his jawline. 'I think I should have stayed snug in your great hall, with my feet stretched out towards the fire.' He laughed, running his gauntleted hands along the bridle, lifting the leather reins to turn his mare alongside his friend's stallion.

A pained look crossed Simon's sharp, angular features. 'Forgive me, Lachlan. I should have thought.' He touched his forehead in consternation. 'Are you sure you're well enough to ride? You're only just out of your sick bed.' He searched Lachlan's vivid features for any lingering signs of illness.

'Christ, Simon, if I had to spend another day, let alone another moment, in that bed, I would have likely killed your physician!' Lachlan stuck one hand through his flame-coloured hair, darkened to a deep copper by the rain, his blue eyes twinkling. 'I thank you, from the bottom of my heart, for bringing me back from France, for tending to me, but, rest assured, I am well on the way to recovery.'

'But how does the wound feel, now you're in the saddle?' Simon asked.

'Not bad.' Not good, either, if truth be told. The long line of cat-gut stitches pulled continually across his right thigh, but he wasn't about to tell Simon. He wanted to leave sooner rather than later, however painful the ride north might be.

'You want to go home, I know,' Simon pushed his wet hair out of his eyes. 'You haven't seen your family in years.'

Family. The word reverberated around Lachlan's skull. He hadn't seen what was left of his family for a long time. He had his uncle, his father's brother, and his wife, and their children. His cousins. His uncle had travelled north, to Scotland, to fetch him after that awful day and had brought him up as his own from the age of eight. They were his only kin now, after what had happened to his parents and sister. They were all dead.

Lachlan hitched forward in the saddle,

wincing slightly as the stitches stretched across his healing skin. 'They would be pleased to see me, I'm sure. And I will see them, as I travel north. But I need to go back to Scotland.'

'You would avenge your family's deaths?'

'And take back what is rightfully mine—the castle and estates at Drummuir? Yes, I would.'

'Even after all this time?'

'I have the King's blessing to take my home back from those cursed Macdonalds. Whatever it takes.'

Simon gathered his reins together in one gloved fist. His horse sidled gently beneath him. 'How similar our situations are, Lachlan. You want your castle back and so do I.' He glanced up at the towering rain-soaked walls, the vast, iron-riveted door at the top of the castle mound. 'But I have no wish to hold you up with what is happening here, Lachlan. Please...you must go if you want.'

'I wouldn't be able to ride the distance,' Lachlan admitted. 'Not even to my uncle's castle. My leg is too painful. So you have me for a couple of days more, if you think I can help you.'

'You can. You can help me find a way into that castle. That's all I ask of you.'

'It's the least I can do, after what you have done for me.' Lachlan flicked his attention to his friend. 'Bringing me back from France; looking after me.' Irritation streaked through him. He had been injured in a local skirmish, catching the swipe of a sword blade across his leg. Not a large battle, but a group of untrained mercenaries who had decided to attack a village. He had been sloppy, inattentive, possibly believing that they would win with a few brief strokes of their blades. Christ, he hadn't even been wearing chainmail!

'It has been a pleasure having your company, despite your injury.' Simon shook his head. 'And listening to your advice. I'm at my wits' end. My petitions to the King have fallen on deaf ears. He is more interested in fighting the French than listening to my woes, so he will not help me. And yet he has decreed that other young widows be married again and has taken their estates back to be given to the rightful heirs.' He wiped the rain from his face with the back of his leather glove. 'It is so unfair, for they were scarce married! That castle, all that land…' he swept his hand along the valley towards the pasture fields, a patchwork quilt across the lower slopes '…she inherited on his death.'

'How long were they married?' Lachlan raised his eyes to the castle, perched on an outcrop of rock on one side of the wooded valley. Beyond, almost invisible in the grey veil of mist, were the shifting outlines of the moor, a vast open plateau of undulating peat bogs and fast-flowing streams.

'Three months! They were hardly together. Peter left Okeforde to join the King's campaign in Brittany shortly after they were married. But she made sure she was carrying his child, clever girl!'

'Was he injured in France?'

'Aye, it was a bad head wound. He never really regained consciousness.' The saddle leather creaked as Simon leaned forward, his narrow lips turning down at the corners. 'She tended to him, of course, but I'm not sure she grieved overly when he was gone. If it wasn't for this baby she is carrying, I am sure the King would have found time to listen to me.'

'Because the baby is Peter of Okeforde's child and will inherit everything.'

Simon grinned, raising his sparse eyebrows. 'But only if the baby is a boy. So I have a chance of regaining what is rightfully mine.'

'Have you seen her at all?'

'Only at my brother's burial. And that months ago. Her guards turn me away at the gates, me, Simon of Doccombe, who grew up in this very place! She pays them well for their loyalty, with coin that should be mine!' His voice rose with an edge of desperation. 'I am not going to let her get away with this! And if the King won't help, then I will sort it out myself. But they won't let me in. Every guard in that place knows my face.'

'But they don't know mine,' replied Lachlan, a slow smile spreading across his generous mouth.

'My thoughts exactly,' replied Simon.

* * *

'Isabella! Can you hear me?' Worried, Cecily twisted around, clambering to her knees beside her sister. The mattress dipped beneath her slight weight. Leaning over in the semi-darkness, she seized Isabella's shoulders, giving her a little shake. 'Isabella,' she demanded, 'please, talk to me! Look at me!'

It was nearly dawn. Already the faint grey fingers of light stretched into the chamber, lightening the deep red velvet curtains around the bed, the elm floorboards, darkly polished. Outside, the rain continued to pound down, driven against the thin window glass on a howling wind, rippling down in swirling spirals. As the chapel bell had tolled midnight her mother had fallen asleep on the low truckle bed by the fire; a peaceful hush had descended on the chamber. The firelight had flickered in the small iron grate, bathing the roughly plastered walls in a pink-orange glow. With a sigh of relief, Cecily had removed the hated feather pillow bump from around her middle, crawling on to the bed next to her sister.

But something had woken her up.

Was it the increasing light from the window, or a change in Isabella's breathing? Cecily couldn't be sure. All she knew was that her sister was staring blankly at her through the gloom, her eyes darting wildly, unfocused. Her skin was clammy, shining with a sickly unnatural light. Straggling out across the pillow, her blonde hair, unfastened, was dark with sweat, like strands of seaweed netted upon white sand.

A faint hiss, sibilant and lisping, emerged from Isabella's cracked lips. A whisper. Cecily leaned closer, catching the sour scent of her sister's breath. Was the baby coming? Yet her sister did not appear to be struggling in labour. Cecily had little knowledge of such things, other than it involved much pain and a lot of screaming, yet her sister lay on the bed calmly, despite her frenzied look.

'My waters...' Isabella stuttered out. 'I'm...all wet.'

The tension in Cecily's body eased. 'I think that's supposed to happen,' she said, smiling. She pushed back a damp tendril of hair from her sister's cheek.

'I want to get up, Cecily. I want to move

around. Will you help me?' Isabella's fingers knotted themselves around Cecily's forearm; her knuckles white and rigid.

'Of course.' Jumping down back off the bed, Cecily swept the bed furs aside, the linen sheet.

Her eyes widened with horror.

Blood pooled beneath her sister's thighs, soaking into the sheet, the mattress beneath. Her nightgown spread out in soggy folds. In the dim, cocooning light of the bedchamber, the patch of blood appeared as a huge black stain across the bed, shocking, terrifying.

Cecily clamped down hard on the scream that rose in her gullet. 'Mother,' she said, a steely urgent thread entering her voice. 'Mother, wake up! I think the baby is coming!'

'Please, can you help me?' Isabella repeated. 'I want to get up.' She reached for Cecily's hand, grabbed it. Her fingers were cold. As she hitched up the bed slowly, rolling from side to side, Cecily turned, intending to swoop around and shield Isabella from the horrific sight between her legs. But before she had time, Isabella glanced down and saw. She began to scream, and scream.

'Lord have mercy upon us!' Her mother reached the bed, wrapping her wimple around her chin, her hair, clamping her circlet down quickly to secure the cloth. 'Christ in Heaven, Cecily, why did you not wake me? Fetch the midwife…now!'

'Are you insane, Mother?' Cecily narrowed her eyes towards Marion. 'I cannot go out, even with the bump attached to me! I am supposed to be in labour!'

Her mother stared at her, green eyes hazing, frantic. 'Then I will go and find Martha, and send her,' she gabbled out, grabbing her shawl from the end of the bed. 'She is the only servant who knows where the midwife lives.' The door clicked behind her.

Running to the oak coffer beneath the window, Cecily threw open the lid. The thick wooden planks banged heavily against the plastered wall. She bent over, riffling hurriedly through the stack, tearing out a heap of linen sheets. Bundling them up against her slim stomach, Cecily raced back over to the bed, throwing back Isabella's sheets, trying not to wince at the devastating pool of blood widening out across the bottom sheet between Isabella's legs.

Her sister was sobbing now, gentle hiccoughs that heaved her juddering chest. Cecily touched her shoulder softly. 'Listen to me, Isabella. I am going to lift your legs and stop the bleeding. Do you hear me? Mother is sending someone for the midwife and she will be here very soon.' Tucking the pile of sheets carefully around and beneath Isabella's legs, she managed to raise her sister's legs up, hoping to staunch the flow of blood.

Isabella reached out one shaking hand, her fingers snaking around Cecily's wrist. 'I am so sorry, Cecily,' she whispered. 'I was a stupid, foolish girl. I should never have...' Her hand drifted up to her pale forehead before she dropped it again. 'I should never have fallen in love...' Her voice faded away, and her eyelashes fluttered down.

'No! No...wake up!' Cecily shook her sister's shoulder, her fingers rough. 'Talk to me!' Grimacing, Isabella opened her eyes. 'Good girl.' Cecily smoothed the back of her hand over Isabella's heated cheek. 'Now listen to me. You have done nothing wrong. You were going to marry Guillame.'

A single tear rolled down Isabella's cheek. 'Yes, I was. But I should not have lain with him before we were lawfully married. And now…now he's dead and will never see his child.'

But at least our mother is happy, thought Cecily. *The baby is the key to us staying here, at the castle. The baby, if it is a boy, will secure our future.*

She jerked her gaze towards Isabella. 'You mustn't think like that, Isabella. The child will always be a reminder of the love you had with Guillame.'

The door slammed back on its hinges. Marion stood in the doorway, panting, her gaunt features flushed with colour. 'I cannot find that foolish Martha anywhere. I think she must have gone to the village to see her family!' She strode forward, arms stretched out towards Cecily, fingers kneading frantically at the air. 'Only Martha knows where the midwife lives and I cannot run as fast as you. You must go…and now!' She cast an anxious look towards Isabella, lying, pale as wax, against the pillow. 'It's so early, there's no one about yet. If you see anyone, just hide until they have gone! Make sure you aren't seen!' Bundling a cloak into Cecily's arms, she shoved her towards the door. 'We cannot deal with this…this bleeding alone! You have to run, Cecily, run as fast as you can and fetch the midwife. Greta's the only one who knows the truth. I have bought her silence; she will not betray us.'

Seizing the cloak, Cecily swept it around her narrow shoulders, her fingers fumbling to do up the vertical row of tiny wooden buttons. Her mother pushed her from the chamber and out into the darkness of the stairwell. With one hand against the gritty stone wall of the spiral staircase, Cecily stepped lightly down as quickly as she dared, slipping out quietly into the cobbled bailey.

To her relief, the courtyard was deserted.

Rain slapped across her face, cold needles against her fire-warmed cheeks. The howling wind snared the hem of her cloak, snapping the fabric out behind her. Cecily shivered, gripping her cloak closely about her as she hurried across the bailey. In her haste to help her sister, she had forgotten to change her slippers for sturdier footwear; as she headed towards the main gate she might as well have been wearing no shoes at all. The supple kid leather gave her no protection against the lumpy cobbles of the yard, nor the puddle after puddle through which she sloshed. No wonder no one was about yet. The weather was horrendous.

Large iron bolts secured the main wooden gates, but cut into the high, iron-riveted planks was a much smaller, narrower door which was easy to open. Darting her gaze around the bailey, she twisted the wrought-iron handle and stepped outside. Doubt slipped away, replaced with a new-found purpose and energy; her sister was in danger and she must fetch help. That was all that mattered at this moment. The rippling gathers of her cloak covered her belly enough to maintain her deception.

Wind snared the generous hem of her gown, whipping the voluminous fabric around her stocking-covered legs. Down below, in the river valley, the tree tops swung about, branches clashing. Leaves tossed in the air as she crossed the bridge over the moat and hurried down the hillside, fast-paced, nimble, through the treacherous mud.

In this horrible weather, the safest route to the village was by way of a stony, well-marked track. But following the high, tree-lined bank around the pasture would take too long. A quicker way was to cut through the woods and cross the river by the stepping stones. Cecily bit her lip. The river would be higher now, because of the rain, but would it be impassable? Probably not. She could wade across. Her feet were wet already; it was only a matter of time before she was completely soaked.

She hurried towards the woods, long grass clinging to her hem. A line of mud crept steadily up her gown, soiling the silk. Cecily didn't notice; all she cared about now was finding help for Isabella. By the time she had reached the woodland, she was running, lungs burning with exertion. The trees swung violently in the wind, branches clacking menacingly together, the last leaves shaken down by the storm whirling down before her. Branches cracked and fell, but she kept her head low, praying none would land on her. This track would lead her to the stepping stones and she followed it, feet sinking into the thick golden leaves, confident of her path.

Lachlan thumped his pillow one more time, driving his fist deep into the feather-filled sack, then rolled the whole thing into a tight little ball, to try and change the angle of his head when he lay flat again. He stretched out on his front, then twisted on to his side. No better. Irritated, he sat up, his strong fingers kneading the sore skin around his wound, the puckered line of stitches. Sleep evaded him. His whole body, his nerves and muscles, fizzed with energy. He was fed up of lying around in Simon's manor house, the enforced recuperation like chains holding him against a wall. He wanted to be up and out, fit enough to ride long distances, to go back to Scotland. To fight for what was rightfully his.

He threw back the bed furs, limped over to the window and peered out through the gaps in the shutters. The wind howled, an eerie noise whipping across the wooden slats. The rain coursed down, continuous horizontal lines. Over to the east, the first glimmers of a grey dawn lightened the dull horizon. He was missing the battles, the fighting, that was it. That was the cause of all this restlessness. Bereaved and lonely, beset with guilt, it was his uncle who had suggested that he become a knight and he had thrown himself into the profession with a desperate need. He had fully believed that throwing himself into the furore of battles for lords and kings would have been enough. Enough to drown out the memories of the past and make them fade away.

All those battles and yet the memories continued to grip him, the vivid images rampaging through his head as if it were yesterday. The terror of the past stalked his dreams, prowled through his daylight hours until he had reached a point where he could no longer bear them. He believed now that the only way to rid himself of them was to return to Scotland and confront his enemies. If it wasn't for this dammed leg wound, he would be there by now.

His clothes lay in an untidy heap on an oak coffer at the foot of the bed. He had worn his shirt to sleep in and now pulled on the rest of his clothes: linen drawers, woollen braies and a sleeved surcoat that fell to mid-thigh. Lachlan picked up his sword; the semi-precious stones glinting in the hilt, then placed it back on the coffer. He was only going for a walk; he had no need of a weapon. Flinging his cloak around his broad shoulders and sticking his feet into leather boots, he left the chamber.

Hitching his right leg slightly as he walked, he strode across the inner bailey, the wind driving hard against him. He breathed in the swirling, volatile air, loving the energy, the power of the breeze that drove away the thick, stultifying feeling in his brain. Simon's home, as befitted the inheritance of a younger son, was a large manor house, a fortified building with ramparts around the roof where guards could be positioned in case of any threat. The house lay a couple of miles to the east of Simon's childhood home of Okeforde, the castle that he was so desperate to regain, separated by a woodland.

Raindrops spattered against his cheeks as Lachlan walked into the woods. Beneath the whirling tree canopy, the air was quieter, the wind filtered, slowed by the ancient trees. The muscles in his leg were sore, but bearable; the pain was not becoming worse with walking. For the first time in a sennight, he could feel his strength returning, the familiar power of his body. The sky had lightened significantly in the time he had been walking; he could now discern the individual tree trunks, the criss-cross of branches against the pale grey backdrop of the sky above and the wooded landscape, sloping down in soft folds from the castle to the river in full spate after a night of rain. In front of him, the raging white froth was visible through the trees.

A movement caught his eye. A ghost, flitting through the woods up ahead? Nay, it was a girl, petite and slim, dressed in a dark green gown, barely discernible through the mass of trees. She moved with purpose, strides swift and determined, moving along the path at an impressive pace, despite her diminutive figure. Where was she going, at this early hour? The river, by the looks of it.

Intrigued, curious as to her direction, Lachlan watched her progress from a distance, propping his shoulder against a tree trunk. His injured leg burned and throbbed.

At last, Cecily broke out from the churning shadows of the trees and on to the bank of the river that flowed down the valley towards the village.

And stopped.

The river that she knew so well, the river that wove around tumbled sets of huge moss-covered stones, that flowed gently through calm pools before picking up the pace once more, had changed beyond all recognition. Now, a great surging current of white water spewed and frothed upwards over barely visible stones, a gigantic torrent surging down the hillside with a terrible force.

Nausea washed over her, sickness coupled with panic. Her mind scrabbled for solutions, but found none. She had no wish to turn back, to retrace her steps and go the long way round. She thought of the blood on the mattress, her sister's screams, her own feeble attempts to staunch the bleeding. No.

She must cross this river. She would do it. Otherwise Isabella would die and it would all be her fault. Again.

Cecily scanned the heaving rush of water, searching for the stepping stones beneath the sliding green flow, the huge plates of flattened rock that normally provided an easy route to the other side. There was no rope or wooden rail to guide her, but she knew where they should be and, yes, if she looked carefully, she could just spot them through the sluicing water, those great flat surfaces, her route to the village and to the midwife beyond. Her sister's salvation.

Cecily picked up a sturdy branch that would support her. Then she sat down on the wet bank and slid her feet into the water. Warning voices clamoured in her head; she shoved them back, resolute. Determined. The river gripped her calves, the water cold, pummelling her skin. Her gown and cloak floated up to the surface, swirling impossibly around her. Biting her lip, she dug the branch firmly out into the raging flow and lurched forward. Despite the icy water around her legs, sweat trickled down from her armpits, but her foot had found the first large flat stepping stone. Thank God. She took another step forward, using the same method, then another. The agitation in her belly, the fluttering nerves, settled a little. She had found the crossing beneath the water.

'What the hell are you doing?'

The man's voice seared through her. Shocked, her head whipped around to the source of the sound, her toes curling beneath the surging current, teetering. Scrabbling for balance, she wavered.

A man stood on the bank. A man she had never seen before, a stranger. Her heart plummeted. Burly-framed; huge. Through the slanting net of rain, his hair was startling: bright red-gold like the kernel of a flame. A dark blue surcoat stretched across his chest, emphasising his shoulders, bulky, muscular curves. Clad in calf-length leather boots and buff-coloured braies, his legs were long, planted astride in the long, wet grass.

He tipped his head to one side, his piercing gaze narrowing upon her, curious, incisive. Fierce. And although he stood some distance away, Cecily realised immediately what kind of character he was. A man who would never stop asking questions. A man who would not be fobbed off with lies and half-truths. A man she had no wish to meet.

'Stay there!' he called out. 'I will help you!' He stepped forward. Towards her.

'No!' Cecily yelled above the roar of the water. 'Go back! I don't need your help!' Christ in Heaven, what was this man doing, wandering about so early in the morning? She could not be recognised, not by anyone, not even a stranger. She needed to reach the other side, to set some distance between them, quickly. She took a hurried, unplanned step forward.

Into the deep, churning water.

Chapter Two

Down, down into the churning green river. Water blocked her ears and eyes, her nose, blinding her, cutting off all sound. The spouting rush of current grabbed her gown and cloak, tore the leather slippers from her feet, spinning them away downstream. Her elbows and knees knocked against rocky edges, sharp pincering bites into her soft flesh, as the river turned her round and round in a powerful, tumbling embrace.

As she attempted to draw breath, her mouth filled with water, half choking her. Visceral panic gripped her innards, slithered through her veins. Was this it? Was she to die out here, because of one foolhardy action? Because of him? That stupid man had distracted her, causing her to lose her footing. Sadness blanketed her chest at the image of her sister, lying in that blood-soaked bed. All their subterfuge, all these months of lying, of keeping Cecily's late husband's brother away from the castle...all of it would have been for nothing.

No. This would not happen! Thrusting her chin above the waterline, she drove the self-pitying thoughts from her mind. Rising anger fuelled her. Isabella needed her help; she would not let her down. Striking out with her hands and arms, Cecily fought and shoved against the force of the water, finally managing to draw the fresh air into her lungs. Her knuckles scraped against a rock and she clutched wildly at the unwieldy mass, digging her nails into the gritty, moss-covered stone, anchoring herself.

The current tugged at her legs and she clung to the rock, her muscles tearing painfully with the effort. Coughing and spluttering, she blinked the stinging water from her eyes, assessing her surroundings. The river bank was not far away, a strip of small white stones collected in a straggly line, backed by a verdant patch of smooth grass.

But how was she to reach the bank? Her

arms shook with the effort of gripping the rock. The water was deep beneath her; she had no foothold, her legs swinging randomly around. Stretching one arm high, she scrabbled to find a handhold further up, a crevice in the rock, a crack, anything into which she could dig her nails and haul herself up. But the water dragged at her skirts, pulling her back down, hampering her. Frustration coursed through her; she wanted to howl. She was not strong enough to pull herself out. Closing her eyes, Cecily pressed her forehead against the dank mossy rock, the air from her lungs emerging in short, truncated breaths.

Then, above the raging onslaught of the water, she heard a voice.

'Give me your hand!' a voice bellowed at her. A tough, masculine voice.

Her head knocked back; she blinked upwards, water streaming down her face. A huge boot was planted on the rock above her, the leather stained with old water marks across the toes. Criss-crossed leather straps secured fawn braies to sturdy shins. The hem of a blue surcoat swung close as a man crouched down, balancing his large bulk on the narrow lip of rock with surprising ease. It was him. The man who had startled her. The man who had made her fall.

'Go away!' Cecily yelled. 'I don't need your help!' Lifting one arm, she batted the air forcefully, indicating that he should go. How on earth did he come to be there? He must have followed her tumbling progress downstream.

He seized her flailing hand in a fierce, bear-like grip. Hand over hand, as if her arm was a rope, he pulled the whole soaking mass of her upwards, slowly, slowly, out of the water, until she flopped, exhausted, on to the rock beside his feet. His thick arm came round her waist, a muscled rope tucking neatly beneath her ribcage, hauling her into a standing position. A lifeline of blood and sinew, clamping her to a solid masculine flank. Her heart jolted in an odd, flickering beat. She wobbled on the rock beside him, clenching her teeth together to stop them chattering. Her belly warmed at the unexpected intimacy of the situation. The closeness of him.

'Follow me!' he ordered her in a gruff voice, faintly accented. 'Place your feet where I put mine.' Dropping his arm, he gripped her hand, crushing her fingers within his.

Clamping her lips together angrily, Cecily realised she had no choice. Hanging on to him with one hand, she lifted her unwieldy sodden skirts with the other. The rough surface of the rock pinched and chafed her stocking-covered feet. The water-soaked garments hung off her shoulders like several sets of chainmail; her feet tangled in the trailing hems, threatening to tip her back into the boiling mass of water. Kicking out her skirts with one foot, she tried to step across to the rock he had just vacated, gripping his hand with grim tenacity, but the fabric bundled unhelpfully around her ankles, and she pitched forward.

'Hell's teeth!' the man cursed, turning swiftly. He caught her as she fell forward, big arms bracing against her back. 'I'll carry you!' he bellowed at her above the roar of the river.

'Don't you dare!' Cecily gasped back at

him, outraged. How was this happening? In her desperation to keep away from him, she was being dragged ever closer. She shoved his chest away with flat palms, pulling herself staunchly upright with determined resolution. 'I can lift my skirts higher, out of the way.' She pushed a long tendril of wet hair from her eyes. The water had ripped her veil and circlet away, and the neat knot of braids at her neck had been dislodged, sagging dismally. One plait had fallen free, hanging down past her waist like a dark rope.

The man's grip tightened on her hand. *His eyes are of the deepest sapphire*, she thought, *shimmering with blue fire*. Sparkling with an energy that stabbed at her, catching her by surprise. Ignoring her protest, he leaned forward, curving his arm around her spine and tipped her over his left shoulder. Honed muscle ground into the soft flesh of her belly. He had slung her over his shoulder as if she were a sack of grain in the market! She was winded by the forceful movement, her breath punched from her lungs. Blood pumped in her ears; her head spun, a sickening jolt of stars sweeping across her vision. Reaching down to the concave dip of his spine, she grabbed a bunch of his surcoat, her knuckles white against the blue cloth. A musky smell rose from the fabric, the aromatic scent of wood-smoke mingling with a fresh, floral smell. Incongruous on such a rugged figure. She shivered, a tingling delight scything through her chilled flesh. He swung around, trudging purposefully from one rock to another.

Cecily's chin bumped lightly against his shoulder. Furious, she clenched her jaw in frustration. Her hands itched to thump against his back. She wanted to kick him, but he held fast on to her legs with a tight, unwieldy grip. Below her, the river flowed and rippled, the water splashing the back of the man's legs, his sturdy leather boots, rounded out by muscular calves. His stride hitched slightly to one side, as if he carried an injury, but he still managed to navigate the oddly placed rocks with ease.

He stepped up on to the grassy bank with her and at once Cecily began to wriggle frantically, squirming in his solid embrace, acutely conscious of his thick arm caught against the back of her thighs. 'Put me down!' she yelled, beating his back with small fists. The thick fabric of his surcoat muffled her voice. 'Put me down right now!' Reaching her hand behind her, she managed to grab a handful of his bright red-gold hair and tugged viciously.

'Christ in Heaven, woman!' he growled, seizing her wrist and pulling her hand away from his head. 'What the hell do you think you're doing?'

'Put me down, you brute! Now!' Shoving her fists into the small of his back, she thrust her head up violently, levering herself up. Her loosened plaits swung down, the wet curling ends brushing the ground.

'I'm going to put you down, you silly woman!' Lachlan roared at her. 'Stop twisting about, will you!' Annoyed, he released his arms, let her go abruptly. She slithered haphazardly against the muscle-hewn length of his body, her soft curves nudging him. As her feet touched the moss-strewn grass, she staggered back, immediately raising clenched fists, as if to ward off an attack.

Lachlan tilted his head to one side. What

was happening here? Did the maid think he was going to physically fight her? For the first time in a long time, he wanted to laugh. What sort of behaviour was this, coming from a noble lady? For she was a noble, he could tell that from her fine clothes, her arrogant, dismissive manner. He had expected some thanks at least, maybe some tears after the experience she had been through, but, no, there was nothing like that. Just a bright mutinous face glaring at him with irritation. Long plaited ropes of glossy hair swinging down across her breasts. And stunning green eyes, blazing with liquid fire.

Lachlan's heart jolted. Oh, she was a beauty, all right. Through the spinning raindrops her wet skin gleamed, holding the lustre of fresh pouring cream. He had a sudden urge to touch, to press his thumb into the velvet plushness of her cheek.

He shook his head abruptly, dismissing his fanciful thoughts. 'Put your hands down. I am not about to attack you.'

Tilting her head to one side, assessing him, Cecily slowly lowered her hands, folding them defiantly across her chest. The rain was gradually ceasing; every branch dripped, leaves shedding droplets, splattering the leaf-strewn woodland floor. Her stocking-covered feet were slowly sinking into the spongy undergrowth.

'What in Odin's name were you doing? You could have drowned, trying to cross like that!' His voice thumped into her with all the finesse of a charging bull. A muscle flexed beneath the high, slashing angle of his cheekbone.

Cecily took a step towards him, cheeks flaming with colour. 'I wouldn't have fallen in if you hadn't startled me! This is all your fault.' She jabbed him with one pointed finger, deep into the middle of his chest, her expression haughty, scornful. 'This is your fault!' Her hand fell away and she spun on her heel, intending to walk away.

Her dismissive tone stung him. Without thinking, Lachlan grabbed her arm, preventing her forward movement. Rude, arrogant chit! What was wrong her? Aye, he had caused her to fall, but he had also pulled her out again. A bad situation made good. She could be a little more grateful. He pulled her close, hard up against his front, and bent his mouth to her ear. 'A small thank-you wouldn't go amiss,' he murmured.

Cecily shivered, but strangely not with fear. His hot breath sidled across her earlobe. Strings of fire lanced through her neck, her chest. His fingers burrowed into the tender flesh of her upper arm. 'Thank you,' she chanted out melodically. The false clang of her voice echoed through the damp woodland air.

'Say it like you mean it,' he growled in her ear, angling his head away so that she wouldn't catch the twitch of his smile. Christ, the chit had a stubborn streak!

'My God!' Cecily whirled around to face him, her emerald gaze sparking fury. 'Who in hell's name are you, sneaking around at such an ungodly hour? Your behaviour is despicable! Why will you not let me go?'

His hand, holding her upper arm, was trapped against her breasts. The hard imprint of his fingers burned through the sodden material of her gown. Her cheeks flushed at the sudden intimacy and she stepped back hurriedly. To her relief, his arm fell away.

'I could say the same about you,' Lachlan replied. The outline of her breast, sweet and yielding, seemed embedded on his palm. An unexpected fire flicked through his loins. 'I could say the same about you.' His thick, vigorous eyebrows raised in question. 'Why were you trying to cross the river when the water is in full spate?'

Drops of water hung, suspended like tiny crystals, from the tips of his coppery curls. Cecily's heart twisted, a warm knife deep in her chest. She took a step back. What was she doing? In her irritation towards this man, she had forgotten her purpose. Why was she talking, arguing so much? Her sister needed her, needed the midwife. A huge shiver coursed through her slender frame and she lifted first one leg, then the other, trying to drive the creeping coldness away, trying to warm up her muscles. She needed to go.

'I was in hurry,' Cecily said pointedly, taking another step back. And yet her body seemed stilted, as if it had forgotten how to move. Energy leached from her slender frame.

'That's no answer,' the man rapped out. 'I asked you, what are you doing?'

'It's none of your business!' Her retort was brusque, violent. The strength sapped from her knees, her muscles like wet wool. She wavered on the spot. Water dripped down her face, from the incessant rain, from her hair; she licked her lips, tasted blood. Lifting her hands to her forehead, she touched her hairline, almost in disbelief.

'You're bleeding,' Lachlan stated bluntly. In the dim, rain-soaked daylight, her pale green eyes shone out, a delicate chartreuse colour, like glass beads. The blood, mingling with the rain, tracked down through the wet tendrils of her loosened hair, trailing down her cheek to drip off her chin. Her skin held the patina of rich pouring cream, emphasised by the incessant rain, the moisture in the air. His loins jolted.

'Let me look.' His hands felt too big, too clumsy to be performing such a delicate task, moving awkwardly over the wet, clotted strands, pushing her hair to one side, exposing the wound, a ragged cut about an inch from her eye. 'It's not too bad.' His knuckles grazed her cheek, a fleeting touch, the brush of a moth's wing. Christ, her skin was like silk.

At his touch, Cecily sucked in her breath, dragging air deep into her lungs. A desperate longing drove sharp and hard into her belly. The lick of desire. She gasped in shock, lifting her arm, a jerky, haphazard movement that knocked his hand away. Who was he, this stranger, to appear from nowhere and make her feel like this? As though he trespassed on her heart?

'Leave it!' she admonished him, quickly dousing the delight that flickered in her belly. 'It is barely a scratch.'

'Make sure you see to it, then, when you return home.' His glittering gaze raked over her. 'I'm assuming home is somewhere nearby?'

'Yes, yes, it is.' Cecily turned, summoning her last vestiges of strength to walk away from this man.

He stared at the proud, neat set of her head, the creamy curve of her cheek, flushed with colour. Despite her outward show of bravado, the disdainful look on her face, he had traced the fear in her beautiful eyes, as though she was hiding something.

'Can I take you there?' Lachlan offered. For some reason, he was reluctant to let her go, just yet. He jammed his hands into his leather belt. He wasn't so heartless as to leave this woman alone in the woods after such an ordeal. He had time, after all. 'You've had a shock this morning.'

'No, no!' She shook her head violently. 'It's fine. I'm fine. Thank you, you can go now.' A faint blue colour tinged her lips, but she managed to turn and walk away from him through the spindly birches with a slow, dogged gait. Her wet clothes hampered her, dragging on her slender frame. She must be freezing. The pink flesh of her heels, her unshod feet, flashed beneath her hem. Her hair was a mess, plaits dislodged, straggling across her cloak. When she had gained some distance from him, she twisted her head, looking back, and realised that he hadn't moved. Her bright eyes blazed at him, shedding sparks of resentment. If looks could kill, he thought, he would be dead.

* * *

Lachlan stood for a long time, watching until her dark-cloaked figure vanished into the shadowed trees of the woodland. Curiosity nibbled at the edges of his brain. The woman mystified him. Who was she, this noblewoman on a servant's errand? Skipping across the river on nimble, dancing feet, clad in a fine emerald gown. He remembered the silk velvet beneath his fingers as he lifted her from the water, the way the material clung to her slender frame; the lightness of her. Her firm breasts sliding against him as he lowered her to the ground. His belly twisted, a strange sensation.

When was the last time he had held a woman? His heart, reduced to a frozen lump within the packed muscle of his chest, was starved of tenderness. After what had happened to his family, he was incapable of feeling any emotion. It made him a skilful fighter, a man who was prepared to risk everything. He simply did not care what happened to him, whether he lived or died. And so, in battle, he would fight longer and harder than anyone, gaining him notoriety, a demand for his fighting skills. And with every battle, he hoped, prayed that this time all the raging, all the bloodshed would drive out the bad memories, and make him whole again.

But, no. It hadn't happened.

'Christ, man, it's only just light now!' Raising one arm, Simon slid another arrow from the leather holster strapped to his back, holding the feathered shaft in place across the bow. 'What were you doing out so early?'

The metal arrowhead gleamed dully in the watery sunshine. The looming bundles of grey cloud thinned slowly, as the weak sun rose, vanishing into a washed pale blue sky. Rags of white cloud floated above their heads, all that remained of the earlier heavy rain. Simon focused on the huge red target, set at a distance across the field, and let the arrow fly. The glinting point hit the target, dead centre. Satisfied with his performance, Simon switched his gaze to Lachlan, drawing his thin eyebrows together, waiting for his friend's answer.

'I couldn't sleep. And I needed some exercise.' Lachlan rubbed his thigh—his stitches had stretched painfully when he'd dragged the maid from the water; he was lucky that the wound hadn't opened up again. More fool him, he thought. He should have left her, ungrateful chit.

'And the maid? Why was she there?'

'I have no idea.' Lachlan's damp cloak began to steam in the sunshine. 'She said she had to reach the village.'

He recalled the desperation in the maid's voice, the flash of guarded anger in her leaf-green eyes. The agitation in her slim frame had been palpable, yet, for some reason, she hadn't tried to run away. In her heavy water-laden clothes he would have caught her in an instant, even with his injured leg. But he would have caught her if she had been wearing nothing.

Desire slammed into him, a sudden, fierce longing at the surprising trajectory of his thoughts. He jerked his gaze up, forcing himself to focus on the target, the large circles of black and white, the painted red bullseye, set before the hawthorn hedge around the field. Above him, a flock of geese honked loudly, held in a loose arrow formation as they flew across the luminous sky. What, in heaven's name, was wrong with him?

'Lachlan!' Simon said, resting his bow against his side. His brown eyes narrowed, hawk-like. 'Did you hear what I said?'

Lachlan laughed, shaking his head to rid himself of his thoughts. The powerful memory of her. Why did it stick with him so? 'No, I'm sorry.'

Simon clapped his hand against Lachlan's shoulder. 'I'm curious about this maid. Did you ask her anything at all? Where did she come from?'

A pair of huge green eyes sparkled across his vision. 'She spoke little and, when she did, was possibly the rudest chit I have ever met. I sincerely hope I never have to meet her again.' The lie soured his tongue; chipped at his conscience.

'She must have had a shock at the sight of you.' Raising the bow and arrow on a level with his ear, Simon took a single deep breath and immediately released his fingers on the taut bowstring. The arrow flew through the air, straight and true, hitting the centre of the target again. He turned to Lachlan. 'That's the reason she was so anxious to escape; she was probably scared to death!' Simon laughed.

Nay, she had not been frightened of him. That was the odd truth. She had been frantic, desperate to escape him, but not *because* of him. Because of something else.

'To be fair, I probably ruined her morning,' Lachlan said slowly. 'She was crossing on some stepping stones, but the river had flooded and they were underwater. I called out to her...startled her. And she fell. It was the least I could do to pull her out again.' His long legs had carried him alongside the river, his eyes pinned to the maid's rapid, tumbling progress through the foaming water. The pale green flag of her cloak as it flew in the air, the stark white of her face as she turned in the water. Thank God she had managed to cling to that rock. She had closed her eyes and leaned her head against it, exhausted, and for a moment, he wondered if she might slip off again before he reached her. His heart plummeted, looped with the memory.

'Wait. Where did you say she was crossing?' Simon drew his eyebrows together, puzzled, bringing his bow down to rest on his side.

'By the stepping stones,' Lachlan repeated.

Simon groaned. 'She's from the castle,' he supplied grimly. 'That is the way we always use…always used,' he corrected himself. 'It shortens the distance to the village by a couple of miles at least.' He clapped one hand to his head. 'I should have told you. If I had been there, I would have held on to her, questioned her about that woman in the castle. She might have helped us gain access, if I had offered an appropriate bribe.'

'I doubt it would have worked.' For some reason he was relieved that he had let her go, if only to spare her Simon's questions. But why would he want to spare her? He didn't ever know her name.

Simon pushed one hand through his hair, his eyes narrowing. 'We need to go back out there, Lachlan. Let's see if we can catch her before she disappears back into the castle. We might be able to stop her on the way back from the village. Can you remember what she looked like?'

A pair of twinkling eyes, the colour of new leaves in spring, flashed through his mind. Piercing. Intense. *Oh, yes*, he thought. *I remember what she looks like.* He would never forget.

Chapter Three

Cecily plodded through drifts of dead, curling leaves, steps dragging, the soles of her feet cut and scraped by sharp little stones hidden underfoot. Her stockings were ripped to shreds, mud-stained. Puffing with exertion, she pushed herself through the woods. The trees overhead were quieter now; the wind had stopped, the rain easing. Vicious brambles, arching cruelly, snagged at her cloak and her loosened hair like desperate, clasping hands, trying to prevent her forward movement. The boggy ground threatened to sink her every step. But by keeping the river on her right and concentrating on putting one foot in front of the other, Cecily persevered until she emerged from the woods at the town bridge.

Towards the east, a strip of light blue sky

inched wide, and a single shaft of sunlight broke free from the horizon. And yet no smoke emerged from the huddle of cottages in the town; it was too early for the townspeople to be awake. Slipping across the stone arches that spanned the foaming surge of water, Cecily hurried along the track that would take her up on to the moor, to the midwife's cottage. Some said Greta was a witch and would not let her live among them, but, despite their reservations, her healing skills were renowned, and even those who denounced her were quick to call on her services if a birthing began to go awry.

The breeze stiffened as she climbed, plastering her already wet clothes to her body, slowing her stride. Shivering, Cecily stepped away from the track, plunging through the bleached tussocky grass. She headed for the tumbledown shack surrounded by a copse of small trees, hawthorns, their tops stunted, bent by a fierce wind. Reaching the cottage, Cecily banged on the door, leaning her elbows against the damp, rotten planks, exhausted. Water trickled down on the inside of her sleeve.

'Is it time?' The door opened a crack and two beady eyes emerged from the shadows. The midwife was tiny, her face wizened, scoured with deep lines. She peered at Cecily with a shrewd, knowing expression.

'Yes.' Cecily's eyes searched Greta's wizened face. 'And she is bleeding. Can you come now?'

The old maid ducked behind the door to seize her shawl, wrapping the threadbare material around her head and shoulders. 'Here, carry this,' she ordered, thrusting a grimy cloth bag into Cecily's hands. 'I have all I need in there.'

The weak sun rose, gradually penetrating the hazy mist that rose in a veil of white steam from the soaked ground. Water droplets hung, suspended like miniature diamonds on the grass tips, turning the moor into a breathtaking expanse of shining, twinkling light.

'What happened to you?' Greta glanced curiously at Cecily's wet clothes, the bloodied mark on her forehead, as they hurried, side by side, back down the hill.

Cecily grimaced. 'I tried to cross by the

stepping stones, but with all this rain, the river was up. I thought it would be faster that way, so I took the chance.' A pair of sparkling blue eyes nudged into her brain. She chewed fretfully on her bottom lip, annoyed that…that man should intrude upon her thoughts so.

'You were lucky you managed to pull yourself out. Many have lost their lives in that water.'

'Oh, I…er, yes, I was,' Cecily agreed limply. She hugged the midwife's bundle closer to her chest. Even as the horrors of her morning's escapade began to fade, the memory of her rescuer remained doggedly persistent. The warmth of his fingers as he gripped hers, rough pads powerful against her forearm. The jolt of his masculine scent as he tipped her over his burly shoulder. Piercing fragments of delight leaped through her mind, like fireflies in the twilight.

'Forgive me, my lady, but aren't you taking a risk, coming out to fetch me like this?' The old maid repeated, peering significantly at Cecily's flat stomach. 'Did anyone see you?'

Only him. The tall stranger with hair of flaming gold.

Cecily took a deep breath. The air left her lungs with a shudder. He must have been a traveller, a knight riding through, en route to another town, another place. 'I…well, a man pulled me out of the river. But I've never seen him before, so I'm—…'

'Don't tell your mother, my lady, or she'll…' Greta stabbed the knobbly stick she used for walking into the ground. Her thin lips pursed with worry.

Cecily shivered. 'I have no intention of telling my mother anything. I made a mistake this morning. I should have come to you on the lane instead.'

They were approaching the castle now and walked up the stony road towards the gatehouse, heads bent low and hoods drawn down over their foreheads, elbows touching. Despite her advancing years, Greta matched Cecily's pace, step for step.

Jerking her eyes upwards, Cecily searched for her sister's window in the south turret. Her heart lurched. 'I pray to God we're not too late.' She glimpsed her mother's white face through the open shutters, obviously looking out for her. She wanted to shout up, to ask how Isabella was, but from this distance her mother would not hear.

Two guards were at the castle entrance, red tunics fluttering over their chainmail, standing either side of the massive wooden gates. Cecily's heart sank. She was too late to slip back to her chamber by the normal route; most of the servants would be up and about by now. No one in the castle must guess that she was not the mother of the baby about to be born.

'You go on,' she said to Greta, tugging self-consciously at the edge of her hood. 'I will go in around the back, through the cellars. Go on now, please be quick.'

The old maid squeezed Cecily's hands, reassuringly. 'Don't fret, my lady. All will be well. Go back down the track, as if you're returning to the village. Those guards will not suspect a thing. Remember, mistress, everyone wants this baby to be born. No one wants Lord Simon to be the lord of this castle. They like you being in charge.'

A cold fear scythed through Cecily. 'You… you've not told anyone?'

'Nay, mistress, your secret is safe with me.' Something caught her attention over Cecily's shoulder; a flicker of movement. 'You had best go now, my lady…there are horsemen coming.'

Twisting her head, Cecily caught the telltale flash of chainmail, the sound of bridles jangling carrying on the breeze. Her heart thudded with panic and, for a fraction of a moment, she wanted to give up, to surrender. The fight was draining out of her, the fight to keep up this ridiculous charade. The temptation to sink to her knees and confess everything to the next person she met was overwhelming. How long must she keep going for? Until her mother finally forgave her?

'Go on, then.' Greta jogged her elbow. 'You'd better move now, otherwise they'll catch up with you.'

Cecily pushed the cloth bundle into the old woman's arms and walked briskly down the track until she was out of sight of the guards on the gate. Then she stepped neatly sideways into the long grass, forging a path around to the back of the castle, to the cellar door hidden in the undergrowth. The thud of hoofbeats grew closer. The edges of her chest folded inwards, creating an ever-tighter box of despair, a feeling of desperate entrapment. She knew, without looking, that among the approaching horsemen was Simon, Lord of Doccombe. That man would never give up.

Stumbling and slipping, Cecily made her way around the steep slope to the north side of the castle. The ground was more treacherous here, falling away down an almost vertical slope towards the frothing river. Her stocking-covered feet were numb with cold and pain, but she forged on, the muscles in her knees and thighs straining to keep her body on the precipitous slope. Her wet cloak swung round awkwardly, catching at her feet.

A movement behind snagged her eye. She turned, heart rising into her throat, blocking her gullet with fear. Two men, squat and thickset, were silhouetted on the brim of the hill against the clear blue sky. One man raised his arm, shouted out to her. The silver skin of his chainmail rippled, the individual links glinting in the sunlight. Simon of Doccombe's men, no doubt, sent to chase her.

She whipped her head around, grimly facing forward and increased her pace. Cold sweat trickled down from her armpits. The cellar door was not far. Lifting her skirts, she broke into a stumbling run, her gait awkward, lopsided, due to the steepness of the slope. Gasping, trying to catch her breath, Cecily rounded the final corner of the castle wall and...there it was. The narrow iron door. Her salvation.

The key was hidden behind a loose stone in the wall. She had placed it there when this whole stupid plan had started, using the route into the castle to avoid being seen on several occasions throughout her supposed confinement. Her hands shook against the gritty stone, seizing the heavy iron key and jamming it into the lock. Turning the key, she fell against the riveted metal, turning the circular handle, pushing her body weight against the iron panel. It opened and she plunged into the dank darkness of the cellars. Pushing the heavy door shut, she shoved the key into the lock, turning it swiftly. Her fingers shook with fear.

She heard the men approaching. One tried the handle, the latch clicking up and down violently. A fist thumped against the iron door. 'Open this door. Lord Simon wants to speak with you!'

A bolt of panic shot through her; she leapt away as the man continued to pound on the door. These henchmen of Lord Simon were far too close, separated by a thin sheet of metal. The blood pounded in her ears, the gasp of her breath sounding raw and loud in the dark corridor. Could they hear her? The thumping had stopped and now there was only silence. She prayed they had given up.

Wrapping her arms around her shivering body, she crept away quietly, tiptoeing through the darkness, towards the narrow steps in the north turret that would lead her back up to her sister's chamber. Relief stole over her, a gradual reclaiming of her sanity as she walked away. Fear leached away from her slight frame. Fortune had been on her side. This time.

* * *

'Go and change,' her mother snapped, peering coldly at the water that Cecily trickled about the bedchamber. 'And then come back to help your sister.' Sitting at Isabella's bedside, Greta glanced up at her and smiled encouragingly.

'How is she?' Cecily asked. Isabella's face held a waxy sheen, cheeks glistening with perspiration. The heat in the chamber was incredible. Two charcoal braziers glowed with coals and a fire burned in an open grate, between the two windows.

'She's fine, for the moment,' Greta replied. 'The blood loss stopped quickly enough; you did the right thing by propping her legs up. The babe has not suffered. Do what your mother says and find some dry clothes.'

After the warm fug of Isabella's chamber, her own room was chilly. Exhaustion clogged her brain, making her thought process slow, unpredictable. Her eyes touched on the familiar objects around her, as if she saw them for the first time: the rich velvet drapes around the four-poster bed; the oak coffer beneath the window, intricately carved by one of her father's carpenters; the earthenware jug and bowl set on a small elm table for washing.

Cecily removed her cloak, spreading the saturated wool over the back of a chair. The light green fabric was smeared with mud, twigs and dead leaves snared in the heavy folds. The legacy of her morning's escapade. Her fingers fumbled with the knot on her belt ties; once loosened, she pulled the open-sided gown over her head. This she placed alongside her cloak. Her fitted gown beneath was more of a struggle to remove. Tiny buttons held each sleeve tight to her arm and it took an age to release them, the wet fabric making the process difficult. But at last the buttons were released and her sleeves hung open. Once she had struggled out of the close-fitting gown, removing her chemise, undergarments and stockings was a great deal easier.

She almost wept at the state of her stockings. The fine silk was reduced to a mass of torn holes, ragged filaments, destroyed beyond repair. Her feet were not much better, her heels and the underside of her toes gouged and scratched. Bleeding. A reddish bruise darkened the edge of her right foot, spreading from her ankle to her toes. Plucking a linen towel from the end of her bed, she scrubbed at her damp skin. Her flesh burned, turning pink beneath her brusque treatment.

She allowed herself the smallest sigh of relief. Despite her foolhardy escapade, that of leaving the castle without her disguise of pregnancy, she had avoided suspicion. This plan, the plan instigated by her mother, might have a chance of succeeding. The castle and the estates would be secured, and her mother would be happy. In truth, that was all she wished for. She was to blame for what had happened with her brother, Raymond. By doing this, by lying, she would be able to make amends.

Her mother had been so happy at Crekelade, their family home when her father had been alive. She had often watched from the upper window of the solar as Cecily, Isabella and Raymond had ridden out on their little ponies with their father, their smiling faces beaming with excitement. Sometimes

William had accompanied them when their father could not. He had worked in the stables at Crekelade and was the same age as Cecily. Until her mother had sent him away.

Pulling on clean woollen stockings and linen underdrawers, she secured them around her slim waist with a pink satin ribbon. Rummaging through the oak coffer, she found a practical underdress of plain light blue wool and a full-length sleeveless tunic of a darker blue. Although she possessed expensive gowns, the ones she had chosen were the garments that she preferred to wear as she carried out her daily chores around the castle. Hard-wearing, serviceable clothes. She slipped these on over her linen chemise, relishing the wonderful feel of the dry fabric against her skin.

They had had a good friendship, she and William. He had been her refuge, a place of safety and security, away from the vengeful rages of her mother. He had often been in the stables, or in the yard, working with her father's horses. She missed him. She had nobody to turn to now; she was completely alone.

She dashed away the self-pitying thoughts, annoyed at her maudlin self-indulgence. Fitting the woven girdle around her waist, she knotted the leather ties across her stomach, pulling her sleeveless tunic into soft gathers. They were almost there, her mother, Isabella and she. As long as the baby was delivered safely, and was a boy, then all would be well. Unwinding her braids, she dragged a comb through her messy, matted hair, before plaiting it efficiently back into two long braids. Coiling them into a bun at the nape of her neck, she secured the heavy bundle with long silver hairpins. A plain length of linen around her head served as both a wimple and veil. She would have to find another circlet later. Donning some soft leather ankle boots, she left her chamber to return to Isabella. Soon, all this would be over.

'I can't do this! Please, let it stop…now!' Isabella gave a long wail as another heavy contraction gripped her. She thrashed her head from side to side on the sweat-dampened pillow. The midwife crouched at the foot of the bed, a pile of linen cloths and a bowl of water on the floor beside her.

Tiredness reddened Cecily's eyes, as she gripped on to her sister's slippery hand. How much longer would this labouring go on? Since she had returned to the chamber, the day had waned to twilight, dusk and, then, full night. Throughout the long hours, Greta had sat patiently by the bed, watching Isabella closely as she either dozed fitfully, or woke, screaming, with another contraction. But now, just before dawn, with a fingernail of moon and the bright star of Venus shining delicately through the window, Greta had moved instinctively to the foot of the bed and thrown back the sheets, peering closely between Isabella's legs.

'You're almost there, my lady,' she announced. 'I can see the head. One more big push now.'

And then the baby arrived in a sudden, glistening rush, straight into the midwife's hands, the little red mouth open almost immediately, crying. Deftly, Greta wiped the mucus away from the baby's nose and mouth, smiling as the pale skin began to pink up. With a flash of a blade, she cut the cord that attached the baby to his mother.

'Here,' she said, handing the squalling, writhing bundle up to Cecily. 'You'd better get used to this. Wrap him up tightly now.'

Grabbing a linen cloth set aside for the purpose, Cecily took the baby into her arms. Him. Isabella had been delivered of a boy. The little scrunched-up face nestled against her breast, the baby's skin like that of a rose petal, exquisitely soft, pink. His light blue eyes held a hint of green. The same green of Isabella's eyes. And hers.

Exhausted, spent, Isabella collapsed back, her head buffered by the mattress, her lank hair pillowed in the bed furs. Her arms lay limply at her sides; her nightgown and thighs were stained with blood.

'A boy! A boy!' Marion clapped her hands in glee. 'Oh, well done, Isabella.' Bending over, she planted a kiss on her younger daughter's head. 'Simon of Doccombe will never claim this castle now. He will have to leave us alone. Your sister's unfortunate engagement with your husband's house knight has saved us, although I never thought that at the time.'

'And I suppose his death was fortuitous, as well,' Cecily murmured. In the same battle that Peter had been wounded, Guillame had died. How mistaken her mother was in her thinking. How blinkered. Isabella had truly loved Guillame. Had her mother forgotten that they were to be married?

Marion shrugged. 'It made things easier.' She stretched out her arms. 'Give me the baby now, Cecily.'

At the bottom of the bed, Greta knelt on the floor, packing up her cloth bag. With one hand on her knee, she levered herself slowly to her feet. 'I will go down and ask the servants to bring up some hot water. I will tell them to leave it at the door...' she glanced pointedly at Cecily '...so you can prepare yourself.' Her slight, wizened figure slipped through the door and into the stair-well beyond.

She means until I have swapped places with my sister, Cecily thought. Guilt swung over her. How could she do this? How could she take this baby away from his mother?

'Can I hold him?' Isabella's voice called faintly from the bed. 'Mother, please may I hold my baby?'

Marion nodded abruptly at Cecily, pursing her lips. But Cecily was already carrying the tiny baby over to her sister, laying him in her arms. A huge smile broke across Isabella's face as she stared down at the child in wonder. The glowing, pearly perfection of a new-born. The small, puckered mouth, the snub nose. Biting her lip, Cecily dipped her head away. Tears of sadness brimming in her eyes. She hadn't counted on this. She hadn't counted on how she would feel when the baby was placed in the arms of his rightful mother. What the hell was she doing?

'This is not right,' she hissed at her mother. Moving around to Marion, Cecily touched her mother's elbow, drawing her away from the bed so Isabella wouldn't hear her words. 'We cannot go on with this ridiculous plan.'

'What?' her mother hissed, her thin lips curling. 'Don't you dare do this, Cecily. You cannot back out now! We are so very nearly there!'

'Look at Isabella, Mother. Look at how she

holds the baby. We cannot take that child away from her.'

'We are not taking the child away from her!' Marion snapped. 'Isabella will be here, with the boy, as he grows up. But we have to go through the charade for Lord Simon to make the whole thing believable and then he will leave us alone. You cannot back out now; not after what you did.'

'It was an accident.' A shudder of memory rose in Cecily's chest.

'Whatever it was, my girl, this is the debt you have to pay. On that day, the day your brother, Raymond, died, you took away our livelihood and now you need to give it back to us.'

The thick air of the chamber, the smell of sweat and blood, pressed down on Cecily. Her head thumped in pain. She touched the sore spot on her forehead where her head had hit the rock, remembering. That man's careful hands, moving over the injury. Her skin smarted, burned.

'And remember, Cecily,' Marion's tone softened, adopting a cajoling tone, 'that if you do this, what the rewards will be. I will tell you where William is. And maybe, maybe, I can forgive you for what you have done. We can be a proper family again.'

And there it was, the bribe. The chance that her mother would love her again.

Cecily half closed her eyes. She needed to think, to escape the fug of the chamber. If only for a moment. 'I must… I need some fresh air.'

'Open the window, then.' Her mother's voice was shrill. 'You need to stay here, with me, and help with Isabella. As soon as we clean her up, you can swap places with her.'

Cecily's hand was on the door latch, pulling the door ajar, listening out for any activity on the stairs.

'Where are you going?' Marion's eyes rounded in horror. 'You cannot leave! Come back here at once!'

'I will be back in a moment.' Ignoring her mother's pleas, Cecily slipped out of the chamber.

'Wish me luck.' Lachlan grinned at Simon as he kicked his booted foot from the stirrups, thudding down on to the leaf-strewn ground. His leg wound ached painfully with the force of the landing; he winced. Bringing the worn leather reins over the horse's head, he handed them to one of Simon's men. Some of them carried torches, the bright flares holding back the dark, seizing the horsemen in a circle of light.

Leaning down from his saddle, Simon knocked his fist against Lachlan's broad shoulder. 'You'll do it. Try and find out as much information as you can, then come back out to us. I want to know what those women are up to, and whether the baby has been born. If it's a girl, then the castle's mine again.'

'How many men are there to defend the castle?' Lachlan asked. In the shadows, his eyes were a deep, iridescent blue.

'Christ, the woman has a whole army up there. She must pay them well to keep them so loyal. Far too many men to keep three women safe.'

'Three?'

'Aye, my brother's widow, Cecily, her mother and her younger sister, Isabella. They all came to live here when Lady Cecily's father died.'

'Have you tried to fight your way in?'

Simon shook his head. 'I don't want any violence. Especially against women. If the King should hear about it...' He trailed off, shrugging his shoulders. He glanced at Lachlan. 'This way is better.'

'The sneaky approach,' Lachlan finished for him. 'In that case, look after my sword and belt for me. It would be better if they think of me as a humble traveller, not a man nosing about for information.' He handed them up to Simon, moving around to his horse's rump to extract a large hooded cloak from one of his saddlebags. He swept the coarse patched fabric around the wide heft of his shoulders.

'What do you think?' he asked, tugging the voluminous hood low over his bright hair.

'I think, Lachlan, that you are a true friend, to help me like this. If only there was something I could do to...' Simon cleared his throat, pale cheeks reddening '...after what happened to you.' He searched the terse angles of Lachlan's face. 'I wish there was something I could do for you,' he said finally, limply.

'It was a long time ago, Simon.' Lachlan's jaw hardened imperceptibly. 'And there's nothing you can do or could have done. I scarce think of it now, anyway.' But as he turned away and strode off through the birch trunks gleaming in the darkness he realised he was lying. Simon's words scoured him, whips of memory flaying his skin. The ground before him shimmered, a blur as the past rushed through him. Horrific, vivid images lifted to his mind's eye, the familiar monsters that plagued him, day and night. The acrid smoke on his tongue as if it were yesterday. He heard his family's screams.

Lachlan shook his head roughly, dispelling the unwanted images. Despite his awkward gait, his long legs, honed from years in the saddle, powered up the steep slope to the castle gatehouse. It was so early; before dawn. Stars twinkled above him in the blue-black sky. The chilly air stung the inside of his throat, catching his breath. Now was not the time to dwell on what had happened; now was the time to fight back, to return to Scotland and make sure that justice was done. Two more days, he thought. Two more days and he would be fit enough to ride north.

It had been a mistake to let the maid from the river walk away from him. He should have hung on to that slender arm and marched her straight to Simon. It would have been a lot easier than all this skulking around in the dark. He smiled, imagining her reaction if he had done such a thing. Spitting at him like a cat, no doubt. That fiery beauty, half-drowned, sopping clothes clinging to her slim frame, raging at him. Her fine skin, like the inner curve of a pearl, glistening with raindrops. So beautiful and yet so hostile.

His breath hitched. Awareness rippled through him, a heightened sense of feeling. The beat of his blood, slowly gaining pace. He frowned, drawing heavy, etched brows together, realising that his hand was poised before the large, double-height door, yet he had failed to knock. Thoughts of the maid had snared him, tangling his usual, rapier-sharp logic. Lifting his great fist, he hammered on the chunky wooden planks.

Nothing. Not a sound. The door remained shut. He thumped again, harder this time. Surely they wouldn't leave the gate unguarded during the night? Taking a step back, he tilted his head, his luminous blue gaze sweeping up the towering granite wall, his eye moving from window to window. Candlelight flickered high up in the east tower; he could see a shadow moving on the interior wall of the chamber.

Raising his fist once more, he almost staggered forward in surprise when the door opened abruptly and a young lad peered out, holding a rush torch in his small fist. The light flared and crackled. The lad wore chainmail that was far too big for him and a helmet that tilted alarmingly. Where were the many house knights that Simon talked about? Were they all still abed?

'Yes…?' the lad asked. His voice quavered with doubt.

'Good day to you,' Lachlan said, bowing his head. 'I have come for food, if possible.

I have been travelling all night and my body is weary.'

'The mistress doesn't...' The boy began to close the door.

Lachlan stuck his booted foot in the gap, before the door was slammed shut on him. 'I'll be no bother,' he said. 'I can eat in the kitchen. Your mistress will never know I'm here.'

A dubious look crossed the young guard's face, his pale eyes staring down miserably at Lachlan's large foot planted imperiously on the threshold. 'All right,' he said finally. 'But you had better be quiet. The mistress has been labouring all night and has just been delivered of a child.'

'Girl or boy?' Lachlan asked as he stepped inside. Up ahead was another archway that led into the cobbled bailey.

'A boy,' said the lad, pushing the iron bolts back across the door to secure it. 'A blessed day for us all. At least Lady Cecily will not lose the castle now.' His timid eyes assessed Lachlan's rugged face. 'She is a widow and her brother-in-law is determined to have this castle back.'

'Your mistress is good to you?' Lachlan asked conversationally.

The boy nodded, a smile breaking across his thin face. 'Aye, she's a fine woman. A hard worker, too. We celebrated the day when our lord, God rest his soul, married her. She managed this whole estate while he was away fighting in France.'

Lachlan raised his eyebrows. This wasn't the story that Simon had been telling him. He had given the impression that his brother's widow had let the place go to rack and ruin, but even in this shadowy light he could see how neat and tidy the place looked. Firewood was stacked in an orderly fashion against the castle walls, protected by a thatched roof; the cobbles of the bailey, slick now with a coating of ice, were swept clean. A smell of fresh straw rose from the stables over to his right.

Lachlan hesitated. There was no real need for him to go into the castle. In the eyes of the law, Simon had lost and the castle would pass to his new-born nephew.

And yet... A pair of emerald eyes, sparkling with hostility, danced through his mind. She was here, somewhere. The girl from the river. It would be worth staying a little longer, just to catch another glimpse of her, before he headed north.

'Point me in the direction of the kitchens,' he said to the lad, lifting his cloth bag more securely on to his shoulder.

Chapter Four

With a quick, light step, Cecily walked along the corridor, breathing in the damp, chill air, a blessed relief after Isabella's over-heated chamber. The ladies' solar was at the far end, in the south-west turret of the castle, accessed down one level on another spiral staircase. A bright, light-filled room reserved only for her mother, Isabella and herself. No one else was allowed access; it was their private sanctuary.

Opening the door, Cecily headed for the wide low window, sinking down on the wooden windowsill. Her mind jumped all over the place, fatigue slowing her thoughts, making them sluggish. If only she could sleep. Reaching up, she twisted the iron latch, pushing open the wooden shutter. Outside, it was barely light, only the faintest lightening of the darkness to the east indicated that dawn was about to break. A single star twinkled above the horizon.

The early morning air bathed her heated face, softening the creeping sadness that coiled around her heart. Her breath emerged in puffs of white mist. She closed her eyes, allowing her mind to drift, to catch at the sadness that always lingered on the fringes of her thoughts. The loss of Raymond would always be with her. She would do anything to go back in time, to forcibly stop her brother from going out on to that frozen pond. Why had she not put up with his spoiled protests, the incessant whining, and stopped him doing what he wanted to do, instead of giving in to him?

Sighing, she leaned her forehead against the smooth wood of window frame. Now was not the time for regrets. Now was the time for healing wounds. For making things right between her and her mother. This rift between them had gone on too long; for Isabella's sake, for this new baby's sake, she had to pay her debt and make her mother happy again. And Marion was right, she wasn't taking the baby away from Isabella; the three of them would raise the boy, together, as a family.

Cecily rose slowly, smoothing down her ruffled skirts, wrapping her linen scarf back into place around her head. She would go back into that chamber now and swap places with Isabella in the bed, so that Lord Simon could visit. The next few hours would be tense, but as long as she held her nerve, they might succeed with their plan. Chewing her bottom lip, deep in thought, she wrenched open the door.

A man stood in the corridor, his back turned towards her.

Christ in Heaven! Cecily shut the door hurriedly, but he had heard her. Heart pounding, she listened to his strides advance decisively towards the solar.

'Mistress?' His voice was muffled as he tapped on the door. 'Can you help me a moment?'

'Go away!' Cecily shouted. 'I am indisposed!' She leaned back against the solid oak door. There was no key; she had no defence against him. Without warning, the door was pushed inwards, a hefty shove. With a cry of disbelief, Cecily sprang away, into the middle of the room.

'How dare you!' she yelled out at the man. 'I did not...' Her voice faltered as he raised his head and stared straight at her. The air punched from her lungs, leaving her staggered, gasping. The man from the river stood in the doorway. The man with piercing diamond eyes and flaming hair. Fear cut through her like a blade. His vast shoulders filled the doorway, a knowing gaze moving over her. His square-cut jaw hardened in recognition. What in hell's name was he doing here?

'So we meet again.' Lachlan smiled slowly, his gaze raking the plain cloth of her gown. 'I wondered if I would see you.'

'Get out!' Cecily yelled at him, flapping him away with outstretched arms. 'I did not give you permission to enter.'

He ignored her. 'You were at the river this morning.' He moved with the easy athleticism of an animal, a supple flex of power carrying his body forward, despite a slight limp.

'I have never met you before!' she spluttered.

He frowned heavily. 'Why are you lying?' He cut off her speech, hard, with a voice of steel as he stood before her. Towered over her. His gleaming eyes roamed over her slim figure. 'I pulled you out of the river. I carried you to the bank. Beneath your scarf is a cut on your forehead.' Unbelievably, he tapped the spot on her head. 'Shall we have a look?'

Cecily reared back, wincing. The raw, musky scent of his skin swept around her, softly tantalising. His boots budged beneath the hemline of her skirts, an intimate intrusion. His body loomed over her, overbearing, intimidating, a snug surcoat encasing the heft of his shoulders, embracing the bulky muscles beneath. She wanted to scream at him to leave her alone, to push at those heavy muscular arms, to shove him away. But her mouth was too dry, devoid of liquid. Instead, she took a hurried step back, her hip banging painfully against the wooden arm of a chair.

Lachlan read the fear in her eyes. His gaze narrowed upon her. What was going on here? Why was the maid pretending that she had never met him? He traced the finely sewn seam around the neckline of her gown, the elegant fit of her sleeves around her slender arms. 'You remember me.' His voice was deep. Blunt.

Christ, how could she forget? The humiliation of that broad frame nudging hers, the sensual press of his limbs. The tangy smell of him. Her heart lurched dangerously, a staggered, rising flutter. Who in Christ's name was he, to keep barging into her life like this? He could reveal her identity and jeopardise her mother's whole plot, for he had seen her twice now, without her disguise. Disconcerted, she raised her hand, touching the tender spot beneath her linen veil.

Lachlan noted the movement with satisfaction. Oh, she remembered him all right. 'It is you, isn't it? Who are you? Tell me your name.'

Beads of sweat flecked her palms. 'It's none of your business!' she responded shakily. She smoothed her hands down the front of her gown. 'The guard should not have let you in.'

'The guard who is a boy of ten winters. A mouse could gain access to this castle.'

Cecily moved behind the chair, using the polished elm as a makeshift barrier. 'What do you want?'

'I understand that Lady Cecily has had her baby?'

Her mouth slackened, dropping open at his question. How did he know? How, in heaven's name, did he know the name? *Her* name? She had thought he was a passing traveller, but… Oh, my God, he must be with Simon of Doccombe! Christ, was he one of his knights? Terror blocked her throat. She backed away, shaking her head, not wanting to reply. Not knowing how to reply. She had to get away from him. Now.

'Yes, yes, she has.' Cecily's voice was a hesitant mumble as she slowly circled the chair. If she could lead him into the centre of the room then maybe, just maybe she could run to the door and be out of the room before he saw too much of her. 'You need to leave, now.'

Cecily strode over to the door, her head held high, acting as if she were about to show him out. Pulled open the door slowly, as if she hadn't a care in the world. The corridor stretched out before her; if she ran along that then he would surely catch her. But if she sprinted down the stairs, she might have a chance of losing him. Blood roared in her veins with the effort of keeping her features set, expressionless. He could not know that she was planning to run.

Without warning, she took off, diving down the spiral staircase, down, down, as quick as her feet would take her, until she reached the narrow door at the bottom, the door to the storerooms beneath the castle.

'No, stop!' His loud voice roared down the stairwell after her.

He tore down after her, his steps thumping heavily on the stone, and she wrenched open the door. Vanished into the darkness. She had to hide from him, hide away until he had gone. If he was connected in some way to Simon of Doccombe, then the chance that he could unwittingly reveal their whole deception was a definite possibility.

'Come back!' he yelled. 'I only want to ask you a few questions!'

Panic bubbled in her stomach, a frothy, whirling tide of desolation. The strength sapped from her legs, debilitating; the resulting weakness making her steps jerky, haphazard. There was no bolt on the inside of the door and she had no light. But she knew her way around this catacomb of chambers, a vast labyrinth of linked vaulted rooms created to house the castle stores. And the man on the stairs did not.

Threading her way around a stack of barrels containing salted meat for the winter, she clambered nimbly over a pile of grain sacks. Her wide skirts tangled around her legs and she kicked the hem down angrily; the bulky cloth hampered her. Her breath expelled in quick, truncated gasps. Behind the sacks was an opening in the wall, low down, and she crawled through the tiny space into the next chamber, stacked high with more grain sacks. Once through, she allowed the breath to leave her lungs, a deep sigh. There was no way such a big man would be able to crawl through such tight space; she was safe, for now, at least. She would hide at the far end, behind the heap of sacks, and crouch down in the darkness until he became bored with searching and left.

Lachlan stared, slack-jawed, as the maid twisted away. What kind of fool did she take him for? Did she not realise that by trying to avoid him, she simply made him more suspicious? This maid, with her dew-soft cheeks and luminous green eyes, had something to hide. And he owed it to Simon to find out what it was.

He jumped down the shallow steps after her, five at a time. Kicked open the thin-planked door that she had so recently closed. He stood, listening, hearing the hurried patter of the maid's feet, the nervous bustle of skirts as she fled into the darkness. Excitement gripped his loins, crazy, haphazard. His mouth twisted ruefully. If truth be told, he was not pursuing her solely for Simon's sake. For the first time, in a long time, he felt alive.

She crashed against something, a wooden crate maybe, then cursed. Lachlan smiled, a slow easy smile. He plunged forward, weaving around the barrels, squeezing with difficulty through a low crawl space into the next chamber, his shoulder scraping the wall above him. Granules of stone dust flecked his tunic. He saw her then, in a gratifying flash of stocking-covered legs, climbing determinedly up a heap of grain sacks, a huge pile that rose almost to the vaulted ceiling. Lachlan sprang forward, stretching out his body to full length, reaching out to grab her.

'Come here, you little wretch!' he yelled triumphantly. His blunt fingers rasped against her delicate stocking, pinioning her slender shin, below the knee. She screamed in outrage, annoyance, kicking her leg upwards in a determined effort to break free. He grabbed her other leg, reaching up to seize the embroidered girdle at her waist, muscular fingers digging into her back. He hauled her down roughly. A mass of fabric billowed out over his face and shoulders, enveloping him in a delicious scent, lavender mingled with the enticing smell of her skin. Her perfume.

His senses shuddered, rippling with fierce awareness. The rigid clamp on his emotions, held tight for so long, cracked open for a tiny moment. The heat of her leg seared his calloused palm, the rough pads of his fingers rasped against her fine woollen stockings. Her warm sensuality, so close, burned through him, melting the solid lump of his heart. He had forgotten. Forgotten what it was like to be so close to a woman. His belly quivered, innards turning to liquid fire.

'Let go of me, you oaf!' Cecily screeched at him, her voice muffled by the grain sacks. 'You have no right to treat me like this!' Kicking backwards with her heels, she struggled in his fearsome grasp, wriggling her hips to try and break free. Face pressed into the grain sacks, the tangy smell of wheat rose in her nostrils. Hot tears of anger, of frustration, seeped from her eyes. Defeat washed over her, the dull tide of humiliation. The man pressed against her, shoving her against the sacks, holding her there, his chest a slab of iron against her back and shoulders. His heavy legs ground into her hips and thighs, an intimate cradle.

Her brain leaped with startled awareness.

Sensation whipped through her, a scythe of blinding light. A visceral stabbing. Exhilaration flooded her veins, dancing flames of intense delight. She had never experienced anything like it. Her wedding night had been a rough, shameful affair. Peter had been drunk, barely lucid, and their coupling had been hurried, painful. She remembered Peter's foetid breath, the stench of his sweat as he collapsed upon her afterwards. Her blood, staining the white sheet, displayed in the great hall for all to see, the morning after. Evidence of their consummation.

The corrosive memory drove her into action. 'Get off me now!' Cecily jammed her elbow back into the man's ribs. The pressure of his heavy body released, allowing her to turn. It was a mistake. Braced over her, the man's arms imprisoned her upper body, his legs encasing the slender curve of her hips. His chin brushed the top of her head, inadvertently. Her mouth was inches below his.

Cecily dragged her gaze downwards, forcing herself to focus on his chest. The buckle on the leather strap that crossed his tunic, glinting dully. The row of neat stitching that held his sleeve to the body of his tunic. He smelled of soil and sunshine, rich earthy scents that spoke of a quiet powerful energy, waiting to be unleashed. A wild animal pacing silently around a cage. Her senses reeled. For one single, insane moment, she yearned to lift her arms around him, to pull him closer. To claim his lips in a kiss.

The air between them slowed, filled with a thickening expectancy.

The sensual lines of her body pillowed against Lachlan's hard limbs. Her hips, the soft flesh of her thighs, sealed against his own. Logic told him to move, to lift himself away. But his brain seemed incapable of sending that instruction to his muscles. He hung above her, arms locked straight, tracing the delicate curve of her mouth, the parted lips. Her eyes sparkled with a strange intensity. A longing. Need.

Desire, buried deep in a choked-up well of self-restraint, burst forth. Blood pumped, obscuring conscious thought, blurring the lines between what was right and what was wrong. Reason fled, chased by a torrent of longing. Lachlan collapsed against her, his mouth claiming hers in the darkness, seizing her lips in a long, hard kiss.

Beneath the impact of his mouth, Cecily's arms lifted, a distracted protest, then dropped again, palms falling open like delicate flowers against the hessian sacks. Any resistance fell away, vanished. His mouth was fierce, relentless against her sensitive flesh, roaming her lips with delicious exploration, bombarding her with wave after wave of sweet, rolling emotion. Her heart rate whipped along, a dangerous, heady beat, pooling her belly to liquid. Building steadily. Yet she had not the slightest inkling of where she was headed. Unknown territory.

Then, as quickly as the kiss had begun, Lachlan ripped his mouth away, standing up abruptly. His eyes shed sparks of fire. He stepped back, jerkily, his mind scrabbling with the impact of what he had done. God in Heaven, he had chased and assaulted a woman in her own home! Had he truly lost his wits, out there on the battlefields of France? This was no way to treat a woman.

'That should not have happened,' he mumbled thickly.

'No, it should not have.' Cecily's voice shook from his kiss, from the sheer, heated intensity. 'You should be ashamed of yourself! How dare you attack me like this!' And yet she had welcomed the touch of his mouth like a lover. What had she been thinking?

Shame washed over her, a hot churning tide of humiliation. Cecily scrambled to her feet, adjusting her clothes, snapping down her skirts, smoothing her hands over her bodice. Her linen headscarf had become dislodged, revealing the brown silk of her hair, gleaming in the shadows. Angrily, she rewound the cloth around her face and neck. Mouth burning, she shoved past him, head held high, marching back.

Lachlan lifted his head as she bustled past him, his eyes, vivid blue, blazing over her. 'I am sorry.' But he was not sorry. Not really. His body hummed with the power of their kiss, shimmering with new-born intensity. The intense contact with this woman had jolted him, driving hard through the armour plating around his heart. After years and years of cold, icy numbness, the taut strings around his chest, his ribcage, loosened fractionally. Lachlan turned to follow her, this maid whose name he did not know, his heart dancing with a sparkling energy.

At the bottom of the spiral staircase, Cecily grabbed the rope banister that spiralled upwards. The rough fibre grazed her palm. The man's big body crowded into the space after her, intimidating, overpowering. She thought of her mother, fretting upstairs, pacing across Isabella's chamber. Cursing her.

'I am needed elsewhere.' Cecily placed one foot on the bottom step, fighting to keep the betraying wobble from her voice. 'And I think you need to leave. The main entrance is through the great hall.' She lifted one arm and pointed. 'That way.'

'I will go…if you tell me your name.' In the gloom of the hallway, his hair glinted, whips of flame. He leaned against the wooden frame of the cellar door, folding his huge arms across his chest. Annoyingly, he seemed in no hurry to leave.

She chewed fractiously at her fingernail, annoyed by his lack of action. 'Sweet Jesu, why do you plague me so? Haven't you done enough?' Lacing her arms across her chest, Cecily tried to slow the race of her heart, the devastating legacy of his kiss. Her lips smarted. Burned.

I haven't even started yet. The thought snatched at him, unbidden. He stared at her mouth, reddened by his kiss. His belly tightened with quick awareness.

She tilted her chin up, green eyes darkening, flicking sparks of anger towards him. 'You barge in here without so much as a by your leave, attack me with your questions, intimidate me and then you…then you…' Her speech trailed away, floundered.

'And then I kissed you.' His voice hitched with unspent desire.

Cecily picked at the coarse rope of the banister. 'God only knows what you're going to do next!' she muttered, without thinking.

'Nothing is going to happen next.' His eyes twinkled over her, deep pools of iridescent blue. 'You flatter yourself, dear lady. I might not have any manners, but credit me with some self-control, at least.'

Christ! What was he talking about? Cecily clapped her hands to her flaming cheeks, an image of the two of them rolling together on the grain sacks. 'I didn't mean that! You know I didn't!' Was he deliberately seeking to provoke her? 'I mean that you...' She shook her head. What harm was there in asking him outright? 'Did Simon of Doccombe send you?'

'Yes.'

She had known, she supposed, yet the terseness of his reply stabbed into her chest. Her hand clutched the banister like a lifeline, her fingers clenching and unclenching, forcing herself to remain calm.

'What does he want?'

'He wants to see Lady Cecily. And the baby.'

And all of a sudden, she saw her way out, a way to make him leave. Lifting her eyes, she traced the lean line of his jaw, a faint glinting shadow of beard dusting his skin. The coarse stone of the wall, dull grey, framed the fiery springiness of his hair.

'He can.' Cecily's mind sprang through the possibilities. 'Tell him to come on the six o'clock bell, this evening. That will give my lady a few hours to recover before she is able to receive visitors.' Her sharp gaze drifted across his face, the defined angles of his cheekbones, hollowed out with shadow beneath, his jaw, a square-cut slashing line. But this man could not come again, not if he was a knight of Simon of Doccombe. For then he would see her, with the baby, and uncover the whole deception. 'And only him, mind,' Cecily said hurriedly. 'Only Lord Simon. No one else. She doesn't want a room full of men.'

'Who would?' Lachlan threw her a taut smile.

She flushed. 'As long as that's clear.' Her tone was over-bright, bossy. 'The six o'clock bell, this evening.'

Cecily had climbed two steps, when the man gripped her arm. 'And who should I say told me? Lord Simon is bound to ask.' A heady feeling slid up her arm, to her shoulder, heat splaying out through her bones, her muscles.

'I... I'm a companion to Lady Cecily,' she supplied hurriedly. 'A cousin.'

'That was some risk you took this morning. What was so important that you had to cross the river when the water was so high?'

'I was fetching the midwife for Lady Cecily. I needed to find her and fast.'

'So you thought you'd take a shortcut. A dangerous one.'

She remembered the blood on the sheets, the helpless panic in her sister's eyes. Who wouldn't take such a risk for their own family? She nodded. 'It took longer in the end... because of what happened. But all is well.' She moved up a step and his arm fell to his side.

'You were lucky,' Lachlan said. His eyes slid across her slender frame, the svelte lines encased in the blue woollen gown, before he nodded sharply in farewell.

Cecily slumped against the cold stone wall, listening to the sound of the man's footsteps fade away along the corridor. Sweat ran down from her armpits, trickling down the inside of her gown. She had been lucky. Up to now, anyway.

Chapter Five

'Where have you been?' her mother rapped out, moving rapidly around the bed, her thin mouth contorting in vague disgust. 'What happened to you?'

Cecily lifted the wooden plank across the door, settling the ends into the iron brackets either side, preventing any access from the corridor. She traced the knots and whorls in the wood of the door, desperate to rest her head against those cool planks, unwilling to turn and face the critical stare of her mother, her constant questions delivered in a high-pitched needling whine.

What had happened down there, down in the cellars? Her mind stuttered, bereft of thought. Her body thrummed from the stranger's kiss, as if his physicality, the solidity of his energy, had stuck to her body, leaving an impression she was unable to scrub out. 'I'm not sure…' Her voice was muted as she turned to face Marion.

'What do you mean?' With a swift flick of her head, her mother glanced towards the sleeping Isabella, to make sure the sharpness of her voice hadn't woken her. The baby snuffled beside her sister, wrapped tightly in a woollen blanket, the perfect skin of his brand-new face glowing with pristine freshness in the sunlit room. 'You didn't meet anyone, did you?' Her mother's clawlike fingers wrapped around a carved bedpost. Beneath the slack blue-white skin of her hands, her knuckles were visible, white bone.

'Yes.' Her voice wavered. Bright blue eyes pierced her conscience.

Her mother staggered a little, gripping the post for support. 'Who?'

'I've never met him before.' The lie dropped easily from Cecily's lips. She picked at a tight knot in her girdle. She couldn't even begin to explain what had happened down by the river. 'But…but he said he had been sent by Lord Simon…'

'Christ in Heaven! How did he manage to get past the guards?'

'I've no idea.'

Marion sat down, abruptly, the strength leaving her bones. She lifted a shaking hand to her pale temple. 'This is what comes of you flouncing off in a temper, Cecily.' The straw in the mattress rustled beneath her slight weight, the bed fur gathering into plush ripples.

'That man that I met…he could reveal our whole deception.' A sense of entrapment, a hostile snaring, wound itself around her, slowly tightening. 'Mother…maybe…maybe we should stop this now. Tell Lord Simon the truth.'

'Are you completely insane?' Marion's pale eyes rounded on her. 'Everything is going in our favour. Isabella has given birth to a boy. We are so very nearly there. Don't you dare say anything.' Marion tipped her head to one side, listening. Footsteps were coming up the stairs, fast.

'Mistress…my lady!' It was Martha, calling to Cecily through the barred door. Gasps punctuated her frantic speech; she had run up the steps. 'It's him, it's Lord Simon! He's at the main gates with his men, wanting to see you! He knows about the baby. He's… he's threatening to break the door down!

Cecily's heart plummeted; she stared wildly at her mother, her mind clouding with despair. 'But Lord Simon was supposed to come later. On the six o'clock bell!' Had that wretched man simply ignored her instructions? 'He will have to wait!'

Marion shook her head. 'We should let him in, Cecily. What difference will a few hours make? At least this way he will stop harassing us. He needs to see you in that bed, cradling that child.' She called out to Martha, 'Tell Lord Simon to make himself comfortable in the great hall, bring him food and something to drink. I will come down to escort him.'

'Yes, my lady, thank you!' Relief softened the girl's voice as she turned away.

'Quick!' Marion ordered. 'Change out of your clothes and into a nightgown!' Her fingers grabbed at Cecily's girdle, tugging savagely. 'Hurry up! I wouldn't be surprised if

Lord Simon ignored Martha and came up here on his own.'

Cecily brushed her mother's hand away, fear driving her to action. 'We must move Isabella from the bed. Take her to the bed in the antechamber. Put the baby in the crib; I can take him when I've changed.'

As her mother helped Isabella across the room, Cecily unwound the linen from her head, pulling out hairpins to release her plaits. Gleaming ropes of ash-brown hair swung down past her waist. On impulse, she unwound the braids, releasing the full silken curtain of her hair. Hopefully Lord Simon would be so embarrassed by her state of undress, he would leave quickly once he had seen the baby. Unknotting her girdle, she wrenched her sleeveless tunic over her head. The fabric tore against the cut on her head as she dragged it off. Her fingers fumbled with the tiny bone buttons that secured the tight-fitting sleeves of her under-gown; in desperation, she ripped at them. Several loosened buttons scattered, rolling across the floor. She unrolled her stockings quickly. Wearing only her chemise and undergarments, she stuffed everything else, including her boots, into the oak coffer under the window and pulled on a white nightgown, so vast that it completely obscured her undergarments. She jumped into Isabella's bed, tugging the sheets and bed furs up to her chest.

'Ready?' her mother said, coming out of the antechamber. 'Isabella is already fast asleep; she's exhausted, poor thing.' Dipping down, she scooped the sleeping baby from the crib and placed him, snuffling warmly, into Cecily's arms. Startled at the sudden movement, the baby's eyes flew open. He stared into her face for a moment, then settled back to sleep.

Thank God, Cecily thought. She drew in a single breath, deep and shaky, shaking her loose hair forward so that it tumbled around the sides of her face.

'I will fetch Lord Simon now.' Marion's voice hardened as she lifted the wooden bar from the door. 'Be ready.'

'I will be, Mother.'

As the door clicked shut, the enormity of Cecily's imminent deception gripped her heart as an icy claw dug into her conscience. Her head whirled as she clutched at the comforting warmth of the baby against her chest. What would Lord Simon do, if he found out? He had the ear of the King; it was well known, so the penalty would be harsh. She shuddered, clamping down on her worried thoughts.

Voices rose in the stairwell. Her mother's voice, raised and strident, echoed upwards. For all Marion's outward confidence, her bluff and bluster, Cecily detected the overlying twitter of nerves. A deeper, masculine voice emerged. Lord Simon, followed by a heavy tread of leather boots, a posse of house knights, sticking to their master's side, preventing any harm to fall on his precious soul. *Oh, God,* she thought, gripping the baby tightly. *Please don't let them in. Don't let him in.* Panic squeezed through her veins, constricted to bursting point.

The door opened. Pinpricks of sweat broke out over Cecily's chest, beneath her chemise. Drawing the baby close, she hunkered back into the pillows, wanting to disappear. Marion swept into the chamber, skirts snaking across the polished floorboards, and threw a curt nod towards her daughter in the bed, an order to make ready. She stood aside, her thin, bony fingers curled around the door latch, waving Lord Simon into the chamber with a ceremonial sweep of her arm.

Lord Simon was tall, as her husband Peter had been. Dark brown hair, smooth and shiny, fell forward over his brow; lines of worry creased his forehead. His face was lean, the skin stretched taut over his cheekbones, emphasising the narrowness of his mouth. He hesitated in the doorway, brown eyes sweeping across her, then the baby. A muscle twitched in his hollow cheek. Behind him, in the shadows of the stairwell, Cecily sensed the shuffling press of other men, his house knights, jostling to enter the chamber, to catch a glance, to peer at the scene within. Yet Lord Simon prevented them, his tall, gangly frame filling the doorway.

'Pray, leave your men outside in the corridor,' Marion said. 'My daughter needs some privacy at this time.'

Lord Simon nodded, throwing a command back to his men. But he left the door slightly ajar as he moved into the chamber. Was he there? The man who had kissed her? Cecily lowered her gaze to the sleeping baby's face. The silky curtain of her hair fell forward across her cheeks.

'Thank you, my lady, for agreeing to meet with me…like this. So soon after…' His voice cracked slightly, then trailed away… unsure. It was as if he suddenly remembered that it was he who had barged his way into the castle. A stretching tension filled the air, his discomfiture palpable. She supposed it wasn't often that he was greeted with a scene such as this; he was probably unsure how to deal with it. With her.

'Come, come in,' her mother encouraged him, seizing Lord Simon's arm and ushering him towards the bed. 'Please, don't stand on ceremony, come and see the baby. He looks just like your brother, the spitting image, I think you'll agree.'

Cecily's heart plummeted. Her mother's sham exuberance echoed with a false note. Surely Lord Simon would suspect? The baby looked nothing like Peter; in fact, being only a few hours old, his crumpled face bore little resemblance to anyone in the family. Marion was overacting. Her smile was too wide and forced, her eyes overly bright.

Lord Simon approached the bed, too fast. His knees knocked awkwardly against the bedframe and he stepped back, embarrassed. A slight flush stained his gaunt cheeks. He peered at the baby's face, framed by a white woollen blanket. Cecily caught the whiff of horseflesh as he leaned over her. 'Very…nice,' he murmured. He stepped back abruptly, clasping his hands together. 'A boy, if I heard your servant correctly?'

'Yes, the baby is a boy,' Marion declared triumphantly. 'So…that means…' She allowed her sentence to trail away delicately.

'I'm well aware of what it means, Lady Marion,' Lord Simon stated tersely. 'And you know I'm not happy about it. But in the eyes of the law, I can do nothing.' He stared solemnly at Cecily, lying in the bed, then switched his gaze towards the door. 'Are you coming in?' he called to someone in the corridor. 'Come and see the baby.'

'Oh, I really think…' Marion darted a

worried look towards the door, then at Cecily's terrified expression.

Lord Simon hastened to reassure her. 'He's a friend, Lady Marion. Not one of my men. He will be respectful.'

Almost before the shape broke out from the shadows, Cecily knew the identity of the man who walked into the chamber. A large hulk of a man, with broad muscular shoulders. The stranger who had pulled her from the river. The man who…had kissed her in the darkness of the cellars, plundering her mouth to leave her wanting more.

The surrounds of the chamber, her mother, Lord Simon, blurred and slipped away. Blue eyes met green, the man's shining eyes riveted upon her, at once incredulous, condemning. The edge of his top lip curled acidly.

The breath stopped in her lungs, colour draining from her face.

Lachlan noted the ashen pallor of her face with satisfaction. Little wretch! In a moment, her whole deception became clear, her continual avoidance of him, the hostility at his questions. All to throw him off the scent. And, she had succeeded. How had he not realised that she was Lady Cecily of Okeforde herself? It was a credit to her ingenuity that she had managed to convince everyone that she was the mother of this baby. He remembered the slim feel of her body against him as he had pulled her from the river. It was not possible.

Cecily eyed him warily, her expression guarded. Vulnerable. He had the power to reveal the truth, the astonishing magnitude of the risk she had undertaken. She clasped the swaddled baby to her breast to present him to Lord Simon as her own, green eyes luminous, patched with shadow. Her hair was loose and long, magnificent, with a pale brown sheen like silken cloth, spilling over her shoulders, curling down over the pristine white bedlinen. His heart leapt with a grudging admiration at her courage, her daring, however misplaced.

An older woman bent over the bed, talking in a high-pitched tone to Simon, keen to show off the baby, her stiff, rigid fingers plucking at the woollen shawl to reveal the child's face. What a sham, he thought. He should denounce them both right now and reveal their duplicity to Simon. That would be the right and proper thing to do.

And yet...

The consequences for such fraudulent behaviour would be huge. Simon would take great umbrage at being duped and immediately involve the King and his court in such a case. As Lachlan stared at the woman's face, stricken with fear, he wanted to give her a chance. He suspected there was far more to this story than what he could see here, this day, in the bedchamber. He wanted to give her a chance to tell her side of the story. A sense of protectiveness settled on his shoulders: he wanted to help her.

Fear stuck in Cecily's throat. She made a supreme effort not to press back into the pillows, to cower in his presence. She read the condemnation in his eyes, the disapproval. She could barely breathe, her lungs twisting in panic, her limbs paralysed, rigid. Sweat rose from her flesh, sticking the flimsy layers of chemise and nightgown to her skin.

When would he denounce her? She traced the firm, tense outline of his mouth. Would it be now, in front of Lord Simon, with his men listening outside? Or would he wait, leaving her to guess, suspended in a tense ball of anxiety until he decided on the moment? She must speak with him, now. Persuade him, somehow, not to reveal their treachery.

In panic, she threw back the covers, struggling to hold the baby at the same time. 'I must…must…' The words blurted from Cecily's mouth. What must she do? Her brain struggled to think of a plan, of a way out of this untenable situation.

Marion's gaze flicked sharply to her daughter, sensing her wavering behaviour. She placed a hand on Cecily's shoulder, pressing down firmly, her fingers pinching through the nightgown into her flesh, preventing her from moving.

'Lachlan, come over here and see the baby.' Lord Simon beckoned to the man in the doorway.

Lachlan, she thought numbly, as the word echoed out into the heated fug of the chamber. So that was his name. The hard, lilting consonants spoke of a land far to the north, matching his wild hair and flashing blue eyes. He came over to the bed, a slight hitch to his long stride. His blue woollen surcoat stretched across his chest, ending at mid-thigh. Beneath the tunic, he wore buff-coloured woollen leggings, the cloth cut close to his legs, revealing the powerful honed muscles of his legs.

He leaned over the bed, peering down at the baby. Cecily held her breath, the air snared in her chest. She lifted her chin, tracing the firm contours of his profile. The rugged jawline, lean and raw-edged. The hollow of his cheeks beneath his high cheekbones. The generous profile of his mouth, the mouth that had claimed her own. Then he turned his head sharply, blue eyes locking with hers, a ferocious onslaught. Mocking. She flinched as if he had hit her, rearing back in to the pillows, her clammy fingers clinging desperately to the poor baby for support.

There was only one way out of this situation. She had to speak to him, in private. Her mind worked rapidly. Maybe…just maybe, she could persuade him, somehow, to keep her secret. Lifting the baby away from her chest, she pushed him into her mother's arms, throwing back the covers.

'Please forgive me, my lord,' Cecily muttered to Lord Simon, her hair swinging around her face. 'I am a little indisposed… I must visit the…er…' She allowed her sentence to drift away, hoping Lord Simon would realise that her plea was of a delicate nature. That she needed to visit the garderobe. Except that she didn't.

Lord Simon coughed, then cleared his throat, flushing heavily. 'Ah, yes, of course. Er…do you need any help?'

He was playing right into her hands. 'I am a little wobbly,' Cecily confessed, making a great show of lowering her feet to the floor and levering herself out of bed slowly, grabbing hold of the bedpost to hoist herself up.

'For God's sake, Cecily,' her mother hissed under her breath. 'What are you doing? Have some decency! Cover yourself, at least!'

'Allow me, please.' Stepping around the bed, Lachlan swept up the velvet cloak from the fur coverlet, settling the soft fabric around Cecily's shoulders. His knuckles brushed against her hair. She shivered at the brief touch, fear slicing through her like a knife blade. Nay, not fear, she realised. More a heady exhilaration, an expectant breathlessness. What in God's name was wrong with her? This man affected the very workings of her brain, sending it into disarray!

'Thank you,' she managed to say, her fingers fumbling to close the front of the cloak, to take the silken cord from one metal boss to the other. The collar was lined with fur and the feathery tips tickled her chin.

'Leave it, Cecily!' Marion snapped, her voice sharp, needling. Had her mother forgotten that she had an audience? 'Be as quick as you can, Daughter, for your baby needs you.'

'Shall I help you, my lady?' Lachlan offered.

Cecily tensed at the sarcasm in his voice. He knew what she was up to. 'Yes, yes, please,' she murmured. She flinched when he wrapped his arm solidly around hers, the heavy muscle in his forearm pressing against hers as he marched her through the door, his limp forcing his hip to bump awkwardly against hers.

The thick door swung back into place behind them, the latch rattling back into the iron bracket, and they stood together in the cool shadows of the corridor.

'That was quite a performance you gave in there,' he remarked drily, unwinding her arm from his and stepping back from her. 'I think you are perfectly capable of walking unaided.'

Her heart sank. 'I probably can,' Cecily replied faintly.

'You can.' His reply was clipped, stern. 'Please, don't bother to keep up this charade on my account.'

Ignoring him, Cecily threw him a wan smile and lurched along the corridor, deliberately making her steps slow and faltering. He watched her for a moment, a wry smile twisting his lips, before following. How much of a fool did she think he was?

Chapter Six

The long corridor was lit by rectangular windows, open to the outside, with oak frames set into the thick stone walls. As Cecily moved through narrow strips of light, the sun snared the shining length of her unbound hair, turning the pale brown to a glorious, golden mass. At last she reached the end, a wooden-planked landing. They were far enough away from the chamber not to be overheard. An arrow-slit window let in the breeze and a strip of light, shone through the rising dust motes.

Cecily turned to face Lachlan, the floorboards gritty and rough beneath her bare feet. The velvet cloak gaped open, revealing her white nightgown, diaphanous linen, beneath. Glossy ribbon ties dangled down from her ruffled neckline. She grabbed both halves of the cloak with her fingers, yanking them together, wrapping them across her stomach. Defensive.

The light green colour of her eyes turned silver in the half-light. 'I know you think the baby doesn't belong to me. But he's mine.' She fought hard to keep the betraying wobble from her voice.

Lachlan leaned back against the wall by the window, crossing his arms over his broad chest. The blue wool of his surcoat wrinkled with the movement. His manner was languid, nonchalant, sitting easily in his big frame. Self-confidence oozed from him, a knowing awareness of how their conversation would progress. 'Forgive me, my lady, but he most certainly is not.' A smile shimmered across his generous mouth.

'But I—'

'Don't treat me like an idiot.' He cut off her protest, his voice stern and sharp. 'When I pulled you from the river yesterday morning, you were not pregnant. When you sprinted away from me, faster on foot than most knights under my command, you were not pregnant. There is no way you were carrying a child.'

'You barely saw me this morning. It all happened so fast...'

'Nay!' Lachlan thumped his hand against the window frame. 'Stop pretending. Christ, look at you! How could you possibly have had a child? I doubt you have even lain with a man!'

His words slammed into her, rough and accusing. She flushed heavily at his crudeness. The jibing intimacy. Her hand fluttered upwards, touched her forehead, then her chin, a gesture of uncertainty. Was it so visible, her inexperience? The fumbled consummation of her marriage? Was it imprinted, like a red flag, across her forehead, for all to see?

'How dare you speak to me like that? You know nothing about me! And nothing about my marriage.' Drawing herself up to her full height, she braced her slim legs as if to do battle. To her chagrin, her chin barely topped his shoulder.

'I know what I've heard.' His knowing eyes drilled into her. As if he could read the truth beneath her skin. 'That you were married to Peter of Okeforde for a scarce three months, most of which he was either away, or incapacitated. I agree, you could have conceived a child in the few days after your marriage, but...' he shrugged his shoulders '...we both know that you did not. You are trying to trick Lord Simon into believing that the baby...' Lachlan jerked his calloused thumb towards the bedchamber '...is Peter of Okeforde's heir.' He pushed himself abruptly from the window, towering over her in the small space, huge, intimidating. 'And I want to know why.'

Desperation sliced through her chest: layer upon layer of compounding wretchedness. She was caught, like a rat in a trap. There was no way out of this impossible situation. She had nowhere to turn.

She shivered. 'And what will you do if I say nothing?'

'So you admit it, then.' His head jerked up.

'Yes,' Cecily replied, clamping her lips together. 'Yes, I admit it.' Was there no way out of this mess? Simon of Doccombe would drag her before the King for his judgement. Would she be hung for her crime? A grinding panic pierced deep into her chest: a barbed arrow, twisting slowly. What could she do to persuade this man to keep his mouth shut? 'Do you need money?' she blurted out suddenly. 'I can give you money.'

Lachlan's eyes glittered down at her, gilded sapphires, his mouth softening slightly. 'So now you're trying to pay me off.'

'Do you blame me? If it hadn't been for you, seeing me at the river, then we would have succeeded with this!' Cecily wound the ribbon tie of her nightgown round and round her forefinger, tightening the narrow strip of fabric until her fingertip turned white. 'My future…our future is in your hands. There must be something that you need. There must be some way I can persuade you not to tell Lord Simon.'

Her eyes rose, meeting the fiery intelligence of his expression, then dropped to trace the firm outline of his lips, the mouth that had so recently claimed hers. Her heart skittered, then raced. An idea that was so dishonourable, so outrageous, grasped her mind in such a way that she spluttered aloud with incredulity. Yet it might be the only way. The only way she could persuade him to keep silent.

'Or...' Cecily cleared her throat, curling her bare toes inward. A shiver whipped through her spine, yet her skin was clammy. 'Are you...are you married?'

Unprepared for her question, Lachlan looked up sharply, a muscle twitching in the tanned leanness of his cheek. He frowned. 'No.' His reply was blunt, stark. 'What of it?'

'Mayhap I could offer you something else.' Her voice dropped to a whisper, as if the stone walls would condemn her for what she was about to do. But as the words fell from her mouth, she realised the whole hideous wrongness of them, the blasphemy. She was not that sort of woman, a seductress. Her experience was limited, a few fumbled couplings with her husband. She clapped her hands across her mouth, her cheeks burning with embarrassment.

'Are you serious?'

'I... I...no, sorry. It was nothing.' She knotted her fingers, distorting them savagely until the skin stretched over her knuckles bone-white. 'Forget I said anything. I made a mistake.'

'Are you offering me your body…in return for my silence?' He stared down at her, incredulous, the low velvet burr of his voice echoing around the confined space. Her skin was the patina of fresh pouring cream, a lustrous, satiny texture. He folded his arms firmly across his chest. 'Do you have any idea what you are doing?' Christ, he thought, what would it be like to lie with this woman? To peel that vast, voluminous nightgown from her velvet skin, to test the sleekness of her flesh against his own?

'No…no,' Cecily stuttered out, staggering back so that her heels jabbed painfully against the stone wall, lifting her arms to ward him off, to push him away, if need be. 'I told you, I made a mistake.'

His eyes flashed over her, blue fire. A shower of sparks igniting her chest. Her breath caught in her chest, then plummeted, looping unsteadily. His pulse beat slowly in the enticing hollow of his neck, his skin honed and taut over the corded muscle. A shiver of sensation, the slow burn of excitement stacked, layer upon layer, in her belly. What was happening? She closed her eyes in shame, unwilling to look at him.

'Maybe not.' He placed one fingertip on the point where her pristine white neckline met her skin. Touched gently.

Fire shot through her, a dagger strike. The flutter of contact made her gasp, raw intimacy galloping through her veins like wildfire. Yet she did nothing. She could not move.

He traced around her neckline, up, up, to the tremulous hollow of her throat, until his hand opened, cupping her cheek. His palm was rough, the skin calloused from years of riding, yet his touch was infinitely gentle, his fingers splaying out along her delicate jaw-line. Her ribs acted like a cage, compressing the air in her lungs—she could not breathe. Her dark eyelashes drifted down, brushing the curving fullness of her cheek.

Against his fingers, her skin held the texture of fine silk. He was so tempted. It had been a long time since he had lain with a woman. He had purposely thrown himself into every battle the King offered him.

The constant fighting kept the demons of his mind at bay and stopped him thinking. Thinking about the past. It kept him sane. His eyelashes dipped. He inhaled her fine scent, the perfumed smell of roses. Lust coiled slowly: a treacherous animal awakened, pawing the ground. Waiting.

'Lachlan!'

A shout at the end of the corridor. A door opened; an iron latch clacked upwards. Lachlan's hand flew from Cecily's cheek, a reluctant retreat, and she stumbled back against the stone wall, shoulders hunching forward. A blade of sunlight cut through the window chink, striping across the velvet nap of her cloak. She lifted one shaking hand to her forehead, allowing it to drift to her ear, her chin, self-consciously, as if she were trying to hide her face from him.

'Lachlan! Where are you?' the voice demanded. 'Bring the woman back, now! Be quick!'

He stared at the slender figure pinned against the stone, the pulse at her throat bumping rapidly above the low, dipping collar of her nightgown. What in hell's name was the matter with him? Something about this woman was leading him astray: was it her delicate beauty, or the determined flare of courage he saw burning in her eyes? She seemed so alone, caught between a spiteful mother and Simon's vengeful wrath when he found out the truth. He wanted to comfort her, to turn her into his chest and hug her tightly, yet he should be marching her back to Simon with no hesitation. Logic chivvied him, yet he stamped it down.

His mind grappled with the enormity of what he should do. The consequences of the maid's actions would be huge. There was a chance she would be condemned to death for her betrayal. What a waste. As Lachlan's gaze swept over the delicate angles of her face, the lustrous curve of her bottom lip, he saw the vulnerability in her expression. The false bravado in the determined tip of her chin. It was a look he recognised. The language of his childhood after he had lost his family, after he had lost everything. Was that how she felt? How could he consign her to such a fate?

'Go on, then.' Cecily's voice was dull,

clagged with defeat. 'You'd better take me back and tell all.' Her mouth hardened in challenge, as if willing him to do his worst.

Hesitation swept over him. He was caught, between a loyal friend who he had known for years and this maid, who he had not known above a day. There should be no question about his course of action. But she forced him to pause. As if she had wrought a spell on him, scattering his senses.

'Lachlan!' the male voice was strident, hectoring, as it bounced along the stone walls of the corridor. 'Get a move on, will you?'

A muscle twitched in his jaw. Disloyalty jagged his conscience. Cecily pushed herself away from the wall, lifting her chin at a defiant angle. The smooth curtain of her hair swept beneath her chin, falling over the high curve of her breasts. She took a step forward. 'We may as well get this over with.'

Lachlan snared her forearm, strong fingers manacling her sleeve. The warmth of his fingers seared her chilled flesh. With no intention of committing the maid to her words, he grasped at the one thing that would gain him a little more time, time to find out the true circumstances of the situation. 'No.' His response was terse, hurried. 'I shall say nothing for the moment.' His eyes flicked over her, steely, determined. 'And neither will you. You have bought my silence with a promise.'

A sagging weakness gripped her knees; as she swayed, his fingers tightened on her arm: a support. Relief flooded through her. 'I... I...' she stuttered out, unable to find the words.

His eyes gleamed over her. There was no time to tell her that his intentions towards her were completely honourable. 'You can thank me later.'

The door to the bedchamber was ajar. She placed her hand on the knotted wood and pushed. After the chill of the corridor, a wall of heat hit her, thick and foetid, laced with the last clinging remnants of childbirth.

She stopped, so abruptly that Lachlan crashed into her back. His arms lifted instinctively, cupping her shoulders, steadying her for a moment before falling away.

A vast trembling seized her at the sight before her eyes.

Isabella lay in the big bed, cradling the baby, the deathly white of her skin streaked with tears. Her mother was beside her, fussing with the woollen shawl around the baby's face. At Cecily's entrance, her thin face jerked upwards, her features rigid, taut with hostility.

'She's the one you want!' her mother declared, jabbing one bony finger towards Cecily. Her cold stare swivelled around to Lord Simon. 'She dreamed the whole plan up. Threatened to turn us out with nothing if we didn't dance to her tune!'

Cecily gaped at her mother in horror. What was she saying? Her whole world tilted crazily, the ground beneath her feet wavering, unreliable. Her brain clawed at the air; she lurched back in shock into a wide, broad chest supporting her. A hand gripped her elbow, bracing her upright. Lachlan. The stranger who had been prepared to help her. For a price.

'It's not true,' she whispered. But her voice went unheard.

Simon turned stony eyes upon her. 'Now it all makes sense,' he said. 'This is the reason you've been keeping me from the castle all these months! My poor brother must be turning in his grave at your trickery. Thank God he didn't live to see this. Did you help him die, as well?'

'Nay, I did nothing to him!' Cecily's voice rose in panic, hectic colour flushing her cheeks. 'He was wounded, in France, you know that!' She threw her hands forward, a gesture of remonstration. Of protest. 'I did my best, my lord, I was at his bedside every day, changing his dressings, giving him water, feeding him.' Her voice hitched, then lowered with the memory of her husband's death. 'But the wounds were too deep; they had become infected on the journey home.'

'And then...' Marion stepped forward, her mouth tight '...when she realised that she might lose the castle because she had failed as part of her wifely duty to become pregnant, she decided to use her sister's pregnancy to dupe you, my good lord!'

Cecily's eyes flared across to her mother,

anger rising in her veins. 'Why are you doing this, Mother? It was as much your plan as mine. We are both culpable.'

'You little liar,' Marion said, her mouth clamping into a narrow line.

'Do you truly hate me that much?'

Marion flicked pale eyes over Cecily's face. *Yes*, her gaze spoke. *Yes, I truly do.*

'I would never have known if the baby hadn't started wailing,' Lord Simon said. 'You banished your poor sister, weak from childbirth, into that cold antechamber, but she heard her child. She dragged herself back through, sobbing, half-mad with the grief of being separated from her baby. My men had to help her back into the bed. How could you be so cruel?'

'It wasn't cruel!' Cecily protested. 'Isabella, my mother...we all decided on this plan together! And we would never have been forced to do this if you had left us alone! But you kept on, day after day, sending your men to intimidate us, continually petitioning the King. You forced us into this position!'

'This castle has been in my family for generations, young lady,' Simon roared at her. 'It belongs to my family, not yours! And if the King wasn't so busy fighting in France then he would have ordered you to leave and married you off to someone else.' Simon jabbed his fingers towards a cowering Isabella. 'Where is the father of that baby? What does he have to say about all this?'

'He...he died,' Cecily supplied.

'And they were married?'

'No,' she admitted.

'Hell's teeth! I cannot believe you intended some fallen knight's by-blow to inherit all this! I should send you all to the gallows for this!'

'Oh, my Lord Simon...' her mother stepped forward, her manner obsequious '...surely you can see that it was all Lady Cecily's doing?'

'No, quite frankly, I cannot,' he bit out savagely. A dull, ruddy colour flared across his gaunt cheeks. 'She must have had help. There was no way she could have carried this whole deception on her own.' He sighed heavily. 'But I am prepared to be lenient. I shall place you and Lady Isabella under house arrest, here, at the castle. Lady Cecily, however, must face the King for this and we will hear what he has to say about the whole affair. You shall all be punished, in one way, or another, make no mistake.' He flicked his gaze towards a couple of his house knights, standing by the door. 'John, Walter, take Lady Cecily to the dungeons for the night.' His lips curled in a half-smile towards Cecily. 'That should help you to realise the severity of what you have done.'

The men gripped Cecily's arms, leading her out of the chamber, down the spiral staircase, deep into the bowels of the castle. Constructed below the east tower, on the same level as the river, the thick stone walls of the dungeon seeped with water. In the light of the flickering torch, held aloft by one of the guards, the moisture gleamed, glutinous slimy green trails running down the walls. Wisps of straw, old and broken, covered the flagstones.

The iron-barred door clanged shut behind them, the key pocketed. Without a word to Cecily, the men retreated, the flaming light climbing the walls with every step until at last she stood in darkness, shivering in her velvet cloak and the thin, diaphanous material of her nightgown.

Her breath was tremulous, the air squeezing in and out of her lungs at a juddering pace. She sank to her knees on the wet, mossy flagstones, folding her body forward so that her forehead rested on her lap. And she wept. Great gasps of noisy, shuddering tears, rolling down her cheeks, spilling over her hands cupping her face. Her mother's expression, contorted with hostility, filled her mind. Horrified her. Sweet Jesu, she had never realised how much her mother hated her until now. Despair and sadness cascaded through her. Nothing had mattered to her more than winning back her mother's love after what had happened to Raymond. She had wanted it so much she had been prepared to commit a crime. Only now could she see the full error of her ways.

Lachlan's fists curled by his sides as he watched Simon's men grip Cecily's arms and lead her away. The hulking guards only served to emphasise the slim delicacy of her figure, the sheer vulnerability of her position. But as she walked past him, she lifted her chin and snared his gaze. Despite risking everything to secure her family's future, she had failed, yet he read the determination in her shimmering green eyes, the flash of steely truculence. His heart flared with recognition at her courage—she was not about to give up. Not like he had done, all those years ago.

'Coming?' Simon asked. 'Let's eat in the great hall.' He glanced at Marion, at Isabella and the baby in the bed. 'I will have some food sent up for you two, but you will not leave this chamber, do you understand? A guard will be posted at the door.'

Sitting on the low stool by the bed, Marion pursed her lips. Nodded.

'And what about Lady Cecily?' Lachlan asked, tilting his head in question.

Drawing his dark brows together, Simon scowled. 'She can go without this evening. That should teach her to try and outwit me.'

'That seems hardly fair, when these two are allowed to eat.' Lachlan thought of Cecily, curled into a tight little ball in the dungeon, hungry, shivering with cold. Despite what she had done, this was no way to treat her.

'Why are you so bothered?' Simon narrowed his brown eyes towards his friend. 'She means nothing to you; she's a chit of no consequence.'

Wrong, thought Lachlan. *I think of her all the time. Her green eyes and quick smile stalk my thoughts.* He shrugged his shoulders, forcing himself to appear uninterested. He didn't want Simon asking him any searching questions. 'I think you should treat her the same as the others.' He flicked his gaze over to the bed. 'You've sent her to the dungeons; the least you can do is provide her with food and warm clothing.'

'You're becoming soft in your old age, Lachlan.' Simon laughed at him, clapping him around the back and walking towards the door with him. 'All right, I shall have one of the guards take food and clothing down to her.'

'I will do it,' Lachlan found himself saying.

Simon stared at him, his mouth dropping

open with astonishment. Lachlan shrugged his shoulders. 'You know what your men are like, Simon. Who's to say one of them won't take advantage of her?'

'Lachlan, you astonish me. You are the same Lachlan, aren't you, who charges head first into battle, who wields his sword with infinite dexterity, dispatching adversaries with a swift, practised flick? Why are you bothered what happens to her? Since when did you become so caring?'

Since I pulled a green-eyed angel from the tumbling river, thought Lachlan. *Since then.*

Chapter Seven

Nerves jangling, Cecily lurched to full consciousness. Panic bolted through her, scything her soft flesh; her heart raced. What had woken her? A tiny noise, a rustling perhaps? God in Heaven, was it a rat? Opening her eyes, she saw nothing. Only a thick dark space, black and suffocating, that cloaked her in immediate despair. Her muscles ached from the cramped position in which she had fallen asleep; pins and needles tingled uncomfortably in her legs. She rose to her feet, wriggling her toes, trying to mitigate the feeling.

Someone was coming. Footsteps approached: resolute, determined. Not close, but descending the steps purposefully. The sound that had woken her. She took a deep, shaky breath, stretching her neck to one side, then the other; raising her arms up in the air to exercise the taut muscles in her shoulders. The time had come to stop feeling sorry for herself. The time had come to fight. Her mother did not love her and nothing Cecily could do was ever going to bring that love back. The realisation was harsh, but she had to acknowledge the truth. Self-pity would not help her now and it certainly would not help her to escape her current predicament.

Quickly, Cecily crouched on all fours, crawling, her hand splaying out over the floor to locate something, anything, which she could use as a weapon. Her nose wrinkled in disgust as she encountered slimy stones, unidentifiable debris. Her fingers grazed a pile of loose stones that had fallen out of the wall. A single stone could be a weapon, of sorts. Hoisting a heavy lump to her shoulder, she positioned herself behind the iron gate, waiting. She had nothing left to lose.

The footsteps were close now. Whoever was coming down the steps carried no light with them. Good, she thought. The darkness would conceal her actions. Her blood picked up speed.

A key rattled in the lock and the handle turned. The gate pushed inwards with a clanking squeak and a dark shape moved into the dungeon.

Lifting her arm high, Cecily lunged forward, bringing the stone down with the full force of her arm. Yet before the stone had even started its downward arc, her forearm was caught, snared in a vice-like grip.

'Don't kill me.' It was him. Lachlan. His husky voice stole through her tense body, a gentle invasion. He towered over her, eyes sparkling in his shadowed face. His breath fanned her cheek. 'I come in peace.'

He released her and Cecily sagged back, the stone dropping from her fingers, hitting the dirt floor with a thud. 'What are you doing here?'

'I thought you might need some clothes,' Lachlan announced gruffly. A faint colour dusted the tops of his high cheekbones; his words seemed so intimate, too personal. He was treading new territory here; his life up to now had held no softness, just a headlong cacophony of barked orders; the sickening clash of swords. 'Some food, as well, if you're hungry.' His gaze swept around the dank horrible space, the generous lines of his mouth tightening. It was not right that she had been locked here, when her mother and sister had the luxury of their chamber.

'Why?' Cecily's voice jolted out, suspiciously. Had he come for something else, as well? She took a step back. Her mouth burned with the memory of his kiss in the cellar and she touched her fingers to her lips, wrapping her arms tightly across her middle. Her breath billowed out, a white mist in the chill. 'You are loyal to Lord Simon, are you not? He's your friend. Does he know that you're down here?'

'He knows,' Lachlan replied. He shifted his weight slightly. 'Your mother and sister are allowed food, so why not you?'

'How considerate of you,' Cecily's voice wavered sarcastically. 'To think of my well-being at a time like this. You could have sent a servant down to check on me. There was no need for you to come. It makes no sense.' She paused, waiting for an explanation.

No, Lachlan thought. *It makes no sense at all.* Yet something about the maid drew him constantly, made him reluctant to leave her. By rights he should be thinking about heading north; the pain in his leg had reduced to a dull ache, scarcely hindering him. But the thought of galloping north, alone, while Cecily was marched towards the King, her outcome unknown, filled him with dread.

He cleared his throat. Her hair was the colour of frosted sand. The long glossy ropes fell like a curtain of tumbled silk, framing the sweet oval of her face. A luminous pearl shining out from the darkness.

'It isn't like you to be short of words,' Cecily pronounced waspishly, sensing his hesitation. 'Tell me, why have you come down here? Why have you brought me these things?' She pinned him with her sharp green gaze.

Uneasiness flowed through him. How could he explain himself? She was the prisoner of his friend and she was in the wrong, yet he wanted to protect her. Lachlan thought for a moment. 'I'm not saying I approve of what you have done,' he said slowly, 'but I do feel responsible for this… the situation that you're in now. I told Simon how I pulled you from the river and he realised that you must have come from this castle. That's why he was outside with his men, when the baby was born. He sent me inside, to find out what was happening.' Placing the heap of clothes on the floor, with the food wrapped in cloth placed on top, he took out a short piece of steel and a flint, a stub of candle from the leather pouch attached to his waist belt.

'You feel…responsible?' Incredulous, Cecily glared at him. 'Why on earth do you even care?'

Was that what it was? Did he care? It was a long time since he had felt any emotion, his heart blunted by what had happened in the past. He couldn't explain the feeling, the feeling of wanting to protect her, to make sure that she would be safe, despite what she had done. Was Simon correct? Was the maid making him go soft?

The silence stretched between them. Twisting her fingers in the corded tie of her velvet cloak, Cecily shivered slightly. Why would he not answer?

She cleared her throat. 'You're right, you are partly responsible. But Lord Simon would have barged in anyway, whether you were with him or not, and who's to say that Isabella would not have rushed out when I was still lying in the bed with the baby? You were not going to tell Lord Simon…remember?' A ray of hope flowered in her chest. Would Lachlan be able to help her?

He nodded. 'Yes, it was just after you offered me your body, if I remember rightly.' One side of his mouth tipped up in a wry smile.

'I was in an impossible situation.' Cecily wound her arms tightly across her belly. 'I was desperate.'

Lachlan laughed. The sound was big, gusty, all-encompassing, filling the small, cramped space with a sense of light, frivolity. 'You must have been, to want to lie with the likes of me.' Kneeling down, he placed a small bundle of dry moss on the stone floor. He struck the flint along the steel. Sparks jumped, arcing out into the gloom, catching the moss and turning the bundle into flame. He touched the stub of candle into the flaming ball and the wick caught light.

Cecily stared at the fine wool of his tunic stretched across the muscled breadth of his shoulders, the ridged sinew in his strong fingers as he lit the candle and thought *I want to. I want to lie with you.* Mortification rushed through her and she turned her hot face away to study the darkness.

'I wanted to secure my family's future.' Her voice emerged jerkily. 'We would have been homeless otherwise. Lord Simon was petitioning the King constantly and one day, the King would have listened and demanded that the estate be given to him. I wouldn't be the first widow for that to happen to.'

'I must say, your family don't seem very appreciative of your efforts,' Lachlan raised his blue eyes to hers. 'Your mother barely looks at you. When she does, she stares at you with such hatred. Why did you agree to go through with this charade if this is all the thanks that you get?'

How could she tell him that she wanted her mother to love her again, to forgive her for what happened with Raymond all those years ago? It sounded so ridiculous. Self-pitying. She fiddled with the collar of her cloak, her fingers restless. 'My mother and I have...we don't have an easy relationship. I did this because I wanted her to change her mind about me. To think well of me again.' Cecily lifted her chin in the air, her expression bleak. 'But obviously I failed.'

'Why does she hate you so much?' Tipping the candle, Lachlan dripped a puddle of molten wax on to the floor. He stuck the candle into the hardening wax. The flame cast a weak circle of light over the dismal surroundings, wavering dangerously in the chill draughts that seemed to ooze from the walls. The thick chunks of stone gleamed with moisture, slick and smeared with a greenish decay.

'It was something that happened a long time ago.' Cecily clamped her lips together, unwilling to elaborate. The candlelight flickered over her wan features, her dark eyelashes casting spiky shadows above her limpid eyes. If she voiced her guilt, she would surely weep and she had no wish to reveal such vulnerability. Besides, this man, this warrior with his flame-red hair who had burst so unexpectedly into her life would not be remotely interested in her woes. Her mind scrabbled to change the subject and her gaze fell on the wrapped parcels he had brought. 'Did you bring food?'

'So your mother forced you to do it?' Lachlan undid the knot that secured the cloth parcel of food, his fingers deft, quick, laying back the edges of the cloth, the enticing smell of bread and cheese filling the small space. Her stomach growled.

'No! She used everything she could to persuade me, but in the end I did it willingly. I thought we would get away with it. Yes, it was a risk. But surely you would do the same? You would do anything to help your family, wouldn't you?'

Her words stabbed at him. His brain reeled. He wanted to shout at her. *Nay, I did nothing to help my family. I stood on the hillside like a snivelling coward, shaking in my boots!* Lachlan's eyes hollowed out, black pits of despair. He scrabbled for equilibrium. To push away the memories of that day: the plumes of black smoke, the war cries of the Macdonald clan as they burned his home. If only he had shouted out a warning. He had done nothing for his family that day, nothing at all. And then it had been too late.

'Wouldn't you?' Cecily persisted. Lachlan's head knocked back as if she had hit him. She saw the way he tensed his muscles, the sudden iciness of his expression. Lachlan tore at the bread rolls, segmenting them into smaller pieces and then into smaller pieces, crumbled across the linen cloth. Oh, God, what had she said? 'I'm sorry,' she muttered. 'Maybe…maybe you…' Her voice trailed away. 'I've said the wrong thing.' In consternation, she pressed her palm to her forehead, wondering what she had said.

'I have a family.' Lachlan's voice was cold. He thought of his uncle, Duncan, who had come up from the south to rescue him after that awful day and had brought him up as his own son. He owed that man so much.

Cecily read the hurt, the rawness in his eyes. She sensed him drawing away, distancing himself from her. The ease of their conversation vanished; she wished she could take back her words. Had something happened to his family that he felt unable to talk about?

'Lachlan?' Taking a step forward, Cecily sank to her knees opposite him. She stretched out her hand, laid it gently on his sleeve. 'I'm sorry if I've upset you.'

'You haven't. It's nothing.' His dark eyes were blank as he churned out the answer. The black turmoil clagged his heart, but he felt the gentleness of her hand upon his sleeve, drew comfort from it. Her presence softened the hacked edges of his grief, lifting him from the hell of his own mind. He threw her a terse smile. 'Will you eat?'

Cecily picked up a piece of bread roll. The loose flour dusted her fingers. 'Thank you.' She took a quick couple of bites, chewing hungrily.

'Why don't you tell me everything from the beginning?' he suggested. The rugged angles of his face shimmered in the candlelight. 'Then maybe I might be able to help you.'

She searched his face, the defined contours of his beautiful mouth, the dip of shadow above his top lip, as if someone had left a permanent finger-mark in the middle of his mouth. 'If you want to help me, Lachlan, then let me walk out of this castle now, right now. And I would go, disappear, and no one would ever find me.' Exhaustion dulled her voice.

And I would never see you again. Is that what he wanted?

The candle flame danced, flickered in the draught that sidled down the dungeon steps.

'Don't be naive.' Lachlan stuck one hand through his hair, leaving fronds sticking up haphazardly. It made him look younger, softening the hard angles of his face. 'Lord Simon would hunt you down, like a dog. And he would find you. You would definitely lose your life for that.'

Cecily stood up, so abruptly that the hem of her nightgown swept over the flame, dousing it. 'But surely it's worth taking the chance? At least I would have tried.' Her voice echoed into the sudden darkness, clear and melodic. 'Instead of being led, like a lamb to the slaughter.'

Lachlan struck the flint and lit the candle

once more. One long leg was bent upward; his arm rested upon his knee. 'You might buy a few more months of freedom, but you would be continually on the run, never settling. Do you really want to live like that?'

'What other choice do I have?' she said, nibbling at her nail. 'Let me go, Lachlan. I will survive.'

He stared up at her, at her slim, upright figure, at the assured, confident set of her neat head and thought, *Yes, you, of all people, might just manage.* Every bone in her body, every muscle and ligament sang out with an undaunted courage, a determination and hope that would carry her onwards.

Yet he also knew how cruel Simon could be. How relentless.

'I cannot let you go; I'm sorry. Simon is my friend and I owe him a certain loyalty. But I will talk to him on the morrow. Leave this with me and don't do anything stupid.'

Lord Simon liked to break his fast early. Not long after the sun peeked over the horizon, he marched into the great hall at Okeforde, his childhood home, and swept his gaze over his sleeping knights. Most of them had bedded down on the floor around the fire, rolled into the blankets provided by the castle servants. They had rushed about, preparing food and drink, all anxious to impress their new lord. Simon smirked. He remembered some of them from his childhood. How assiduous they all were now, worried about their positions within the household. Christ, it was good to be back here.

Moving around the hall, he prodded his boot into the flank of every sleeping man, nudging them awake. As they groaned and yawned, Simon leapt on to the high dais, flinging himself into the oak chair, the very chair his father had sat in when he had been a child, sat back and smiled.

'You look very pleased with yourself.' Lachlan strode into the great hall. The icy breath of morning clung to his clothes, his high cheekbones ruddy from the cold.

Simon lifted his chin, acknowledging his friend. 'I am,' he replied. 'And you have helped me to sort out this sorry mess. I thank you for that, my friend. Come...' he held out his hand '...come and help me break my fast.' He scanned the bare tablecloth, briefly irritated, then clicked his fingers at one of his men. 'Go and find someone to bring us some food. And you—' he pointed at another man '—throw some sticks on that miserable fire.' The fire in the grate had burned down to a smouldering pile of ashes, with only the smallest chink of visible orange glow.

'Where have you been?' Simon leaned forward to rest his elbows on the tablecloth, watching Lachlan climb the wooden stairs up to the dais.

'Outside,' Lachlan replied, flinging himself into the chair next to his friend. 'I thought I would check on the horses. I wanted to make sure they had been fed.'

'Good idea,' replied Simon. 'Although I don't intend to travel today. There's too much to sort out here. Only two or three horses will be needed to take Lady Cecily to the King. Two men, I think, to escort her and she can be led on a horse. She can ride, if my memory serves me correctly.

Her name on Simon's lips pierced him like an arrow. Lachlan shifted uncomfortably in his seat. His sleep the previous night had been restless, disturbed, beset with vivid images of her. The slender whip of her body pressed against his as he pulled her from the river, the translucent green of her eyes as she glanced at him. The ash-brown colour of her hair. He wondered how she had spent the night after he had left her, down in that cold, dark cell.

'...don't you think?' Simon was saying. 'Wake up, Lachlan! It's not like you to be half-asleep!'

'Sorry... I beg your pardon?' Lachlan dragged his mind back to the present, to Simon's loud voice rapping at him.

A servant appeared, carrying a tray covered with a cloth. Moving along the front of the table, he placed it before the two men, removing the cloth with a flourish. Bread rolls, slices of meat and cheese, and two bowls of steaming porridge were revealed. Another servant arrived with a jug of mead, plates and goblets.

Simon eyed the food, then switched his gaze back to Lachlan. 'I was talking about the woman... Lady Cecily. Do you think that's a good idea? Two men to escort her to the King? Would she try to escape, do you think?'

He remembered how she had struggled against him as he carried her from the river, how she had sprinted away from him when he had told her to stop. The determined quirk of her mouth when she asked him to let her walk out of the dungeon. *Oh, yes*, Lachlan thought. *She would definitely try to escape.*

'She would be easily caught, if she tried anything. I think two men will be enough.'

Lachlan's heart burst with a pang of despair, of loss, at the thought of her running away, running for her freedom, pursued by two of Simon's thuggish house knights. 'I wanted to talk to you about Lady Cecily,' he said, fixing his friend with his bright blue eyes. 'I will take her to the King for you. I wouldn't trust her with your men.'

'Oh, Lachlan, I couldn't ask you to do that.' Lifting up an earthenware pot, Simon spooned honey into his porridge. The golden liquid oozed over the steaming surface, glistening. 'I thought you would stay a few more days with me, help me sort things out here.'

'I must head home, Simon. My leg is almost better. I am certain I can ride longer distances now. And the King will be in Exancaester in a few days. If I start heading north with Lady Cecily, then we can meet him there.' To his surprise, a faint line of sweat appeared around the collar of his tunic— what would he do if Simon disagreed? She would be safer this way. With him.

Simon compressed his mouth, thinking. 'I suppose... I suppose that does make sense, but...are you sure, Lachlan? I mean, surely you would rather someone else escorted her? It's a massive imposition on you.'

No, it's not, he thought. *Thank God.* At least this way she would be safe. He could protect her. He shovelled another spoonful of porridge into his mouth. 'I will take the road north, anyway. What difference would it make, taking her with me?' But as the words left his mouth, he knew he was lying to himself. It would make all the difference in the world.

As the chapel bell tolled six times, one of Simon's household knights came into the dungeon to fetch her. A young lad, who averted his eyes respectfully as Cecily struggled awkwardly to her feet. Her eyes were crusty, blurred from lack of sleep; her muscles cramped and chilled. She bent down to pick up her nightgown, crumpled into a bundle on the floor. She had changed into the clothes that Lachlan had brought: a slim-fitting dress of pale lilac wool and a looser, sleeveless over-gown of a deeper purple, embroidered around the hem with a silver thread. She had plaited her hair into two braids, securing the ends with thin ribbons from her nightgown. Pulling on woollen stockings, she wriggled her cold toes inside the leather slippers. Her heart twisted with Lachlan's thoughtfulness; he had come down to the dungeon of his own accord to give her food and clothing. It was the first time anyone had shown her kindness in a very long time.

Twitching her skirts so as not to trip, she followed the young man up from the darkness of the dungeons. As they emerged into the open air, into the breeze of the shadowed gatehouse, she staggered, blinking hurriedly, squinting in the bright light. Water streamed from her eyes, coursing down her cheeks.

A hollow fear entered her heart as she followed him across the inner bailey, through a thick-curtained arch and into the great hall. Here, she would learn her fate. Learn what Lord Simon planned to do with her. A tiny pinprick of hope needled her: hope that lay in the form of a giant of a man, with tousled bronze hair and brilliant blue eyes. Her heart lifted with possibility.

Eight large windows in the great hall flooded the enormous space with daylight. Greyish-white plaster covered the double-height walls, stopping at the point where the heavy wooden trusses arched inwards to support the roof. Colourful woven tapestries depicting the many conquests and victories of the Okeforde family hung down from horizontal wooden poles at intervals along the wall. The familiar trestle tables sat in rows before the high dais, the fire burned dully in the grate, puffing out desultory grey smoke.

She eyed Simon's knights, sitting along the trestle tables, laughing, talking to each other, digging into the food no doubt sorted out by

Martha or one of the other servants. Strange how this task, that of organising the kitchens to provide food for the castle inhabitants, had been removed from her hands, alongside all the other countless jobs she dealt with on a daily basis. Isabella had been a great help before she became confined by her pregnancy, but her mother had done little to help her in the management of the estate.

'Keep moving,' the house knight urged her on, reminding her that she must walk forward. He took her elbow and dragged her past the trestle tables to a spot below the high dais.

He was there. Lachlan. Sitting next to Lord Simon, talking to him, in between mouthfuls of porridge. Shock tingled through her. Clad in his dark blue surcoat, the colour emphasising the brilliant red-gold of his hair, he formed a startling, dramatic contrast to his friend, with his brown hair and watery, insipid eyes.

Lord Simon stood up, leaned over the table. His chair scraped across the wooden boards as his calf muscles pushed back against it. His voice was quiet, but strangely menacing, every word that he uttered pulling her further and further down into the depths of despair. 'Today, you will begin your journey to the King, young lady, and he can decide what punishment to mete out for the crime you have committed.' He lifted a roll of parchment, secured with a red wax seal. 'Within this document I have written the full details of what you have done, for the King's eyes only.' He handed the roll to Lachlan. 'You keep that safe, Lachlan.'

Her heart flared, a volatile mix of fear shot through with excitement. Was this Lachlan's solution to her situation? What was he planning to do with her? Take her to the King, or maybe would he let her go? Cecily's head spun.

Lord Simon stood back from the table, his hands resting on his hips. 'She's all yours.' He slapped him on the back. 'Make sure the little chit doesn't outwit you, like she almost did with me.'

Lachlan grinned. 'I don't think she will be a problem.' His hot glance ran the length of Cecily's slender frame and she pulled herself straighter beneath his penetrating look, meeting his gaze boldly.

'I owe you for this,' Simon continued. 'John and Walter can ride alongside you; you'll need some protection on the roads and you can take them further on with you, to travel north, if you like.'

Lachlan grinned, smoothing his hand across the wine-spotted tablecloth. 'It's not that bad, Simon. You speak as if the north is a lawless hell-hole.'

'Isn't it?'

'No. It is my homeland.' Scraping the remnants of porridge from his bowl, Lachlan laid down his spoon, wiped his mouth with a linen napkin and stood up. 'You two,' he said, pointing at the knights who waited below the top table, 'go down to the stables and saddle up four horses.' He turned his bright eyes to Cecily. 'Are you ready to leave?'

Cecily jutted her chin in the air, clasping her hands across her stomach. 'Yes, yes, I am. But can I say farewell to my mother and sister, before I go?'

'I will send someone to bring your mother

down when you leave,' Simon replied, running one hand through his dark hair. 'She can bring anything she thinks necessary for your journey.'

'Thank you,' Cecily replied.

Then suddenly, Lachlan was beside her, his vibrant hair burning like a flame, catching the light in its glistening strands. 'Let's go.'

Chapter Eight

In the watery light of morning, the sun hazed by floating ribbons of dark cloud, Marion's angular figure appeared between two house knights at the top of the stone steps, the main entrance to the castle, her white face pinched and rigid. She hunched her shoulders against the chill wind, holding a leather satchel. The breeze tugged at her skirts, pulling the rich material aside to reveal her bony ankles.

'It was not my choice to come down.' Marion's voice was rigid, censorious. 'Lord Simon insisted upon it.' She clutched the leather satchel like a talisman, as if reluctant to hand it over. Her mouth clamped into a tight line. 'And Isabella begged me to come and say goodbye. To give you her good wishes. I've packed some things for you.' The gold embroidery on Marion's pale blue gown twinkled in the weak winter sun. Against the dark heavy wood of the door, she appeared like a glorious butterfly shining out between the two house knights in their understated livery.

In the cobbled yard of the bailey below the stable lad was saddling the horses with Lachlan. Cecily lifted her gaze at the sound of her mother's voice, squinting in the harsh light. Her hood was drawn up over her plaits, the bulky dark blue wool framing the delicate lines of her face. She glanced around at Lachlan, tightening the girth straps on his stallion, tracing the impressive breadth of his shoulders as he bent down beside the big animal. 'Can I go up…and say goodbye to my mother? She has brought down a bag for me.'

'Go on up,' he replied quietly, as the stable lad handed him the reins. His woollen cloak hung in soft gathers from his wide shoulders to his knees, the cloth secured with a wooden toggle at his neck.

Lifting her skirts, Cecily climbed the shallow steps, the flat stone chipped in places, mottled with patches of dark green moss. She held out her hand for the bag her mother held, clearing her throat. 'Thank you. How are Isabella and the baby this morning?'

'They are doing well,' her mother replied tersely. 'Although she is exhausted, poor mite.' Marion stared pointedly at Cecily's loose braids, hanging down across the open front of her cloak. 'You need to do your hair,' she hissed. 'There's a veil and circlet in that bag for you, hairpins, too. Make sure you use them.' She turned away.

Cecily reached out, scuffing her fingers against her mother's elbow, stalling her. 'Tell me where William is, Mother. What happened to him after we left Crekelade?'

Her mother narrowed her eyes. 'Ah, yes, William. I had forgotten.' Marion's mouth curled with contempt. 'You know I never like your friendship with him.'

Cecily jutted her chin in the air, ignoring her mother's harsh tone. 'Tell me.'

'He went east, towards Dornceaster. Your father sent a letter of recommendation to the Duke of Montague, but I am not certain he is there now.' The wind tugged at Marion's veil, blowing the flimsy material across her thin face.

Relief sifted through her. William was someone she could trust. If she needed help, then at least now she knew where to go. Where to run. William would hide her. From her elevated position on the steps, Cecily stared down at Lachlan's imposing frame as he stepped forward to take the bridle of her dappled mare. But maybe she wouldn't need to run. Lachlan had promised to talk to Lord Simon after he had left the dungeon last night. This flame-haired warrior might be able to help her, after all.

Cecily placed her foot in the knight's interlaced fingers and sprang lightly on to the side-saddle. With practised ease, she twisted her leg in order to hook her right knee around the pommel, giving her a secure seat. Leaning down, she shook out the voluminous cloth of her skirts to fall in a graceful arc over her legs and gathered up the reins. Her mare nickered gently in recognition of her mistress. The stable lad pulled out the back of her woollen cloak so the material spread over her mare's rump.

Lachlan sprang into his own saddle, the stitches in his leg pulling slightly with the movement. He twitched his reins to bring his horse alongside her own. 'Ready to go?' His knee bumped against her rounded thigh.

Sensation flared through her at the fleeting touch. 'As ready as I'll ever be.' Her eyes swept up the steps, but her mother had disappeared, the door firmly shut. She turned her head sharply away, focusing on the track that ran down the steep hill from the castle.

They rode away, away from Okeforde, the place that had been her home for the last year. Had it only been twelve months since she had been married and widowed? It felt like a lifetime. As her horse plodded carefully down the steep stony track towards the river and the village, an unusual feeling swirled through her: a sensation of weightlessness. The burden of responsibility eased away from her strained limbs, her muscles tense from lying to everyone for so long. The truth was out; she had nothing to hide any more. She was Lachlan's prisoner, but curiously she felt free.

'What was your mother talking to you about?' Lachlan tilted back in his saddle as his horse picked his way through the loose stones. The stiff breeze riffled his flaming hair, pressing the fiery strands back from his forehead, revealing the strong profile of his face, the high cheekbones.

'About...?' She would not tell him about William, about her refuge. For if he knew she had a place to go, to hide, then he would keep a much closer eye upon her. Better he thought that she was vulnerable, with nowhere to go. Alone.

'She looked so angry with you.' His piercing blue eyes narrowed with curiosity. 'She was not sad to see you go. Maybe you would tell me now why she hates you so?'

Her mare pitched forward awkwardly and stumbled. Cecily clutched the pommel, steadying herself, trying to regain her balance. Considering the fate that lay before her, did she have anything to lose by talking to Lachlan? Nothing she said now would make the King's ultimate sentence any worse. It was bad enough already.

'It's a long story,' she mumbled.

He shrugged his shoulders, his gaze drifting to the far horizon, the wide rolling moorland stretching away into the distance. A few trees, gnarled and bent over by the force of the wind, dotted the landscape; long, bleached moor grass dominated. 'We have time,' he said. 'We have at least a day of riding to Exancaester.'

Her spine sagged. 'She hates me because…' She stared bleakly at Lachlan, as if scouring his face for a way of putting what had happened into words. His expression was neutral, neither overly sympathetic nor judgemental. She looked away quickly, down at the frothing mane of her grey mare.

'Because…?'

'Because I caused the death of my younger brother.' There, she had said it. Cecily waited for the shock, the condemnation on Lachlan's face, but saw neither.

He watched the shadows dull her beautiful eyes. 'What happened?'

Cecily chewed on her bottom lip, staring

at the wind-whipped trees ahead, the rippling strands of long grass, a buttery yellow colour. She sighed. 'It happened many years ago. When we lived at Crekelade. My childhood home,' she added, by way of clarification.

'To the east of here?'

'Yes, it's further on from Exancaester.'

If they kept going in this direction, she thought, they would eventually reach it. A fortified manor house built from a warm yellow stone, set in acres of fertile pasture and woodland. When the weather was good she and her brother and sister would play outside, running through the gardens, the woods, the fields. Her heart twisted with memory. Until her brother's death, when it had all stopped.

She wrinkled her nose, considering, wondering how to put into words what had happened that day. Her gaze ran over the two knights riding in front of them, every tiny link of their chainmail glinting in sunlight. They wore helmets and carried swords and shields, adequately armed against any attack.

Her thumb rubbed at the worn leather on her reins. 'There was an accident.' She spoke so softly that he leaned sideways in his saddle to catch her words.

They had reached the path that ran on a level beside the river towards the village. A stand of pines marked the crossroads, their frilly silhouettes starkly green against the washed blue sky. Wind roared through the top of the trees, leaves skittering on the track. The knights up front turned right, heading towards the huddle of cottages in the distance, the bridge that they would cross towards the open moorland. Smoke rose in thin trails from the thatched roofs.

'It happened in the winter. The pond had frozen solid, a thick layer of ice on top.' Cecily turned her horse in unison with Lachlan, memories crowding in. 'A clear blue sky, sunshine. Isabella was not well, so she stayed inside.' God in Heaven, how she wished they had stayed inside that day, as well.

She shivered in her cloak, hunkering down in the saddle. The cold seeped into her muscles, numbing her movements, making her limbs feel stiff, unresponsive. Her eyes held a haunted look. Lachlan itched to reach out, to touch her, gather her in his arms. But instead he waited. He could not force her to tell him, but he wanted her to. Because with every word she uttered he began to understand her, just a little bit more. Understand why she had agreed to enter into this mad deception with her mother and her sister.

Dropping the reins, she rubbed her fingers together, trying to warm them. 'I was out, playing with my younger brother, Raymond, by the pond. He wanted to slide across the ice. I told him...' Her voice wobbled with emotion. 'I told him the ice wasn't thick enough.' Her voice pitched higher. 'I told him that. I told him not to go. But he wouldn't listen.' Her teeth began to chatter. Emotion welled in her chest: great, heaving waves of loss, of the grown-up brother she had never had. 'He ran out into the middle before I could grab him, turning to laugh at me. Then the ice cracked open and he disappeared.' A sob tore through her voice. 'I lay down flat upon the ice and pushed my hand down into that freezing water and I tried to pull him out. But it was too late.'

At least you tried, thought Lachlan. He reached over and said, 'I'm sorry.' He curled his big hand over her knuckles, squeezing gently. His cheeks were a dusty red, whipped raw by the relentless wind.

Tears ran down her cheeks and she dashed them away angrily, forcing herself to school her features, to train them into some semblance of normality. 'That's the reason why my mother treats me as she does. She blames me for ruining her life. She wishes it were me who had fallen that day, not Raymond. When my father died, we lost the castle, because my brother was the only male heir on our side of the family. I thought, I thought, by doing this...' she waved her arm angrily back towards the moor '...by pretending to be pregnant to keep my husband Peter's castle, I thought... I thought she would love me again. But I was wrong. She is never, ever going to forgive me for what happened to my brother.' Cecily clamped her lips together, embarrassed. She had said too much, blurting out her life history.

His hand continued to cup her knuckles,

warm, nurturing. 'So you took a risk to win back your mother's love. But it didn't work.'

'Thank you for pointing that out.' Using the back of her free hand, Cecily smeared the tears across her cheek. His fingers tightened around hers, strong and powerful. His nails, broad and flat, were clipped short; the pads of his fingers were rough. A deep sigh welled up from her chest and she sniffed, tugging her hand away and rubbing violently at her nose. 'So now you know.' Cecily threw him a tight little smile. 'I suppose you think I'm pathetic for doing such a thing.'

Not pathetic, Lachlan thought. Cecily was the complete opposite of pathetic. Pathetic was a word he associated with the simpering wenches who hung around the royal court, who wouldn't lift a finger to help themselves. Nay, Cecily was strong and determined. Clever. Even now, she was not bowed by her experience. She rode beside him, her figure graceful, narrow, straight and upright in the saddle.

'I think nothing of the sort.' His eyes flared with a grudging admiration. 'Foolish and rash, maybe. But not pathetic.'

'Thank you,' she said, her generous mouth tipping up at the corners. For some reason, her chest swelled with his faint praise, seizing his words like a talisman. She leaned forward eagerly in the saddle, adjusting her seat. 'So, now we're away from the castle, tell me your plan.'

'My plan?' Lachlan frowned.

'Yes,' Cecily said eagerly. 'Remember, you said you would talk to Lord Simon. That you might be able to help me...?'

'I did talk to him. This is the result.'

'What...you escorting me?' Cecily gaped at him, damping down the fear trickling through her chest. 'That is the plan? I thought you were going to let me go!'

'No, Cecily,' he replied calmly. 'I'm not going to let you go.'

'Why not?' she cried at him. 'You must have something better to do, surely?'

'I do,' Lachlan replied. 'I need to go home, to my uncle and his family. They live to the north of Exancaester. They will be anxious to see me; I have been away in France for a long time. And then, after that...' His voice dropped away. He had no wish to tell of the details of what would follow. The long ride north, the battle that must be carried out in order to avenge his family. It needed to be done for him to have any chance at a proper life. A life without torment.

'Then why don't you go?' Cecily studied Lachlan's craggy profile, the bright fronds of his hair sharply contrasted with his blue tunic and cloak, the dulling of his gimlet eyes. So he had family, of sorts, she thought. She wondered what had happened to his parents. 'These two can take me to the King.' She flung her arm out in the direction of the two knights. 'At least that way I would have had a chance of escaping.'

'Don't you think I don't know that? Listen, Cecily, it's much safer this way. Going on the run is not a good idea. Especially with the mood that Simon is in.'

'So you are taking me to the King,' she cried, outraged. 'My God, I thought you were going to help me!'

'Shhh, keep your voice down. It's better this way. Believe me when I say that I'm trying to protect you.'

'Well, I don't need your protection,' Cecily replied huffily. 'I can look after myself. I've done it for long enough.'

He heard the note of loneliness echo through her tone and wondered at it. She had been surrounded by people at the castle, but who among them had actually cared for her? Looked out for her? Not her family, that much was certain. Not her husband, either, from what he had heard.

'Why don't you let someone look after you for a change?'

Her head whipped around, her green eyes blazing. 'Who do you suggest? Because I cannot think of one person who would do that for me.'

I can, he thought.

He wanted to be there when she met the King. He wanted to be with her. What did he think he was going to do? Plead for her innocence, beg for leniency? Yes, he would do all those things, and more, because he had no wish to see her die, whatever crime she had committed.

They rode all day. Mile after mile, trapped between the knights at the front and Lachlan either beside or behind her, Cecily plodded along on her little grey mare, her limbs gradually solidifying in the icy weather. At some point, Lachlan had handed her a bread roll and she had clutched at it clumsily, forcing her arm to lift the food to her mouth, chewing methodically.

On leaving Okeforde, riding through the town, they had followed a track up on to the moor, a vast expanse of high grassland, where the wind had been strong and fierce, tearing at their cloaks and the horses' tails. Tussocks of grass, bleached to a pale straw colour, were flattened into the soggy ground. It had been impossible to speak or hold a conversation. Words tore away before they had a chance to be heard. The path, reduced to a narrow trail of bare earth, had stretched away into the distance, edges softened with clumps of bright yellow gorse and heather.

Now, bulky grey clouds gathered to the east, obscuring any memory of the sunlit morning. The light became shadowed, crepuscular. They were following a path along a river, the water tumbling haphazardly against the stones. Oak trees gathered around them, the bare, skeletal branches rising up the valley sides, frilling against the grey sky. Beneath the trees, the light was even darker. The air was thick with the smell of dead leaves, of mushrooms and fungus, a dead, rotting scent.

Cecily drew her hands inside her cloak, her fingers unable to work the reins any longer. Her limbs were numb, frozen solid into the one position; it was uncomfortable even to move, for if she moved, the claws of ice seemed only to dig deeper, prise open the very core of her. With every step of her horse, energy leached from her, leaving her exhausted, weak. Desperately, she tried to clench her thigh muscles, to stay upright in the saddle. Were they ever going to stop and rest, these men?

A drop of ice hit Cecily's cheek, then another. Sleet rather than snow, a slushy flake, melting swiftly on her heated cheek, then running down her chin. She licked the droplets away, relishing the cool, fresh taste. The swollen, saturated clouds released a burst of icy rain and the water coursed down, soaking her face, her woollen cloak, her full skirts. The needling rain scoured her skin, a raw, painful kiss. Yet she relished the sensation, for surely, surely, these men would stop now and take some shelter? She twisted round in her saddle, the material of her wet sleeve dragging uncomfortably on her shoulder, and squinted at Lachlan, half-closing her eyes to protect them from the sluicing rain.

'Shall we stop?' Her lips moved awkwardly with the cold. 'We will be soaked through!'

Lachlan narrowed his eyes. The rain dripped off the carved angles of his square-cut jaw. 'No.' His answer was rough, abrupt, grinding into her, a drumbeat of doom. 'We have to keep riding until we lose the light, otherwise it will take us two days to Exancaester, rather than one.'

'I don't care if we take all year!' Cecily replied, irritated by his censorious tone. Her teeth chattered. 'I want to stop now. I'm freezing and I need to warm up!' Over her head, the branches swayed and clacked together. A shower of brown leaves spiralled down, spinning around her head.

Lachlan steered his horse's nose on a level

with her own. His warm breath tipped out into the rain-soaked air. 'It's not long now until sunset. Your horse is still fresh.' Drops of sleet landed on the dark wool of his cloak, white flakes that melted instantly to leave wet, irregular circles. 'Stop trying to delay us,' he muttered. 'Go on now.'

Angry at his commandeering response, Cecily wrenched back round in the saddle. So that was it. He thought she was pretending, a deliberate attempt to slow up the journey. An uncontrollable shivering gripped her body, rippling violently through her flesh.

Time condensed, then dissipated. Sleet fell sporadically; a relentless, grinding cold pierced her bones. Snared in a frozen web, Cecily lost track of time, scarcely noticing as the sky gradually inched into twilight. She pinned her eyes to the shiny chainmail of the knights in front, the flexing metal skin acting like a beacon, a lodestone, to hold her on her horse, to keep her awake. Her little mare was trustworthy and would follow the horses without any instruction from her mistress. All Cecily needed to do was stay in the saddle.

Her eyelids fluttered and drooped; Christ, how she longed for sleep. That wonderful soporific state where she could be warm and safe. A lightness danced in her head, lifting the heavy weight of her shoulders from the wretched lump of icy flesh that formed her body. Awareness dropped away; she swayed violently, then caught herself in time, lurching upright once more.

'Cecily!' a voice shouted. The sound seemed muffled, as if reaching her ears through a padded cloth.

'Hey! My lord, watch out!'

Dimly, Cecily heard the warning before she fell. A slow graceful plunge, pitching forward out of the saddle, senseless, unable to save herself. Flakes of sleet, sparkling like gemstones, spun before her vision. But before she hit the ground, she was scooped up, snared in strong arms that held her tight.

Lachlan cursed as he swept Cecily's slight figure up against his chest, one arm beneath her hips, gathering up the bulky layers of her skirts, the other cradling her slim back. Thank God he had been quick enough to catch her. He had been watching her anyway, watching the elegant tilt of her slim figure in the saddle, and saw her swaying. He had known she was about to fall, even before the young knight alerted him to the fact.

Her head rolled back against his upper arm, her eyes half-open, but hazy with confusion. Her lips were blue. Her cheeks held the translucent luminosity of a pearl, deathly white. She had become too cold. She had told him that she wanted to stop riding and had he listened? Nay, he had thought she was shamming, annoyed with him for taking her to the King. He had pushed her too far.

'Cecily, wake up!' His harsh tone jagged into her, jolting her back into full consciousness. What was she doing, lying in Lachlan's arms? Her teeth knocked together with the cold. She touched one confused hand to her head, then pushed a long straggling tendril out of her eyes. The movement seemed to take a great deal of effort and she let her arm fall slackly.

She was shivering now, her whole body quivering with the effort of trying to keep warm. Her eyes narrowed on him fiercely. 'I told you I was cold.'

He glared down at her, guilt flooding through his chest. 'I thought you were…' Was this what his behaviour had been reduced to, after all these years of battling? A husk of a man, incapable of understanding others' needs, so wrapped up in his own self-pity and loathing that other people, other women, meant nothing to him?

'You thought I was pretending.' Cecily's voice was muted. 'You can put me down now.'

Removing his arm from beneath her hips, he allowed her legs to slide to the ground. 'I was wrong.' In the twilight, his eyes glowed over her.

Her feet were numb, unresponsive blocks, and she was forced to clutch his upper arm for a moment to regain her balance. 'We need to find shelter. I cannot go on like this.' Hopping from one foot to the other, trying to drive out the cold, she folded her arms rigidly across her chest.

'Tie the chit to her horse, my lord, and then we can continue!' one of the knights shouted out. He nudged his companion, who laughed. They had dismounted up ahead; one of them had stepped forward to take the bridle of her horse.

What? Was she to be slung over the saddle like a sack of grain? Cecily's cheeks flamed and she lifted her emerald gaze to Lachlan. 'You dare...' she whispered.

Sparkles of sleet clung to Lachlan's cheeks, giving him an otherworldly appearance, shimmering in the half-light. 'Have no fear, Cecily, I've no intention of doing anything like that.' He cast his gaze about him, to the shadows of evening closing around them, to the treetops blowing wildly in the wind and the valley below, caught in a low-lying, icy fog. 'We will find somewhere. But you're not going back on your horse. You can ride with me.'

'I will not.' Cecily pushed away from him, teetering on the frozen lumps of her feet. Her lips pursed, a mutinous line. 'I will ride my own horse.'

Lachlan stroked his palm down the side of his horse's head. The animal's nose wrinkled, appreciative of his master's touch. 'I am not going waste time arguing with you, Cecily. We are all cold and tired and in need of rest. You are in no fit state to ride. I will put you on my horse, one way or another. You can make this as difficult or as easy as you like. Which is it to be?'

Cecily. Was it the first time he had called her thus? Her name echoed strangely from his lips, caught in the slight inflection of his accent. An accent that spoke of the far north, of windswept cliffs and a raw, rugged landscape. A landscape that suited him.

'I suppose I have no choice.' She tipped her head back to look at him. Her hood had dislodged with her fall; the cut on her forehead had scabbed over, flowering into a bluish bruise along her hairline.

'No, you don't,' Lachlan replied calmly. 'You can ride in front of me.'

Hands planted about her waist, he lifted her up to his saddle. She swept one leg over the horse's neck so she could ride astride, spreading her skirts. The sodden material hung in great swags around the horse's neck.

In a moment, Lachlan was behind her, vaulting on to his horse with a speed that left her breathless. His chest knocked against her spine, his hips cradled hers, and she gasped at the sudden intimacy, crouching forward.

'Nay, lean back,' he said. 'It will be too awkward to ride with you pitching forward like that.'

'But…' Her body hummed with his closeness, every nerve ending tingling with a sudden, flooding expectation. 'You're too…too near me!'

He chuckled. 'I'm sorry. There's no other way.' She jumped as his hot breath caressed the lobe of her ear, her jawline. 'Surely you rode like this with your husband sometimes?'

'You are not my husband,' she replied grimly. She flushed, a great heat climbing through her cheeks, Lachlan's solid thighs pressing into her legs through her skirts.

'Thank Christ.' Lachlan's voice rumbled above her ear. 'Being married to a chit like you would be hard work. Argumentative. Stubborn. Always wanting your own way.'

She flinched at his words, staring stonily ahead. 'Aye, you have it right, Lachlan. That's exactly what my husband told me, too. But he liked the large dowry I brought with me, so there was some compensation for my behaviour.'

Annoyance flecked her tone. But he heard the note of anguish, too. Guilt flooded through him. Why had he said such things to her? He hadn't meant to be deliberately nasty; he had thought to be more teasing than that. But he had obviously hit a nerve and she had taken his words to heart.

The sleet was falling more heavily now. 'Move back,' he ordered her. She leaned tentatively against the strong pliancy of Lachlan's chest, the breath squeezing from her lungs.

'That's better,' he murmured. He placed a firm hand on her belly, winching her even closer to him. The possessive gesture sent a flood of intimacy pulsing through her blood, her veins, pushed every nerve ending to a tingling, almost unbearable, awareness. Was this what it was like to have a man hold you safe, to take care of you? Her body craved Lachlan's touch, savoured it.

She took pleasure from being near him and yet he was completely unaware. She closed her eyes in shame.

Chapter Nine

The younger knight spotted the dilapidated barn through the trees, the roof drooping precariously to one side. Bright green moss spangled the oak shingles. With a shout of glee, he spurred his horse onwards through the spindly trunks, then jumped down. He peered through the wide, open entrance, a roughly hewn piece of oak forming the low lintel above his head. 'It's dry inside, my lord,' he shouted back to Lachlan. 'There's a stack of hay and some wood to light a fire.'

A great shudder rose in Cecily's chest. The feeling of relief. Slumped back against Lachlan, his strong fingers splayed across her middle, holding her secure, she wasn't certain how much longer she could have carried on. She was cold, but also exhausted from trying to hold herself away from him. Every time she bumped back against him, excitement sparked her chest, and, God forgive her, her belly and loins. She needed to peel herself away from him, regain some sanity, some sense of equilibrium. A place where she could gather her scattered thoughts.

The evening darkened to night. The falling sleet turned to snow, great fat flakes spinning lazily to the ground. The branches, hanging low, were dusted with white, sparkling, ethereal. Lachlan pulled on the reins; the firm, rounded muscle in his upper arms squeezed tightly around her shoulders. His horse swung to a stop in front of the barn. Lord Simon's knights were already inside, sparks striking upwards in the gloom as they started a fire. Smoke billowed out, puffing fitfully, before being sucked up by a hole in the roof that acted as a makeshift chimney.

'This will do for tonight.' The comforting cage of Lachlan's arms fell away and he leaned forward to dismount, his solid chest pushing heavily against her back. The heat from his body left her suddenly; Cecily shivered, feeling strangely bereft. She shook her head. This was not right. Where was the woman who managed the vast estates at Okeforde gone? Her incisive logical brain, the one that made clear, precise decisions, that never wavered—where had that gone? Lachlan had turned her world upside down; her mind and body were struggling to cope.

She tried to find the energy to dismount. Something that she had done a thousand times before. Feather-light flakes of snow landed on her eyelids, her cheeks, chill kisses that melted swiftly. Cecily rubbed the snow from her eyes, as if focusing more clearly would give her the physical power to dismount.

Lachlan stood on the ground beside her, one hand splayed across the animal's neck. The snow had settled on the dark blue wool of his cloak, dusting the vivid brightness of his hair. 'Shall I help you down?' His eyes shone out, brilliant sapphires in the gloom.

Cecily bit down desperately on her bottom lip. 'I… I can do it.' Go away, she wanted to shout at him. Why did he make her feel so vulnerable? She had told him she was used to looking after herself, so why couldn't she do it now? She needed some time, time to unfreeze her limbs.

'Can you?'

Cecily slumped forward, crunching her frozen hands into small fists on the horse's neck. 'No,' she admitted, staring at him helplessly. 'I think… I think I'm too cold.'

Lachlan lifted his arms and grabbed her waist, pulling her from the saddle. She collapsed rigidly against him, unable to put her hands out to keep some distance between their bodies. Their cheeks collided, cheekbones knocking together, and she caught the heady scent of him, fresh, invigorating. Sensual.

Her heart stalled. 'Oh, God, sorry!' Her cheek burned on the spot where she had banged against him. 'I can't seem to…'

'Stop apologising,' Lachlan said softly. 'It's my fault you're like this. I didn't listen. Can you walk?'

'Yes, yes, I can.'

Lachlan kept one arm about her waist to support her and she gritted her teeth, forcing her numb legs and feet to move forward, to walk towards the barn. Inside, the interior was dim, shadowy. Hay bales were stacked up all around, filling the air with the luscious smell of mown grass, dried in the hot summer sun. The knights sat cross-legged on the packed earth floor by the fire, the flames casting a glowing circle around them.

'Wait here,' Lachlan said. 'I'll fetch a blanket from my horse.' He ducked back out through the archway.

Cecily stood silently, cheeks smarting with the cold, aware that Lord Simon's knights both watched her intently. Unnerved, her fingers reached for one long curling end of her plaits, twisting the glossy hair round and round.

'You seem very close to Lord Lachlan.' The younger knight pinned her with his narrow gaze, snapping a long twig between his fingers. He threw the ends on to the fire. 'I suppose you hope to seduce him into letting you go.'

'I think nothing of the sort!' Cecily protested, cheeks flaming. Did Lachlan think the same? She had attempted to offer him her body, after all. A feeble, half-hearted attempt. Warmth blossomed in her chest with the shameful memory.

'We've seen you, mistress, with your simpering ways,' the other knight chipped in. 'Pretending to fall off your horse so you could ride with him—' He stopped speaking abruptly as Lachlan came back into the barn, carrying the blanket.

'Do you want to sit by the fire?'

'No,' Cecily answered, her voice low and miserable. 'I only want to sleep.'

He caught the look of distress on her face, the way her eyes slid away from his, steadfastly refusing to meet his gaze. The uneasy tension in the air. Had one of the knights said something to her? 'What's the matter?'

'Nothing.' Cecily clawed at the ties of her cloak, her throat tight with tears as she fumbled uselessly with the knot below her neck. Her fingers refused to co-operate, refused to execute the fine movements.

'Let me.' Tucking the blanket under his arm, Lachlan brushed her hands away, working swiftly at the tight knot that held the edges of the cloak together. Cecily flushed, conscious of the other soldiers' close scrutiny.

His knuckles bumped against her chin, grazed her jaw.

Sensation lanced through her, a lightning streak of excitement. She drew in a short, sharp breath, a whisper of desire.

'Oh, please, will you leave me alone?' Desperation etched Cecily's voice. She knocked his fingers away, annoyed with herself, annoyed with him for being so attentive. Why couldn't he treat her badly, make her stand outside in the rain or walk barefoot along a stony track? Anything to stop her feeling so attracted towards him. 'Let me sleep, will you?' Grabbing the blanket from him, she stalked off into the opposite corner of the barn.

Throwing herself on to a loose pile of straw, she rolled herself into the blanket, back facing rigidly towards the fire. Why could she not hate this man? It would certainly make life a lot easier. But even now, as she lay here, fighting to control the uneven race of her heart, the liquid puddle of her emotions, she realised it was not possible. Despite the situation, he made her feel cared for, protected, in a way that she had never known before.

Cecily's eyes opened; she blinked, licking her lips. Her throat was sore, scratchy from lack of water. She needed a drink, but her limbs were idle, so reluctant to move. Wrapped in both her cloak and Lachlan's blanket, a delicious warmth slowly started to envelop her, her body pillowed by the dense pile of dry hay smelling sweet. Tentatively, she stretched her legs out, wriggling her toes, enjoying the easy pull of her muscles. The wonderful sensation after so many cold, arduous hours of riding was sublime.

A deep rumble filled her ears. Cecily turned her head on her makeshift pillow of hay, slowly, not making a sound. She had no wish to wake anyone. Tucked up against the opposite wall, two figures were rolled into blankets. Both knights, snoring loudly. And sitting cross-legged by the fire, awake, was Lachlan.

The fiery glow bathed his face in a golden light, flickering over the rugged contours, the hard slash of his cheekbones. He rested his arm on one knee, twisting a stick between his fingers. He stared at the piece of wood, his eyes holding a strange, haunting glimmer. A look of deep and utter sadness.

Her breath snared, tangled in her chest.

She must have made a small sound. Lachlan's head jerked up, a muscle in his jaw tensing, then releasing, when he realised she was awake. He snapped the twig decisively between his fingers and threw both ends into the fire. The flames crackled, sparks flying up.

Cecily sat up abruptly, yanking the blanket around her shoulders. Her plaits tumbled down, over her chest. Pulling the bag towards her, she rummaged inside the soft leather for her circlet and veil, extracting the hairpins. She began to wind her plaits into a loose bun at the back of her head, jabbing the long pins in to secure her hair. She reached for her veil.

'You needn't bother with that.' Lachlan's mouth quirked at her sense of propriety.

'Oh, but...' She glanced over at the knights in the corner.

'You've spent the whole day with your hair loose in plaits, Cecily. Why worry about it now?'

She flushed at his perception. 'My hair has been covered by a hood all day. But now...'

His long eyelashes flickered upwards. 'They don't care about you, Cecily. They are in the employ of Lord Simon and they do as I say. You're a single woman, sleeping alone with three men. It matters not whether your head is covered or not.'

Cecily stood up, moved over to the fire. She knelt down opposite him, shuddering in the waves of heat thrown off by the flames. 'You make it sound as though I should be worried.'

'They won't touch you if I'm here.'

'They wouldn't touch me if you weren't!' Cecily flashed back at him. Her cheeks flushed pink. What was he saying? That if he hadn't accompanied her, they would have raped her?

His eyes narrowed suddenly, pinpricks of light. 'Are you completely naive, Cecily? What do you think happens to most female prisoners? They have no protection, no rights. There is no one to look after them. They are completely at the mercy of their guards.'

Cecily gripped the edges of the blanket, chastened by his words, wanting to weep at her powerlessness. 'What's going to happen to me after you have delivered me to the King? You won't be there then, will you?'

No, he thought suddenly. He hadn't thought that far ahead. *No, I won't.* A chill wrapped around his heart. How could he leave her there, at the mercy of the King's guards?

The silence between them grew, broken only by the crackle of the burning wood.

'Let me go, Lachlan,' she whispered, her fingers playing with the lattice of straw on the ground, picking up wisps and laying them in a criss-cross pattern. 'Can't you say that I slipped away in the night, when everyone was asleep?'

'Everyone would know that was not the truth.'

'Why not?'

He pressed his lips together, a mock grimace. 'Because that would never happen to someone like me. And everybody knows it.'

The arrogance of the man! 'How lovely that you should have such a high opinion of yourself.' Her voice was heavy with sarcasm.

He shrugged one shoulder, staring into the flames, then lifted his chin to meet her scornful gaze. His eyes sparkled blue, perceptive, incisive, drilling into her very soul. 'I am sorry, but it's true. Lord Simon would know that I'd let you go.'

'Oh, my God, you are impossible!' Balling her hands into fists, she resisted the urge to thump down on the hard-packed earth floor. 'I cannot believe that you have never blundered or made an error in your life. Maybe you could make a little one now. Everyone makes mistakes.'

'You're right,' he replied slowly, with supreme effort. 'Everyone makes mistakes.'

'But not you, obviously.'

'Yes, I made a mistake.'

'What…only one?' Cecily scoffed.

'It was a very…' He sighed, sticking his hand into his hair and pushing it back. 'It was a very big mistake.' His eyes darkened, reduced to a glittering sadness.

'There you go, then,' Cecily replied lightly, her voice adopting a persuasive lilt. 'You are just as fallible as the rest of us. If Lord Simon knows of this big mistake, then surely he would not think it suspicious that I managed to escape your clutches?'

The air in the barn shifted, tightened. The flow of conversation dropped like a stone, plummeted to the ground.

Oh, Christ, what had she said?

His eyelashes dipped fractionally at the impact of her words. As if she had hit him across the face or cuffed his ear. Checking that the soldiers still slept, Lachlan rose to his feet, abruptly, in a rush of honed muscle. He towered over her, his shadow thrown huge and monstrous on the wall behind him. 'You need to stop talking, Cecily. You need to stop talking, right now.'

His steely tone, though hushed, hit her with the brute force of an axe. Her chest twisted in fear. Hugging her knees, she curled her upper body over them tightly. A defence against whatever onslaught was about to come.

Lachlan strode to the open archway, planting his fist high on the roughly hewn oak of the frame. His breath puffed out into the cold night air, white billows of warmth. He waited for the memories to come bouncing back, the vivid images to sear painfully behind his eyes, but all he saw and heard was a more muted version, an echo.

Someone touched his arm. Cecily. Her fingers curled gently around his sleeve, pressing against his forearm. The fine bones of her knuckles shone out white. She stood at his side, her neat head on a level with his shoulder.

'I'm sorry,' she whispered. 'I have said something to upset you, but I've no idea what it is.' Her voice was soft, heavy with chagrin.

The sweetness of her apology wrapped around him like a soothing balm. Did she really care that much about how he felt? 'It's nothing,' he replied gruffly. 'Something that happened a long time ago.'

'What was it?' Her upper arm nudged against his.

He watched the slanting snow, the flakes heavier now, settling on the trees, the coarse bleached grass in front of the barn. Had any-one ever asked him that question before? Maybe once, a long time ago, when he had been a snotty-nosed, blethering youngster, his emotions floundering, incapable of deal-ing with the loss of his parents, his sister. Not since then. But now? Now it seemed the most natural thing in the world for this maid, for Cecily, to ask such a question. And for him to tell her.

Her hair brushed against his shoulder. 'Tell me.'

'It was my family. My whole family died.'

She clutched at his sleeve. 'I am so sorry.' Shock reverberated in her voice. 'Don't speak of it, if it makes you sad. You don't need to say any more.'

But I must, he thought. Cecily had offered him a lifeline without realising it. Drag-ging him out from the murky depths of his guilt-ridden past and lifting him up, up into the light, to a place where he could breathe again.

'I must speak of it,' he ground out. A muscle flexed tightly in his jaw. Already he could feel the difference in his body, the lightening of his muscles as the burden of guilt, the guilt that he had carried for years and years, began to dissipate.

He sighed, leaning his head against his raised forearm. 'My father's family originally came from Denmark: they were Vikings who settled in the Orkney Isles. My father travelled south and fell in love with a Scottish maid. It was his undoing. Her family, the Macdonald clan, did not approve; they hated us and swore that they would do anything to get rid of us. My father had enough loyal men to keep us safe, to protect us from their continual onslaughts, until one day...' his jawline was rigid '...one day, he didn't.'

Her hand moved from his sleeve to clutch the fingers of his left hand, hanging by his side. She held her breath, not wanting to speak, or to interrupt the flow of his speech.

He clasped her hand with both of his, searching her face. His expression was bleak, raw. 'They killed my family and set the castle alight. Razed everything to the ground until there was nothing left. And I could have stopped it. I could have saved them. Yet I did nothing. And that was my big mistake.'

'I don't believe you,' Cecily whispered.

'It's true.' His voice was ragged, low, so as not to wake the men sleeping on the other side of the barn. 'I was eight at the time, out on the hills with my dog. High up, above the castle. I saw the men coming, I saw them on the brow of the hill. I should have run then, run to raise the alarm, but I couldn't move; it was as if I was frozen.'

'You were frightened, Lachlan.'

He closed his eyes. The rigid sinew of his fingers wrapped around hers, squeezing painfully. 'I could have saved them.'

'You were eight, Lachlan. Eight years old. Just a baby.'

'It's no excuse.' A few snowflakes had landed on his hair and he brushed them off.

'Lachlan,' she whispered, 'you have to stop blaming yourself. Otherwise you will go mad.' Without thinking, led only by an instinct to comfort him, she slid her arms around his waist and hugged him close.

As her slim frame knocked into his, against his chest, his stomach, Lachlan took a sharp intake of breath. His senses jolted, igniting, his long eyelashes dipping with the sweet sensation, savouring the warmth of her fingers against his chill skin. 'There's only one thing left to do now,' he said, trapping her hand beneath his. His voice trembled with rough emotion.

'What is it?'

'I need to go back up to Scotland and find the people that did this to my family. They need to pay for what they did.' Since his family had perished, he had fought harder and better than anyone else, to be strong and brave and courageous. To never know fear like that again. But his actions had failed to drive the memories away, memories that plagued his every waking moment. He needed to do more.

'You seek revenge.'

'I do.'

'Do you think it will make you feel any better?'

He shrugged his shoulders. 'How can I let them get away with it?' He searched for the anger within that had driven him forward for all those years, but could only find the fleeting dregs of it. What had happened to him? Had Cecily weakened his resolve and made him forget his purpose?

He frowned, stepping back suddenly. Her hand dropped away.

'It won't bring your family back, Lachlan, will it? It won't bring you any peace if you don't stop blaming yourself for their deaths.'

He gaped at her, stunned by her speech. 'You are too bold with your words, Cecily. You forget your place.'

She scowled at him, narrowing her bright eyes. 'Oh, yes. I do apologise.' Her response was mocking. 'A prisoner...offering advice to a lord. What was I thinking?'

'Get some sleep,' he growled at her. 'We've a long ride tomorrow.'

Cecily flounced away, hurt, chastened, throwing herself down on her makeshift bed and pulling the blanket around her shoulders. Her words chivvied at him, sending a spiral of doubt deep into his chest. Why had he told her? Because she had asked? But many others had asked him what had happened all those years ago and he had shut their questions down as fast as they had arisen.

He hunkered down where he had stood, folding his legs beneath him in the open archway, the cool breeze chipping at his cheek. He kneaded the wound in his leg, more from habit now than from any actual pain. The result of Cecily's quiet questioning astonished him: the guilt that clogged his heart seemed eased and his mind felt lighter, somehow. Yet he had punished her for making him feel better, throwing her wise words back in her face, dulling those bright eyes. He had taken her sympathy and then discarded her.

Rising slowly, he stepped carefully over to where she slept, his eyes tracing the rigid, hostile line of her back angled towards him. He crouched down, balancing on the balls of his feet, curling his hand around her shoulder. 'Cecily? I know you're not asleep.'

'Go away,' she mumbled, staring fixedly at the cob wall in front of her. The mud and straw mixture was old and had fallen away in patches, exposing the old straw poking out.

'I shouldn't have spoken to you like that.' Lachlan's voice was gentle.

She rolled over, facing him, her eyes sparkling truculently. 'As you say, I overstepped the mark.'

'I reacted badly,' he admitted, throwing her a wry smile. Trying to make peace. 'No one has ever spoken to me about what happened before.'

'I'm sorry if my questions caused you pain.' Her voice was timid, careful.

'On the contrary.' Lachlan's gaze drifted over her lightly. A wayward strand of hair had become detached from one of Cecily's braids, straggling across her cheek. He took the fine tendril between his fingers and tucked it back behind her ear.

She sucked in her breath.

'Thank you.' Lachlan leaned down, brushed his lips against her cheek. 'Thank you for listening to me.'

Shock waves pulsed through her. As his firm lips grazed her skin, her innards melted, reducing her body to a puddle of intense longing. Her breath punched out, a great, gusting sigh of release, of desire.

'Please. Don't.' Her hands sprang up, her fingers digging into his hair to push him away.

But he had heard her. Heard the intense sigh of longing. Beneath his mouth her skin was like silk. His lips slid down to claim her mouth. To roam along those soft lips, to explore.

Cecily wrenched her mouth away, gasping. 'Please... Lachlan. The guards...they think I'm trying to seduce you...so that you will let me go,' she whispered hurriedly, praying they hadn't woken up to witness what had happened.

'Aren't you?' He lifted his head, the tendrils of his hair spiralling out like a gilded halo, touched gold by the fire. Sat back on his haunches.

'Absolutely not! It's you.'

He stood up. 'It's both of us, Cecily. We are both to blame for this.'

But he managed to walk away from her.

Chapter Ten

'Time to break your fast,' a gruff voice announced. A wave of warm, foetid breath brushed her ear. The younger knight bent over Cecily. Pincering her shoulder with his big meaty hand, he shook her roughly. Eyelids dry and scratchy, she levered herself into a sitting position. The cob wall of the barn blurred before her; she scrubbed hurriedly at her eyes to clear them of the last vestiges of sleep. After the late-night conversation with Lachlan, her body trembling as he wrenched himself away from her, she had thought sleep would elude her, yet she had fallen almost immediately into a deep, dreamless slumber.

Standing up, Cecily smoothed down her skirts, checking that the leather side-lacings on her gown were secure. She secured her plaits at the nape of her neck with the hairpins supplied by her mother, settled the veil and silver circlet over her hair. She picked up her cloak, shaking out the heavy folds, brushing off the loose fronds of straw.

'Will we reach Exancaester today?' she asked.

The knight, John, crouched by the fire, attempting to coax the dead ashes into life. 'Aye, if we ride fast and the roads are in good shape.' His narrow face held a sly expression. 'And if you pull no more of your tricks.' He jerked his head sideways.

Cecily followed his glance. The soldier thought Lachlan had been duped by her. Through the wide archway, he was saddling up the horses with the older knight, his cheeks red, raw with cold. The sun had scarce broken over the horizon; the sky was translucent, a limpid blue. A single star hung low on the horizon, peeking out through the fretted silhouette of dark branches. The temperature had dropped even further during the night. The ground held a light dusting of snow; beneath the trees, a spangled frost coated the dead leaves.

From the shadowed interior of the barn, Cecily traced the hard, lean angles of Lachlan's face, and wondered at his words of grief from the night before, at the sadness, the guilt that he had carried for such a long time. She clamped her lips in solidarity— she knew what guilt felt like. What it did to you. For hadn't she carried the guilt of Raymond's death around, for years and years, like a hard, lumpy parcel against her heart?

Now she knew what tormented Lachlan, what drove him. His need to avenge his family, to right the wrong that had been done to them. If she cared about escaping her own situation at all, then she should persuade Lachlan to seek revenge now, this very day. And yet the thought soured her tongue. She had grown used to his company, his strong, protective presence beside her, which strangely she had no wish to lose. But, however much she liked having him around, it didn't change the fact that he was determined to take her to the King. If she wanted to save her own skin, she would have to do it.

Cecily walked out into the light, skirts

swishing across the rock-hard, icy earth, brushing a path through the frosted leaves. Lachlan was bent down against his horse's glossy flank, adjusting a girth strap. Cecily moved around the back of the animal, the pelt glossy in the sunshine. 'May I speak with you, my lord? Alone?'

Lachlan lifted his eyes at her approach, yanking the girth strap tight, securing the buckle. He straightened up, pushing sinewy fingers through his brilliant hair. 'Go inside,' he ordered Walter, the older knight. 'What is it?' He rested his hand on his horse's saddle. The edge of his cloak flipped back with the movement, revealing the tight sleeves of his under-tunic. The fabric clung to his arm, revealing taut, rope-like muscles beneath.

'Last night...' Blood flowed into her cheeks, reddening the soft skin.

His blue eyes traced her delicate features, the fine curved bow of her mouth. 'We are both to blame for what is happening between us, Cecily.' His voice curled around her.

'Not that!' she whispered, urgently. 'I mean the things you told me about your family.'

'What of it?' he murmured. 'You know my history now and what I intend to do.'

'Yes, and you taking me to the King is holding you up. You could be on your way north, right now.'

'I thought you didn't approve of me seeking revenge.'

'Since when did you care what I thought?' Cecily bit back. 'You told me that I had "forgotten my place", if I remember rightly.'

'And I apologised.' Lachlan ran his thumb slowly around the leather stitching of the saddle.

Yes, he had. She lifted her fingers to her cheek, to touch the spot where his mouth had been.

Lachlan smiled, his bright glance tracking her movement. In the clear morning light, her skin adopted a dewy plushness. His fingers twitched, ached to touch, to test that velvet softness once again. He curled his palms ruthlessly by his sides, fingernails digging deep into his palms. Concentrate, he told himself sternly, focus on what the maid was saying and not what she looked like.

'So, are you going to go?' Her voice was

bright, quick with hope. 'Surely you can see that I am a burden to you.'

'What are you trying to do?' His eyes raised in mocking question. Christ, her eyes shone like emeralds, green flames, devastating, that seared into his soul. Branded him. His breath seized.

'Do?' Cecily asked innocently, folding her arms across her chest. Her cloak rumpled beneath the tight clasp of her arms.

'Give up,' Lachlan ground out. 'I am not going to leave you until I have delivered you to Exancaester, so you can rid yourself of any thoughts to the contrary.' Her long, delicate fingers were white, her fingertips blue. She needed some gloves, he thought.

'But I thought… I thought you wanted revenge for your family.' She ducked her gaze, stared at the ground.

'I do,' he said. But even as the words emerged from his mouth, he realised he did not. His words rang out with a dull clang of uncertainty: a lack of conviction. What was happening here? Where had his rage gone?

'Then seize this moment, Lachlan, and go.'

He shook his head, his mouth set in a firm,

resolute line. 'I have waited long enough to take the journey north. A few days more will not matter. Sorry to disappoint you, but you'll not rid yourself of me that easily.' Rummaging around in his leather saddle bag, he extracted a pair of gloves, woven from coarse grey wool. 'Here,' he said, 'these will be too big, but they will keep your hands from freezing solid.'

Cecily took the gloves, throwing him a half-smile to thank him for his concern. But her shoulders slumped in despair. There was nothing more she could do.

They dropped down from the moorland as the sun reached its highest point in the sky, the horses travelling in single file along a series of earth-packed tracks through the ice-topped scrubby grass and gorse. Far, far in the distance, across the vast marshy flood-plain of the river, the square turrets of the great Norman cathedral in Exancaester rose up from the wreaths of mist floating in the valley, the reddish-purple stone shimmering in the hazy sunshine, as if floating on air.

Before they reached the city though, they

had to cross the Forest of Haldon, a great mass of trees clustered on the lower slopes of the moor, stretching down to the river. The rounded tops of the trees spread out in a huge horseshoe shape before them, dominating the lower slopes of moorland.

Cecily jagged back on the reins, slowing her small grey mare.

'Go on, Cecily!' Lachlan shouted at her from behind. 'Why are you stopping?'

She hitched around in the saddle, the collar of her cloak brushing her cheek. 'We must go around the forest, Lachlan. Outlaws live in these woods. It is not safe to go through.'

The older knight turned his horse around and came back up the hill towards them. 'What's amiss?' He stared dispassionately at Cecily.

'These woods are not safe,' she said again.

'I have travelled through here before,' the knight named Walter scoffed openly. 'And nothing happened to me. The chit is only trying to buy herself some time. It will take at least one more day to go around these woods.'

'We are trained fighters, my lord.' The

younger knight steered his horse back towards them. 'There's not much that we're afeard of.'

'We go through,' announced Lachlan. His tone rang out dismissively.

Her heart sank. Of course he wouldn't listen to her now, not after her fumbled attempts to persuade him to leave early, to head north. But she told the truth. She had heard many bad things about this forest. About people who had entered and had never come out again. And if they did emerge unscathed, there were the stories of strange noises and lights in the darkness; of bad spirits filling the air.

She shivered, squeezing her knees into her horse's belly to urge the animal onwards.

The bare trees closed in over their heads as they entered into the woods in single file, the two knights at the front, Cecily in the middle with Lachlan behind. Spindly twigs scratched against her cloak, caught in her veil; low overhanging branches forced her to duck her head. Brambles snagged, dragging at the hemline of her cloak.

The path was faint, difficult to see, snaking in a vague circuitous route through the trees. The horses up front switched to left, then to the right. As long as they kept heading in a northerly direction they would eventually reach the city, thought Cecily. But it was hard to focus on where north was; the thick mass of branches above prevented the weak sun from reaching the forest floor.

They plodded steadily, silently, around the dark, serried trunks, moving forward through gaps big enough for the horses. The woods were quiet, no birdsong permeated the air. Cecily shuddered, a sense of anxious premonition gripping her heart. The borrowed gloves, too large, had slipped down over her wrists; she pushed the cloth back up to her cuffs, grateful for the warmth. Maybe they would be all right, she thought. Both the knights wore chainmail and carried swords, and although Lachlan wore civilian clothes, he carried a sword at his belt. She allowed herself to relax, just a tiny bit.

The attack, when it came, was swift. Savage.

In the hiss of an arrow, the older soldier up front toppled from his horse and thudded to the ground. In a trice, the other knight was down, an arrow quivering in his neck.

A howl of fright tore from Cecily's throat. Her little mare reared up, front hooves pawing the air.

'Get down!' Lachlan yelled at Cecily, jumping from his horse and drawing his sword. Bunching her cloak in a fierce grip at her waist, he yanked her from her horse, shoving her into the undergrowth. Legs braced, he pivoted lightly on nimble feet, his keen eyes searching the dark woodland, so that he covered a full circle in the space of a breath.

Lachlan had thrown her in front of a massive clump of brambles, behind a thick tree trunk. Cecily hesitated, crouching low, blood thumping in her chest.

Sword outstretched, Lachlan jerked his gaze towards her. 'Hide!' he growled. 'Crawl, make yourself invisible!' Breathing heavily, he swung his lithe body round in another neat circle, his big feet moving with a surprising lightness for a man so tall. 'Do it now!'

His order was terse. She scrabbled forward on her hands and knees. Nettles stung her skin. The woven gloves snagged on the bramble thorns, caught, slowing her progress. She yanked them off and left them. The earth was damp, cold beneath her fingers as she crawled deeper and deeper into the undergrowth, the rotting fungal smell stinging her nostrils. This felt so wrong, this running away. She wanted to be out there, alongside Lachlan, but that was stupid. She had no weapon and no idea how to fight. She was of no help whatsoever. She was useless.

The brambles arched high above her head, but she found a space, in the middle of that dense nest, a space where she could turn and sit, clasping her knees with tightly knotted fingers. Her blood thumped in her ears and she tried to slow it, to still her breathing, in the hope of hearing what was happening to Lachlan.

She heard a shout, then a clash of swords. A volley of cursing. More shouts. Sweat beaded her palms. Cecily had no idea whether it was Lachlan, or someone else. The invisible enemy. The swiftness of the soldiers' deaths had caught her by surprise;

the accuracy of the arrow shots meant that, whoever they were, their adversaries were skilled. They had the upper hand. Deep in her hiding place, thorns catching at her hair, her veil, her clothes, she bent her head to her clasped knees and prayed. Prayed that Lachlan's life would be spared.

Please God.

The image of the two knights, falling swiftly, tortured her inner vision. Dead before they reached the ground. Would Lachlan suffer the same fate?

She hunched forward, resting her chin on her knees. If only she had her wits about her, if only her brain was not befuddled by Lachlan, by his strong, dynamic presence, then she would use this chance to flee and head north. She would go to her friend of old. She would find William. She should keep crawling, crawling away, then straighten up and walk away. Run.

She should.

And yet—she could not.

She had scarce known this man above a handful of days and yet she could not leave him. Her brain screamed at her to go, to flee, but her heart made her stay. Sit still. Wait until the moment when it was safe to go to him.

Her thoughts made no sense, settled on rickety planks that had no support. Emotion tangled with reason. Lachlan was her captor, taking her to a place that she had no wish to go, yet she wanted to be with him. The memory of his voice hummed into her, that low accented burr drilling down to the very core of her. She could not wrench herself away. She had to make sure that Lachlan was safe.

Cecily had no idea of how long she waited, waited until the forest was quiet again. And even then, she hesitated. What would she find, when she crawled out of this hiding space? Would Lachlan be dead? Her heart howled with the thought, a great cavernous hollow opening up in her chest. A chasm of loss. How was it that she couldn't bear to lose him? This man who had turned her whole life upside down.

Working her way back through the brambles, the dead wood and leaves, Cecily eventually emerged into the open space where they had been attacked. She squinted, her eyes watering in the low sunlight. The horses had vanished: either they had been taken by their attackers or had run away. She hoped that her little grey mare had been quick enough to escape capture. The bodies of the two knights lay where they had fallen, crumpled on the muddy, leaf-strewn track. She grimaced, averting her eyes; despite being Lord Simon's men, she had not wished them ill. Her heart tripped and rolled, her eyes searching frantically through the trees for Lachlan—had he been taken?

Then, through the whispering of the trees, a faint groan, so faint she wasn't sure if she even heard it. Tilting her head, Cecily tried to locate the source of the sound, her eye roaming the dense vegetation, peering through the narrow gaps in the trees, searching for the tell-tale flash of fiery hair, or any scraps of blue: the colour of Lachlan's tunic, his cloak.

In the scuffle of breeze, Cecily heard the sound again. She darted through the trunks, her shoulder banging painfully on the solid bark as she barged through. A dust of lichen, pale green, smeared her dark cloak as she tore through.

Lachlan lay in a puddle of brindled leaves, so still. Felled, like a giant oak. His legs stretched out before him, sprawling across the dead leaves; his arms were flung out either side. His beautiful eyes were shuttered, long dark lashes sweeping the top of his high cheekbones.

Her heart plummeted, screwed tight with wretchedness. Flying towards him, she plunged to her knees, sinking into the damp mossy undergrowth. The wet leaves soaked upwards through her gown. 'Lachlan,' she whispered, fearful that the outlaws might still be about, might hear her. 'Lachlan!' She bent her head down to his mouth and his warm breath sifted across her cheeks. Her heart swelled with joy. Thank God!

Cecily patted his cheek, his skin rough and cold. The short bristles on his jawline scratched the soft skin of her palms. Running her hands over his shoulders, his chest, then over his torso and legs, she checked for entry wounds, but found nothing. 'My God,

Lachlan,' she blurted out, half-sobbing into the silence of the forest, resting her palms flat on his chest. 'What have those bastards done to you?'

'They hit me on the head.'

She jumped at the sound of his voice. Dry, laconic. Her eyes sprung to his face. Lachlan's eyes were clear, brilliant. Studying her closely.

'Oh, my God, Lachlan! How do you feel?' Instinctively, she touched his cheek, cupping his chin. Relief flooded through her; relief that he was alive.

'Terrible,' he grunted, turning his face into the warmth of her hand. 'At least they did not find you. You are unhurt?'

'Yes. I found a safe place.'

His eyes sought and held hers: a questioning look. 'I must sit up, yet I fear it may be difficult.' *She had come back to find him*, he thought.

'Let me help you.' Dropping her hand, Cecily leaned forward to hook her arm into his, hoisting his muscular body into a seated position. He swayed against her, his face a deathly white, bracing his straight arms on to his outstretched legs. His massive shoulder locked against her slim frame and she breathed in the heady, masculine scent of him. So close.

'Can I look at your wound?' Cecily asked, tentatively.

He nodded, then groaned, wincing at the movement, narrowing his eyes in pain.

'I'll have to let go of your shoulder,' she explained, 'so I can move around to the back of you.'

'I'll be all right,' he said, through gritted teeth. Christ, how his head ached.

Cecily hitched around behind him, raising herself on her knees. Blood matted his hair, dark red and oozing. With careful fingers, she parted the blood-soaked strands. A gash cut through the white skin of his scalp.

'It doesn't look too deep,' she breathed, deliberately keeping her voice calm, steady. 'I don't think you will need stitches.'

'Someone clunked me with a stone,' Lachlan growled, dropping his head slightly. 'They must have thought they had killed me.'

Thank God they did not. Sitting back sud-

denly on her heels, she traced the strong col-
umn of his neck, the tanned flesh striped
with drying rivulets of blood and thought,
I cannot do without you. He made her feel
safe, protected, for the first time in her life.
And she clung to that feeling, like a lifeline. It was ridiculous, stupid. She wanted
to laugh out loud. Or cry. Her situation was
impossible, untenable.

'Those bastards took everything: the horses,
our provisions.'

I don't care, Cecily thought. *You are alive
and that is all that matters.*

Lachlan twisted his head around, scowled
at her. 'Go on then.' Above their heads, the
bare branches clacked together in a sudden
gust of wind. Crows squawked, lifting from
their perches in a swarming black mass,
wings like flashing knife-blades.

What was he talking about? 'I don't understand.'

'I'm talking about you, Cecily.' His blue
eyes grazed her puzzled expression. 'Why
do you not run, while you have the chance?
The two knights are dead and I doubt I

could run after you. Go now, before anyone comes.'

No, no! 'But I... I can't leave you...like this.' Her tone rose in protest.

His face was tough, incredulous. 'Why on earth not? You have no duty of care towards me. I am nothing to you.'

You are wrong, she thought. *You are so wrong.* His words pierced into her, blunted arrows of rejection. 'You're hurt, injured.'

'Aye, that I am, but I'm not going to bleed to death.' He assessed her calmly. 'And we're not far from Exancaester now. I can walk there. What's the matter, Cecily? Only this morning you were suggesting that I leave to go north and now you want to stay with me?'

A florid colour spread over her cheeks. 'I...er...' Christ, how could she stay with him without revealing her feelings? Her mind scrabbled to find a suitable answer, something with which she could fob him off so that he would never guess her true intentions. He would surely laugh in her face if he realised how much she had come to care for him.

Cecily thought quickly. 'Because…because, as you have so rightly pointed out, if I flee now, then Lord Simon will be for ever snapping at my heels. I shall always be on the run, never able to settle. This way, if I take you to the King, you can plead leniency for me, because I helped you in your hour of need.'

Lachlan laughed softly. 'I should have guessed your motive. But the plan might work, especially if the King sees what the outlaws did to me and did to them.' Lachlan waved his hand in the direction of the dead knights. He reached for her hand, grabbed her cold fingers between his. 'But are you sure about this, Cecily? I cannot predict what the King's decision might be, even if I do plead for you. You could go abroad and live far away from here. Lord Simon might never find you.' His heart sank deep, a hollow opening up in his chest. He didn't want her to go. Already, in these past few days, her bright face had lightened up his days, like a rose, startling the winter gloom with its glorious burst of colour. 'It's a risk.'

'I'm certain,' she replied. 'I have no wish

to live in fear of being caught. It's a risk I am willing to take.'

And I'm willing to take it for you, she thought.

Chapter Eleven

Scrambling to her feet, Cecily bent over to tear a strip of linen from the bottom of her shift that she wore beneath her gown. The white fabric was not exactly clean, splattered with mud from the journey, but it would suffice until they reached Exancaester.

Lachlan turned his head at the ripping sounds. 'What are you doing? Do not ruin your clothes on my account!' He caught the flash of her slender legs encased in fawn woollen stockings; her delicate ankles encased in leather ankle boots, sopping wet. That fleeting glimpse, the intimacy of it, drove a pulse of longing deep into his chest.

'I must bind your wound, Lachlan.' She held up the narrow piece of cloth. 'And now I have a bandage.'

Lachlan hitched forward, intending to rise.

'Nay.' Cecily laid a hand on his shoulder, pushing down lightly. 'Stay for a moment. Your wound is bleeding quite badly.'

'There's no need to bind it,' Lachlan said.

'Do you want to bleed to death?' she snapped back, tearing off a clump of moss from the bark of a tree with which to pad the wound. 'This will only take a moment.'

'If you must, then,' Lachlan replied reluctantly, his shoulders slumping back down. 'I didn't know you cared.'

You don't realise how much I care, Cecily thought, pressing the moss gently over the open cut. 'My petition to the King will not look good if I let you bleed all over the place.' She wound the strip of linen, carefully, tightly, around Lachlan's head, securing the mossy pad at the same time. His hair, silky filaments of red-gold, brushed the back of her hand.

'Ah, yes, of course,' Lachlan said lightly. 'I knew there must be a reason.'

As she ripped the end of the linen into two strips in order to tie a knot, Cecily's cheeks flushed with colour. She wasn't doing it for the King at all. She was doing it for him. For Lachlan.

'There,' she pronounced, standing back from him. 'I've finished.'

Lachlan rolled slowly over on to all fours, his big knees sinking into the spongy, leaf-strewn earth, then clambered slowly to his feet. He swayed, his skin grey and pale, and she darted towards him, grabbing his arms.

'Christ, my head is spinning.' He gripped on to her shoulders.

'Lean on me,' Cecily said quickly.

'I'll be steady in a moment,' he gasped, looping one muscled arm along the back of her shoulders, and she staggered back a little under the force of his body.

'I'm too heavy for you,' he muttered.

'I'm stronger than I look,' she said, relishing the feel of his heavy muscles along her shoulders.

'Believe me, I know.' Despite his aching head, Lachlan chuckled, thinking of the risks she had taken to protect her family, to keep them safe. 'Your fragile beauty is deceptive.'

Fragile beauty? Her heart jolted at his

compliment. What on earth did he mean? Had the knock to his head sent his thoughts awry?

Lachlan saw the flash of bewilderment cross her face, wondering at it. His head was beginning to clear, his sharp intelligence returning, despite the thumping headache those rogues had left him with. Did Cecily not realise how completely stunning she was? That bright, chartreuse gaze, that full, rosebud mouth that stopped his breath?

With his arm around her shoulder, they started walking slowly back to the clearing where they had been attacked. His chin was level with the top of her head. Her white silk veil flowed down in gossamer folds over the mud-stained wool of his surcoat, clashing incongruously. Silk that was exquisite, he thought, like the woman who wore it. Too exquisite for his rough, brash ways. 'What's the matter? Someone, surely, must have told you how beautiful you are?'

Cecily stopped, twisting her lips together in annoyance. 'Don't mock me, please.'

'But I'm not. It's true.' He laughed, his grip on her shoulder tightening. 'And I can't believe your husband never told you, that he never valued you…'

'No! Please…stop.' She turned and laid her palm flat against his chest, as if that very action would stop the words emerging from his chest. 'Why are you saying such things?'

Lachlan shrugged. 'Did he marry you for your money? Is that it?'

'Of course he did!' She gave a hollow laugh. 'Isn't that what most marriages are based upon? My parents arranged my marriage to Peter; they offered him a large dowry to take me off their hands.'

A single burnished leaf fluttered down and landed on her shoulder; Lachlan brushed it away. 'Did he mistreat you?'

'No, nothing like that. I hardly knew him. We were only together for a few days before he went off on campaign. He was a stranger to me.' She took a faltering step forward, gripping his hand that dangled down over her shoulder, so that he was forced to walk with her. 'Come on, we need to keep going before it gets dark.'

They walked slowly, haltingly, back to the spot where the two knights lay.

'This is horrible,' whispered Cecily as she eyed the fallen bodies, then turned her gaze sharply away. Her face was stark white. 'We must bury them.' Tears sprung to her eyes. 'We cannot leave them here, like this.'

He hated seeing her sadness, the swift shine of tears springing to her eyes. In all his years of battling, he had oft seen dead men; this was a familiar sight for him. But for Cecily? It must be difficult and sad for her to see something like this. Lifting his arm away from her shoulders, he brushed the back of his hand against her cheek, a fleeting gesture of comfort. 'I am so sorry it happened, Cecily. I am sorry you have to see this.'

At least it's not you, Cecily thought. *I could not bear to see that.*

'It would take us a long time to dig graves for them,' he continued. 'And we need to cross the marshes and the river before dark. We could send someone back from Exancaester to bring them into the castle.'

'It will take too long,' she protested. 'By that time, the wild animals...'

'There may be another solution.' Lachlan pointed through the trees. 'Look over there.'

Following the direction of his arm, Cecily heard a familiar whinny. Her little grey mare was picking her graceful way through the undergrowth towards her! 'Oh, she's there!' Cecily gasped. 'She must have run away when the fighting started.'

'She has more wits than my horse, anyhow.' His tone held a grim ruefulness.

'I am sorry, Lachlan, that they took him.'

'He belonged to Lord Simon, not me. But he was a good horse and those bastards knew it. They will get good money for him.' He angled his gaze down to her. 'But at least now we can take the knights back to Exancaester with us. We can lift them on to your horse. Think you can help me?' His eyes twinkled. The colour was returning to his cheeks.

'I think it may be a case of you helping me,' she replied, smiling gently. 'Can you stand on your own, while I fetch the horse?'

Lachlan lifted his arm up, away from her shoulders, demonstrating his answer. In truth, his strength had gradually returned as he walked through the forest with her, yet he hadn't wanted to pull away, enjoying the sweet bump of her hip against his own.

Cecily walked over to her horse and took up the trailing reins. Swallowing deeply, she led the mare over to the two men on the ground. 'How on earth do we do this?' she asked.

'If you can grab his ankles, I will lift his upper body.' Hunkering down beside the first knight, Lachlan wrapped his arms around the man's shoulders, hoisting him upwards under the arms. Cecily bent down and clutched at his leather boots, lifting the dead weight. As Lachlan slung the man's upper body over the back of her grey mare, Cecily supported the knight's legs. They proceeded to do the same with the other knight.

Cecily crossed herself. 'Christ, this seems so wrong,' she whispered. Her eyes shuttered briefly, dark lashes brushing her bright cheeks.

'At least, this way, they will receive a Christian burial,' Lachlan replied. 'And their families will know where they are laid.' He swayed momentarily, the exertions of the past few moments catching up with him. His head felt light, and dizzy. He reached out for her and Cecily took his hand, steadying him, his big fingers knotting into hers. The fitted sleeve of his tunic had ripped open, the buttons gone and the buttonholes all torn. Fine golden hairs dusted the bare muscled flesh of his forearm.

'You should not have done that,' Cecily murmured. 'It was too much for you.'

He laughed faintly. 'You talk as if I'm an old crone on her deathbed, Cecily. I've been in far worse situations than this.'

'I can imagine,' she replied, her glance touching the bodies slung over the back of her horse. How many dead men had he seen? How many had he killed? She dropped her gaze to the ice-hard ground. 'Do you think you are able to walk to Exancaester?'

'Of course.' He smiled at her. 'I am not about to collapse on you.'

Colour had flooded back to his cheeks; his eyes sparkled, blue sapphires. 'I suppose... you are looking better,' Cecily said, almost to reassure herself. 'I mean, if you want, we could stay here a while, if you wish to rest.'

'I am feeling better!' Lachlan laughed. 'Besides, I am in no mood to stay in this forest. We are too vulnerable here. Let us move, now.'

From the west, the sun began to sink towards the horizon, painting the land in a luminescent gold. Leading the grey mare, Lachlan and Cecily squinted in the brightness as they emerged from the chill somnolence of the forest, searching for their path across the gently sloping grassland. The track was easy to find, leading down to a wide marshy area alongside the river, then narrowing to cross the bridge into the city. The many spires and turrets gleamed in the glowing evening light.

'We head for that bridge now.' Lachlan indicated a series of pointed arches, initially spanning the marshy ground, then across the river and into the city. A sturdy gatehouse, with a round tower either side of the archway, sat at the city end of the bridge. A scramble of timbered buildings, built from the same reddish-purple sandstone as the bridge, clung to the parapets. Wooden posts, driven into the shallow river bed, supported the backs of the houses which overhung the flowing water. Ribbons of laundry were strung out from the windows over the river.

Even from this distance, Cecily could see people moving across the bridge: loaded carts, horses and packhorses, all jostling for space. Fear pinched at her heart—this city would be the place where her future would be determined. 'I never thought it would come to this,' she said quietly, turning to Lachlan. The crude white bandage on his head stood out incongruously against his flaming red hair. The east wind tugged at her words, cruel and biting, but he heard her.

'You thought you would get away with it,' he replied. She had pulled up the hood of her cloak against the wind; the bulky wool framed the sweet delicacy of her profile, emphasised the velvet bloom of her skin.

'Yes, we did,' she said, lifting her skirts above the muddy track. Ice still clung to the long tips of the grass either side of the path. Her eyes met Lachlan's, bold and brilliant. 'We were stupid. Back there, in Okeforde, it all seemed so easy. But now, when I see the city, all those buildings…' Her voice faltered. 'I'm frightened, Lachlan. Frightened of what is going to happen. I wish I had never done it.' Tears brimmed along the bottom of her eyes, pearly gems of sadness.

Lachlan dropped the reins, wrapping his big arms about her, drawing her close. The golden bristles on his chin grazed the top of her woollen hood. He wanted to tell her it would be all right, that he would make it all right. But how could he reassure her about something of which he knew nothing? True, he had the ear of the King and he had fought for him, advised him successfully on battle strategy on many occasions, but he had little idea of how much influence his relationship would have in the light of Cecily's deception.

'Cecily, you are the bravest woman I have ever met,' he murmured. His deep voice rumbled through her slender frame. 'I cannot think of another woman who would have done what you did, back in the forest. You came and found me. Most women would have collapsed in a heap and cried until someone had found them. But you found me and you treated my wound. You helped me load two dead men on to a horse. Remember that, when you face the King. And I will be there, beside you, every step of the way.'

Her body sagged with relief against his. His speech curled around her: a blanket, wrapping around her. She revelled in the sheer deliciousness of it, of his warm body, against hers. Even when her husband had been alive, she had been wary, always on tenterhooks, unsure of his protection, even though she carried his name. And yet this flame-haired warrior, who had burst so unexpectedly into her life, made her feel cared for. Loved. The word sprang in her brain, a tremulous, flaring spark. Aye, he made her feel loved.

'I...thank you.' The wool of his tunic tickled her cheek.

'Thank me when it's over.' His chin nudged the top of her head as he spoke. 'All you can hope for is that the King is lenient. And I will tell him—' His thoughts stopped suddenly, jerking to an abrupt halt. His mind was heading in a direction that he was not sure he wanted to go. What would he tell the King? That he would take care of Cecily? That he would be responsible for her? After his family had been slaughtered, he had vowed never to be close anyone, ever again. But Cecily was different. Cecily was not just anyone.

As they walked up through the main thoroughfare of the city, a cobbled street lined with merchants' houses, people stared openly at them, at the odd ensemble: a lady and her wounded knight, with two dead soldiers slumped over a grey palfrey. By the time they reached the castle at the northern end of the city, dusk had fallen. Firelight glimmered behind wooden shutters, and the smell of roasting meat and woodsmoke mingled and rose in the cooling air of evening. Above the castle gatehouse, the luminous disc of a full moon rose, illuminating the midnight-blue nap of the sky.

Lachlan reached up, pulled the bandage from his head.

'No, you must leave it on!' Cecily said, watching him stuff the bloodied linen beneath the grey mare's saddle.

Lachlan touched the wound at the back of

his head and winced. 'It's stopped bleeding.' He waggled his clean fingers at her, as if to prove a point. 'And I need to look presentable if I'm going to meet the King.'

'What about me?' Cecily asked in a horrified voice, smoothing her hands down her purple over-gown, staring in dismay at the tide mark of mud around her lilac-coloured skirts. She patted her veil, brushing her cloak down self-consciously. 'Do I look presentable enough, too?'

He sucked in his breath, setting his mouth into a firm line. She looked beautiful. The exquisitely cut lines of her gown beneath her cloak hugged her slim figure, highlighting her firm, high breasts; the neat indentation of her waist. In the chill air her eyes shone out like chips of leaf-green glass, her cheeks glowing with the cold. She took his breath away.

'Lachlan!' cried King Henry, rising from his chair on the high dais. 'Welcome to Exancaester! I didn't realise that you and Simon had returned from France. I hear you decided to stay at Simon's castle in Doccombe for a while?'

'I had no option but to stay. I was wounded in France,' Lachlan said as he climbed the wooden stairs to the dais, gripping Cecily's hand to keep her alongside. Her hemline brushed against his boots as they walked.

'Bad luck, Lachlan,' the King said. 'But your wound has healed now.'

'Yes, it has.'

The King's brown eyes landed on Cecily. His brow wrinkled with interest as he noted her fine pale skin, the expensive cut of her lilac woollen gown and cloak. 'Sit with me.' He beckoned them along the dais. 'Tell me what you have been doing.' He turned to the elderly nobleman sitting alongside him. 'You don't mind moving along a little, my lord? I haven't seen Lachlan in such a long time.'

The older man's mouth tightened in disapproval, before he made a great show of shuffling his chair back and ordering a servant to move his plate and goblet along the table to an empty seat. It was his castle, after all, in which the King was staying and he was spending a great deal of money keeping

Henry and his entourage well fed and watered until they moved on to the next castle.

'Come, come, my dear.' Henry raised his hand to beckon Cecily into the empty seat beside him. His giant rings flashed in the candlelight, the red fire of rubies set into gold. In contrast to his grandiose gestures, his figure, although tall, was thin and gaunt, his hair a faded mouse-brown, drooping on to his shoulders in loose, wispy locks. He wore a plain gold circlet to denote his regal status, which sat low across his forehead. 'Where did Lachlan find you, eh? I never heard that he had married.'

Cecily flushed to the roots of her hair, glancing at Lachlan. He had folded himself into the chair on the opposite side of the King, his strong body a muscle-bound parcel of energy, his gold-red hair acting like a marker of his innate physical strength. Beside him, Henry looked like a child, although they were probably about the same age. 'Oh,' she managed to splutter out. 'No, you have it wrong, my lord... Sire, I am not married to Lachlan. I... I am...'

'I have brought Lady Cecily here on

Lord Simon's behalf,' Lachlan cut across her smoothly. 'She was married to his late brother, Peter.'

'Ah, yes, I did hear of his death. My condolences to you, Lady Cecily.' Henry clicked his fingers and a servant leaned down between the chairs, setting a clean goblet and plate in front of her and pouring a glass of wine. A couple of red drops landed on the pristine white tablecloth, spreading slowly. Slices of meat appeared on her plate, a bread roll, some vegetables, and Cecily stared at them dully, as if in a dream. She shifted uncomfortably, wondering if she should even be sitting at the top table with the King. Surely when he found out what she had done, she would be treated differently. The blade of the eating knife, set beside her pewter dish, glimmered in the light of the many candles, set at intervals along the trestle table.

'So,' Henry said, pushing a slice of chicken into his mouth and chewing hungrily. 'What brings you to my side?'

'Lady Cecily has done something that

Lord Simon is not happy about and asked me to bring her to you to resolve the issue.'

'I'm glad you did,' Henry said, patting him on the shoulder. 'For otherwise I would not get to see you at all.' He swallowed and took a sip of wine, wiping the drops from his beard. 'What have you done, my lady? I'm sure it cannot be that bad.'

Cecily bit her lip. She had to stand up for herself, defend herself. There was no point in trying to hide the truth. She took a deep shaky breath. 'I pretended…' She paused, squeezing a lump of bread between her fingers, pressing the soft crumb again and again. She stared at the tablecloth, the drops of wine. 'I pretended to be carrying a baby, so I could pass the child off as my late husband's heir,' she said finally. 'Lord Simon wanted his brother's castle and lands back and it was the only way we could keep it.'

The King sat back in his chair, bolt upright, visibly shocked.

'Is this true?' He turned to Lachlan.

'It is, my lord. But, without trying to diminish the severity of Lady Cecily's crime, I will say in her defence that on our journey here, we were attacked by outlaws in the Forest of Haldon. I was knocked unconscious and the two knights who travelled with us were slain. Lady Cecily had the perfect opportunity to run away, yet she did not. She crawled through the undergrowth to find me and tend my wound. She could have left me to bleed to death.' Lachlan's eyes sought Cecily's, caught and held. He flashed her a quick reassuring smile.

Henry glared fiercely at his plate, now empty, then took a long sip of wine from his goblet, wiping the drops from his beard. He set the goblet back down on the table with deliberate slowness, running his finger around the ridge of pewter that decorated the goblet base. He sighed heavily. 'This is a serious crime, my lady, one, I might say, of which you do not look capable. I have to tell you that such a crime normally merits a lengthy imprisonment, or even hanging in some cases.'

Cecily gasped at the King's pronouncement. Her head spun, nausea rising in her throat. Sweat coated her spine, sticking the fine material of her gown to her flesh. She gripped the thick edge of the table, knuckles white.

'Normally,' Lachlan repeated the word, loudly. His velvet tones pierced her terror; she snared his bright eyes and clung to them, helplessly. He raised his eyebrows, a warning. Steady, he seemed to say.

'You should be tried, my lady, before my court. I do not have the power to make decisions on your fate alone. But the next court is not for another month or so and I am not inclined to imprison you for that length of time, especially as you had the chance to run away and did not.'

Cecily clasped her hands in her lap. Her mouth was dry, her fingers slick with sweat.

'So…' drawled Henry, 'I am in the mood to offer clemency. A good word from Lachlan is worth three from any other man; I value his opinion greatly. You have been brave enough to face me and face whatever punishment I might have given you.' Henry wrinkled his nose. 'I'm thinking that you need another husband, someone who would keep you in line. Maybe even have a child or two of your own, eh? You're a pretty piece,

I'm sure I can find someone who would be happy to marry you.'

A sudden wave of heat flooded through Lachlan's body; he ran one tapered finger around the neckline of his tunic. The wound on the back of his head throbbed. He hitched forward, listening intently. Why had he not envisaged such a scenario? Why had he been so stupid as to imagine that Henry would let her go on Lachlan's say-so? Christ, the thought of her going to another man, probably one of Henry's old cronies who had worked their way through one or two wives already, didn't bear thinking about. Lachlan watched the colour drain out of Cecily's lovely face, the sparkle die in her eyes, and he thought, *I cannot let this happen.*

'Let me think,' mused Henry, leaning back in his seat and resting crossed arms on the rising curve of his protruding belly. 'Who needs a wife? Can you think of anyone, Stephen?' he shouted past Cecily to the nobleman on her other side, staring at his plate. The man turned to Henry. A lock of grey frizzy hair fell across his lined forehead.

'The Lord of Colcombe has just lost his wife in childbirth.'

Henry clapped his hands. 'Ah. yes, the Lord of Colcombe, an excellent choice!'

'I don't have a wife.' Lachlan's voice emerged suddenly, calm and measured, breaking across the King's high-pitched exclamations, the burble of chatter along the table. 'I will marry Lady Cecily.'

Chapter Twelve

Heat flashed across Cecily's face; astonished, she stared at Lachlan, mind reeling. Her hand flew to her throat, then her neat chin, fluttering undecidedly, her fingers finally settling around her jaw. What in heaven's name was Lachlan thinking? Was he out of his mind? And yet a tiny kernel of hope flickered, deep in her belly. She touched her bottom lip, slowly, remembering his mouth upon hers. Maybe he thought more of her than she had imagined.

A dull ruddy colour touched the top of Henry's gaunt cheeks; he cleared his throat several times, before gulping down some wine. The red liquid dribbled down his chin; he wiped it away angrily with his sleeve. 'My God, Lachlan, you don't have to do this! I wasn't asking you to marry this...'

He sneered at Cecily. 'Why saddle yourself with her when you could do so much better? Let her go to one of my lesser nobles.'

Cecily laid her palms flat upon the white tablecloth; her fingers shook and she tried to steady them *Yes*, she thought, *come on, Lachlan; I want to hear what you have to say. Why would you saddle yourself with me?* She searched his face for clues, but the lean angles of his face remained irritatingly bland, impassive.

Lachlan shrugged, hitching his eyebrow as if the matter was of no consequence. 'I need a wife,' he said. He leaned back in his chair, his arm stretched out over the linen tablecloth, his fingers playing with the stem of his pewter goblet. 'And as you wish Lady Cecily to have a husband, then it may as well be me.' *And I can protect her with my name*, he thought, *even if I cannot give her my love.*

Henry nodded. 'I see. You need someone to produce some heirs, to carry on the family name after…' His voice died away and he clamped his lips tight shut as if to prevent any further words emerging. Lachlan tipped his head to one side, acknowledging the fact that Henry was not going to talk about what happened in his past.

Cecily stared down at her plate, heaped high with food. Her mouth was dry; she had failed to eat even a single morsel. She had no idea why Lachlan had offered to marry her; she hadn't envisaged such a thing before they had approached the King. Biting her lip, she sought out his bright blue eyes along the table. 'Are you sure about this?' She spoke directly to him, ignoring the King in between them. 'It's a big commitment.' Beneath the fizzing nervous energy, beneath the anxiety that came from being in the King's presence, something shifted within her heart. Was it hope?

The King rose between them suddenly, blocking her view of Lachlan. He was incredibly tall, taller than Lachlan, and his bony frame loomed over her. He leered down at her; his hawk-like nose, his face twisting with ferocious intent. 'No one asked you to speak, Lady Cecily. You have no choice in this matter, after what you have done. You should be grateful that Lord Lachlan offered for your hand.'

At the King's harsh words, she slumped back in her seat, clamping her lips together to hold back the tears. What a fool she had been; she should have learned to hold her tongue by now, especially in front of the King. This was a good outcome for her and she would do better for herself if she did not question it. If Lachlan was set on marrying her, then so be it.

'If you're sure you want to tie yourself to her, Lachlan, then I will not stand in your way.' Henry swallowed the last dregs of wine from his goblet and wiped his beard with the back of his sleeve. 'You've been a loyal supporter to me for all these years. But...' Henry lifted his shoulders in an exaggerated gesture, then let them fall again with a deep sigh '...you know you can do much better than that chit.'

'I know,' said Lachlan.

But she's the one I want.

The words popped into his head, unbidden; he blinked in surprise at the thought, his lashes flicking upwards, startled.

'So be it.' The King threw himself back into his chair, throwing his stained napkin into the middle of the table. 'You can be married in the morning, in the chapel here. I will witness the marriage before the lords and barons start arriving here for the monthly parliament.' He snapped his fingers impatiently towards an unseen servant. 'Hester! Take Lady Cecily to the guest chamber and make sure she's comfortable for the night. Lord Lachlan and I have a wedding to plan.'

Flanked by a pair of castle guards, Cecily made her way along the high dais. A weakness invaded her knees, Lachlan's proposal driving all strength from her body. She resisted the urge to grip on to the chair backs as she moved along the top table, but she stumbled on the wooden steps and was forced to seize the banister. Smoke hazed the lower part of the great hall, belching out from an enormous stone fireplace. The air was thick with the smell of roasting meat and honeyed mead, mingling with the sour note of sweat that lifted from the crowds of people crammed together along the trestle tables, peasants and knights eating and drinking hungrily as the roar of their voices rose to the high rafters.

No one paid Cecily any attention as she slipped by them, following the diminutive maidservant, and for that she was grateful. The maid pulled at the heavy brocade curtain that hung across the open archway at the end of the hall and held it aside, indicating that Cecily and her guards should go through. The entrance hall was much cooler, lit by a single torch, slung into an iron bracket by the main door. In the shadows, Cecily made out the stone steps on the left that disappeared up through an arch to the upper floors.

A group of knights stood in the entrance hall, talking in low voices as they pushed back their gleaming chainmail hoods, and handed their gauntlets and shields to their young squires. Jewelled sword hilts sparkled in the gloom as they crowded into the small area, blocking the route to the stairs. A guard gripped Cecily's upper arm, shoving her over to the left, towards the stone staircase so that the knights could enter the great hall.

A rope banister threaded up the steps, hung between iron rings; Cecily clawed at it, her stomach roiling with nerves. The maidservant, Hester, preceded her, lighting the shallow stone steps with a candle in a wooden cup. The guttering flame dipped and swayed along walls that sparkled with damp. Her mind clouded with staggered disbelief at what had just happened in the great hall. Her life had been spared by the King, but only if she married. And Lachlan was to be her husband.

Reaching the first-floor landing, Hester lifted the iron latch on the first door she came to and pushed it open, standing aside so that Cecily could enter. 'In here, my lady. I will come and make the bed up for you.' She cast a steely gaze at one of the guards. 'Make yourself useful. Run downstairs and tell the kitchens to send up hot water for a bath. Now, if you please.'

The other guard dangled an elaborate key from his gauntleted finger, swinging the heavy iron from side to side. 'They won't escape while you're gone, Geraint,' he reassured his friend. 'I will lock them in.' The other man nodded and disappeared back down the stairs.

The chamber was dim. A small charcoal brazier threw out a flickering heat in one corner. Hester shut the chamber door, pressing her hips firmly back against the planks, before walking swiftly around the room, touching her little candle flame to the rush torches set at intervals around the stone walls, before fitting the candle into a iron holder beside the four-poster bed. A glowing, ambient light filled the chamber.

'You must be tired, my lady, after your journey.' Over by the window was a bucket of charcoal pieces. She picked up a couple of lumps and threw them into the hot, molten centre of the brazier. 'They were saying in the kitchens that you have travelled in from the moor.'

Cecily stood by the door. The edges of her cloak, below the row of buttons at the neck, had fallen aside. She wound the ties from the girdle around her gowns round and round her middle finger, pinching the skin. Her head jerked up. 'Yes, I did.' A great shiver passed through her. Questions clamoured in her brain, gnawed at her, making her feel exhausted with the effort of thinking about it all.

Hester glanced at her shyly, clasping her hands in front of her simply cut gown. She was a short, buxom girl of about twenty winters. 'The King has posted guards outside your door,' she whispered. 'What have you done, my lady? They're saying in the kitchens that you murdered two men.'

The arrival at the castle of the dead knights slung over the back of her horse would not have gone unnoticed. The rumours and gossip must have travelled around the castle like wildfire. 'It's a long story,' Cecily sighed. 'I have committed a crime, but I haven't killed anyone. I'm not a danger to you, if that's what you're worried about.'

Hester grinned and shook her head, her soft brown eyes gleaming. 'I know, my lady. I am a good judge of character; I know you're not a bad person.'

Hot tears, sudden and unbidden, sprang to Cecily's eyes. A trembling wave of gratitude flooded through her: a vast relief. How could a few simple words from a maidservant overwhelm her so? Cecily stuck her chin into the air, trying to keep the tears from falling. 'Thank you, Hester. It means a lot to me to hear you say that.'

The girl threw her a quick smile. 'Do you wish to sit while I make up the bed?' She pointed to a plain oak chair, the tall laddered back pushed back against the white-plastered wall. 'I shall not be long.'

Cecily moved to the chair as if in a dream, almost falling into the seat. Hester snapped out the bottom sheet, a fine-woven linen, tucking the fabric neatly in and around the straw-stuffed mattress. She laid another sheet and woven woollen blankets on top, plumping up a couple of feather pillows and placing them carefully against the vast carved headboard. Rummaging about in a large oak chest, she produced a sable fur which she threw across the whole bed.

'There,' Hester said, stepping back, surveying the bed with a satisfied air. 'Now...' she turned to Cecily and clapped her hands together '...now I shall prepare a bath for you. Where are those lazy louts from downstairs?'

As if on cue, there was a tap at the door. Cecily watched hazily from the chair as servant after servant marched in to pour their brimming buckets into a bath that was hidden behind a tapestry screen. Hester chided the servants, scolding them for slopping too much water on the floor, pointing with an outstretched hand to the puddles on the polished elm floor. As the last boy left the chamber and the key turned once more in the lock from the outside, the diminutive, apple-cheeked maid turned to Cecily, rolling her sleeves up to her elbows.

'The water is ready, my lady,' she announced quietly. 'Shall I help you with your clothes?'

Cecily rose unsteadily from the chair, a wave of nausea passing through her belly. Had she eaten too much or too little in the great hall? Her memory of the evening seemed obliterated, except for…except for the moment when Lachlan said he would marry her. Her head lolled, as if iron weights had been attached to the nape of her neck.

She stared down ruefully at the hem of her filthy skirts.

'I will take your clothes and have them washed, mistress. With all the fires going in the kitchen, they will be dry by morning. I can fetch a nightgown for you to wear now.'

'I have a leather satchel with some possessions in,' Cecily explained. 'The bag is down in the great hall, with my cloak.' She removed her circlet and veil and laid them on the end of the bed.

'I will have them fetched for you,' Hester said. 'Now, shall I help you with your gown?'

Between them, they undid the side-lacings of Cecily's over-gown, Hester lifting the gown over Cecily's head. The fabric collapsed in a muddy purple heap on the floor, the spiralling silver embroidery twinkling in the candlelight. Hester worked on the tiny buttons securing the sleeves on Cecily's lilac underdress. When, at last they flapped free, Cecily managed to pull the looser garment over her head without help.

'Thank you, Hester,' Cecily said as she stood before the maidservant in her chemise and stockings. She had already removed her wet leather boots and noticed that Hester had placed them beneath the charcoal brazier, in the hope that they would dry out overnight. 'You can go now, if you like. Or has the King told you to stay?'

Hester dipped her head slightly. 'The King gave me no orders, my lady, other than to help you, but...' The smooth skin on her forehead puckered with worry.

'Say what you want to say, please,' Cecily encouraged her softly. She wiggled her feet in her damp stockings, watching the steam float out languidly from the edges of the tapestry screen.

'Forgive me if I seem outspoken, my lady, but I would not like to leave you alone in this chamber while you take a bath. Not with those men outside in the corridor. You cannot secure the door from the inside and they are free to walk in at any time. They have the key...'

Cecily held up her hand. 'Then stay, Hester. I would like you to.'

The woman beamed. 'I shall sit by the door, my lady, and guard your privacy.'

* * *

Once behind the screen, Cecily quickly removed her chemise, undergarments and stockings and climbed into the wooden tub. She released her hair, unpinning her bun, and shaking out her plaits into long, curling tresses that brushed against the curve of her hips. As the hot water closed over her shoulders, she gasped at the sweet sensation, at the silky liquid caress that eased the tension in her aching limbs. She shuddered, a deep, rippling vibration that started at the tips of her freezing toes and worked its way up her body. Bringing her knees up, she sank even lower, her loosened hair floating out on the water, like silky seaweed.

Leaning her head back against the wooden brim, she traced the colourful images in the tapestry screen that shielded her from the main part of the chamber. The scene was of a forest, depicting trees and elaborate foliage, with wild mythical beasts roaming along in the foreground. The detail was exquisite, with every image, down to the last tiny acorn at the bottom of the screen executed in the finest needlework. She remembered her sister, her mother, with their heads bent over the tapestry frames at home, then in the solar chamber at Okeforde Castle. In her mind's eyes, the scene appeared to be one of cosy domesticity, yet she knew she was lying to herself. Every day had been riven through with tension, her mother's barbed comments and dark looks. How she wished it could have been otherwise. Maybe one day she would see them again. After she had married Lachlan.

After she had married Lachlan.

Closing her eyes, she sank down further into the water. In order to protect her skin from catching any splinters from the wooden sides, the bath was lined with a large piece of linen, and, as she leaned her head back against the brim, her neck was cushioned by the fabric. A deep frown furrowed her brow, a sense of loss and shame. Lachlan had offered to marry her, why, she had no idea, other than a misguided sense of responsibility, because she was a problem to be solved rather than the fact that she was someone he wanted to be with.

Yet she wanted to be with him.

Her eyes popped open. He had looked after her in this last few days, there was no denying that. He had chosen not to reveal her deception to Simon and had offered to escort her to the King so she had not been at the mercy of Lord Simon's knights. She had grown used to that wonderful feeling of protection, of being cared for. She had forgotten what it was like to be alone.

Cecily shifted in the bath. The water sloshed against the sides, a soft gurgling sound. Exhaustion clogged her brain, making it sluggish, unresponsive. On the brink of sleep, her head rolled to one side and she nudged it upright again. Forcing her eyes open, she scrubbed her arms furiously with the linen flannel and white bar of honeyed soap left by Hester on a circular wooden stool by the tub. After she had rubbed every inch of her body with the flannel, rinsed all the dirt and sweat from her skin, she turned her attention to her hair, sinking down into the deep water to wet her long tresses. Bobbing up once more she lathered the sweet-smelling soap through her hair, then slid down again to rinse it.

'My lady?'

Hester's voice made her jump. Her fingers skittered across the rapidly cooling water, causing an eruption of little ripples across the surface. She twisted her head. Hester poked her head around the side of the tapestry screen. One end of her linen head-wrap had come loose; a bright strand of blonde hair curled down in front of her ear.

'Shall I help you out, my lady? The water must be cold by now.'

'Yes, thank you.'

With Hester holding on to her arm, Cecily stepped over the high-sided wooden tub and out on to the sheepskin rug that protected her bare feet from the cold wooden floorboards. Her naked skin gleamed in the candlelight, the water sluicing down her toned limbs. Hester wrapped a large linen towel around her and used another towel to dry Cecily's hair, patting the long tresses gently to soak up most of the water.

'If you sit on this stool near the brazier, my lady, then I can comb your hair for you.'

Cecily scooped up the towel around her naked skin and settled on to the low wooden stool. She wiggled her bare toes into the soft sheepskin. Lit by a couple of candles set into wall niches, the area behind the tapestry screen was warm and cosy, the charcoal brazier throwing off a delicious heat. She tipped her head back as Hester pulled a comb through her wet locks, her fingers deft and gentle.

'I can braid it for you, mistress, when it is drier,' Hester said. There was a sharp rap at the door. 'That will be your satchel from the great hall, my lady. I sent someone to fetch it for you.' She disappeared around the screen.

Cecily heard the click of the latch and Hester's lilting tones, speaking to whoever was in the corridor. The words were muffled, difficult to decipher. Her wet hair was draped over her ears and the spitting coals in the brazier obscured most sound. All Cecily could hear were the high-pitched notes of Hester's voice against the low rumble of a servant in the corridor. Then she heard the door close once more, and the heavy key clunk round noisily in the lock. She smiled, thinking of the maidservant ordering the guards outside to give her that key.

'Was it my bag, Hester?' she called, dabbing a trickle of water away from her cheek with a corner of the towel. Rising from the stool, Cecily flapped the towel open so that she could wrap it around herself more securely. She moved around the screen.

Hester was not there.

Lachlan stood by the door, clutching her leather satchel. The bag looked incongruous in his large, sinewy hands—too small, too feminine to be carried by such a man. He was a warrior and a fighter, not a carrier of bags. His eyes fell on her slim, scantily clad figure; roamed the luscious curves greedily: the concave belly, smooth with a pearl-like lustre, the enticing curve of her breast. She flipped the towel briskly across her naked flesh, angling her jaw up at him in question.

'Why are you here?' Cecily hung back, half-hidden by the screen.

'I...' Lachlan trawled his mind to find something, anything appropriate to say, but the words had vanished from his brain. His head was empty, bereft of coherent speech. He sucked in his breath; tried again. 'I brought…your satchel,' he croaked out. 'I thought you might need it.'

Cecily stood poised, a startled deer about to run. Her eyes were huge, great shimmering discs of green dominating her face. The large towel draped over her; she gripped it fiercely to her throat, her knuckles white. And yet it was not enough. Further down, the fragile edges gaped dangerously, affording him tantalising glimpses of her soft, rounded thighs; the neat indent of her knee. The elegant bones of her ankle. Christ, she was perfect.

Heat thumped through him; sweat slicked the back of his neck, his scalp. His senses snapped, thrust him up to a stark, vivid awareness. The air changed, knife-sharp, a quivering tension. He wolfed down her beauty, a starving man, searching the shadows beneath her towel. Pinned to the spot, incapable of stopping himself. What had seemed in the great hall like a simple act of kindness, taking Cecily's satchel upstairs because he thought she might need something, had now become a hazardous mission. Why had he not just handed the bag over to the maid at the door, instead of sending her and the guards downstairs for their supper? What a stupid mistake.

He should leave, he told himself. Get out, now.

'Lachlan...' Cecily hesitated, as if unsure about moving from the relative safety of the screen. Her glorious hair, the colour of a fawn's pelt, straggled around her in loose curling waves, dropping to her hips. Like the first day when he had met her, down by the river. Her skin was damp, gleaming from her bath, lit by the flickering candles. He traced the curve of her neck, the rapid pulse at her throat.

Lachlan cleared his throat, a wave of heat coursing through his muscular body. 'Here,' he said, holding out the bag towards her, unwilling to move from the door.

'Thank you.' Cecily's voice was quiet, muted. His eye fell upon the hollow at her throat, the sparkling residue of water polishing her skin. She stepped forward to take the satchel.

No, no, go back! His belly clenched with desire, a burgeoning heat, slowly building.

He retreated with a quick step, his shoulder hitting the door.

Cecily glanced at him, a rosy colour staining her cheeks. 'Lachlan, I need to talk to you about…what happened down there. In the great hall.'

'Now is not a good time.' His eyes fell to the cleft on her chest and, sweet Jesu, the tantalising curve of one breast, peeking out from beneath the towel.

'But you'll want to hear this,' Cecily said eagerly, stepping closer to him. His heels bumped against the locked door.

'Later,' he ground out. Shock ran through his body, a swift, zig-zagging jolt that whipped through him like wildfire. Cecily stood inches from him, her beautiful body clad only in the gauzy woven linen, her bare toes, like small pink shells, peeking out from the flowing sweep of fabric, magnificent hair snaking down in glossy rivulets, hair that he wanted to bury his…

'So what do you think…?'

'Wh-what…?' he spluttered, dragging his eyes up to her face. Had she been speaking? 'Christ, woman, will you please cover yourself!' Exasperated, he lurched for the towel, intending to drag it across her naked flesh, in a desperate attempt to hide the shadowy delights that lay beneath.

His knuckle grazed her flesh. Her skin held the patina of velvet, smooth and cool. Sweetly seductive.

Cecily gasped beneath his touch, her mouth dropping open in surprise; he could see her small white teeth, neat and even, the silky roll of her tongue. Desire stabbed his heart, tore at his muscles, twisting them slowly, ever tighter. Her eyes shimmered, translucent emeralds fringed by dark lashes. She tipped her head to one side as if bemused by his behaviour.

Did she have no idea of the effect she was having on him? The candle shone out from the bedside, shining through the linen that she had wrapped around her, highlighting the soft curves of her body: the neat indent of her waist, the flaring curve of her hips.

He thought he would go mad. Air whistled from his lungs. He gritted his teeth, pivoting smartly to face the door, his fingers clawing desperately at the key to unlock it. He had taken the key from the guards and locked the chamber from the inside in order to maintain Cecily's privacy. What a fool he had been.

She touched his arm, stalling him. 'Why will you not talk to me?'

He heard the plaintive note in her voice, the rejection. The key slipped from his sweating fingers, spinning across the floor boards. 'Hell's teeth!' Lachlan thumped on the door, leaning his forehead against the cool wood. He closed his eyes, breathing heavily. Where was his self-control, the restraint that he prided himself on? Where was it now, when he needed it the most?

'What's the matter?' asked Cecily, her eye travelling across the breadth of his shoulders, his bent head. She gazed at the dried matted blood on his hair, marking the place where he had been hit. 'Are you ill? Is your head paining you?'

'Nay, Cecily, I'm not ill.' Despair tugged at his voice.

'Then why will you not talk to me?' She knotted her fingers together in front of her stomach, shivering a little in the cooler air of the chamber; it had been warmer behind the tapestry screen with the brazier burning.

Lachlan turned back, bracing his spine, his legs against the solid oak door. 'Do you really have no idea?' His speech was weary, teetering on a precipice.

She shook her head.

'I'm trying to protect you, Cecily.'

'Protect me? From what?'

'Oh, God in Heaven!' Lachlan growled. 'From me, Cecily. From me.'

A single drop of water trailed down from her ear to the hollow of her throat. He tracked the glistening orb with his eyes, instinct guiding his finger to stop its downward path. Lust flickered beneath the dark crust of his conscience, a banked-up fire that burst forth with ravening thirst. He moved his finger slowly upwards, savouring the satin lustre of her skin, up, up, until he reached the softest spot, beneath her chin. His fingers lifted away, wrapped around her jaw.

Her breath pulled in, swift and fierce. A keening sigh, heavy with need, with longing. Her head tilted, wanting his touch. Wanting more. She would not say a word. She would not stop him.

His jaw hardened. 'Forgive me,' he whispered, 'for what is about to happen.'

Chapter Thirteen

He grabbed a handful of the lightweight towel, tugging her forward sharply. Her slender frame jammed hard against his frame. Belly to belly, chest to chest. A delicious scent rose from her heated skin—lavender—reminding him of the sun-bathed hills of summer. His mouth lowered, lips seizing hers, claiming them in a heady, plundering kiss. His strong arms locked around her, winching her into him, closer and closer. Lust rolled through him, deep and visceral, an unstoppable tide of desire.

Her legs collapsed as she bent into him, arching her slight, graceful figure, fitting herself against him as if it were the most natural thing in the world. Conscious logical thought, the rights and the wrongs of what she was doing, were swept clean from her mind, shocked by the swift, demanding contact of his mouth. Why did she not shove him away, shout and scream for someone to come and help her? Pushed away by her greedy need for him, her self-control had fled. Shame fluttered on the edge of her consciousness. She ignored it.

Arms locked around her waist, Lachlan lifted her slightly, backing towards the bed, his big legs knocking against the base board before they fell together, as one. The dark sable pelt engulfed their twined figures, pillowing their limbs. His mouth claimed hers once more, tracking along her lips, demanding more.

Her limbs melted into his burly frame, her hand running over the rounded muscle of his shoulder, marvelling at the solid power beneath her fingers, the honed ripple of muscle beneath his linen sleeve. Her hand moved up his corded neck to his hair, plunging into his fiery curls. His scalp was hot against her fingers; he groaned at the gentle, sifting touch.

He wrenched his lips from hers, panting heavily. 'There is only one way this is going to end, Cecily, unless you stop me now.' His eyes, midnight pools of flickering desire, sought hers, imploring.

'I will not.'

'Do you realise what is going to happen?' His hands framed the perfect oval of her face. Her skin was pale, like cool marble; her damp, beautiful hair spread out on the bed furs around her. Like a mermaid, he thought. A wild nymph of the sea who had cast a spell over him.

'Aye, I do,' Cecily replied quietly.

'God in Heaven.' Lachlan blinked, shocked, astounded by her response. Desire barged into him like a physical force, all-consuming: a surging fire, claiming his body as if it were not his own.

Cecily shuddered as his lips claimed hers once more, but it was a shudder of delight, not fear. She did not fear him; she wanted this with all her heart. His hands roamed down her back, down to the flaring curve of her hips; she gasped at the intimacy of his touch as he winched her ever closer to him. The edges of the towel fell away; she lay naked before him. A voice of warning chattered in her brain, like a baby bird, but she dashed away the omens, sent them skittering back to the shadows. She cared not. The worry and regrets would come later, but right now, all she wanted was to lie with him, with this man who had come to mean so much to her over the past few days.

Lachlan tore impatiently at his clothes, flinging them haphazardly to the floor. The candle in the wall sconce jumped and flickered, kissing his muscled skin, the shadowy curve of his big shoulders, the sculptured ridging of his chest. He reached out for Cecily and they rolled together on the bed furs, flesh against flesh.

The air in her chest squeezed in sharp delight as the naked, honed length of him pressed into her, his hard angles against her softer curves. The vibrant blue of his eyes darkened to black, fired with a quick, intense energy, a yearning to have, to possess. He found her mouth once more, the damp tendrils of her hair teasing his cheek, then his lips worked downwards, lower and lower, to the dip between her breasts…

'Lachlan, I…?' Excitement consumed her, ripped through her with lightning force, striking at the very core of her. Her body tripped and thrummed in a state of nervous anticipation. A slow-burning intensity flared through her belly, her groin, until she thought she would scream aloud with the piercing ache of longing. She quivered with need, her ribcage flexing with sweet awareness, the knowledge of what was about to happen.

Winding his leg across both of hers, he hitched her beneath him, moving with infinite slowness. His heavy limbs splayed over her, sinking into her soft frame. The short hairs on his legs tickled her calves and she pressed her fingers to his chest, in awe at the beautiful man above her. His longing seared into her, yet he waited, claiming her lips once more, teasing and tantalising as his hand slid along the silken length of her thigh.

Reason fled, torn away by raging desire, left in tatters. Her mind was not her own now, swept up in a whirlpool of desire from which she had no hope of escape. The fiery seduction of his searching hands drove her out into the wilderness, to a place she had never been, to a place where she would truly lose herself. His scorching touch stripped her soul down to the very nub of her being, yet she wanted to yell and shout out her delight at the way he made her feel. Every fibre of her muscles stretched tight with tortuous anticipation; she wobbled on the brink, feet slipping on the loose stones, about to plunge into the unknown abyss.

Carefully, inch by inch, Lachlan slid into her warm, velvet folds, gritting his teeth savagely to bridle the eagerness in his body, the thrusting urge to possess. Shocked at the sudden intimacy, Cecily gasped out in surprise, her eyes enormous, unfocused. Braced above her on his thick arms, Lachlan hesitated. Had he hurt her? 'Cecily...?' he breathed. 'Shall I stop?'

'No!' she cried out forcefully. 'Don't you dare!' Her arms flew around him, drawing him down, closer to her, clinging to the possessive glitter in his eyes.

He chuckled, despite himself. He heard the plea of desire in her voice, the need. Senses inflamed, he reminded himself to go slowly, gradually, yet he seemed unable to hold back, seized by a wildness that he had never known before. An unknown force possessed his flesh, an enchantment. He surged forward in delight, with an abandonment that astonished him, driving into her completely, wholly, utterly. Shifting within her, he began to move more slowly, building his possession of her with gradual movements. Unable to hold back any more, his speed quickened, moving faster and faster, driving into her on the shining sable pelt.

She welcomed the abrupt change in tempo, matching his powerful thrusts with a joyful hunger of her own. The strict, censorious part of her brain, the part that told her what to do and how to behave, ceased to work, flattening out to nothing. Her breath emerged in short little gasps, her slight frame barely able to contain the wave after wave of pleasure that rolled through her limbs. Her eyelashes fluttered down, her belly and groin tightening in heady anticipation. Then she moaned, her body clamouring for a high point, climbing and climbing. The air ripped from her lungs. A white-hot heat surged through her, needles of light slashing across the dark innards of her eyes, a pounding frenzy of sparkling stars crashing through her.

She cried out then, waves of tumultuous passion ricocheting through her at hurtling pace, leaving her collapsed, spent. Reaching his own climax, Lachlan shuddered, throwing his head back to shout out loud. Then his big body sprawled heavily over her naked body, sated and, for the first time in a long time, fully alive.

They lay there for a long time, twined into each other, their panting breaths gradually subsiding. The sweat cooled on their naked limbs. Shifting his weight to one side, Lachlan pulled the bed furs over them, Cecily curling in to his right flank, her softness melding to the hard, muscled angles of his body. Her hair straggled across the curving bloom of her cheek and he smoothed it back, tucking the silky length behind her ear. She gave a small sound of satisfaction, stretching her slim arm across his broad chest, but her eyes remained closed, her dark lashes casting tiny shadows on her cheeks.

What in Christ's name had he done? His eyes searched the linen canopy above the bed, tracing along the many pleats and creases as if he could find the answer written in the fabric. The candlelight flickered on the cloth, wavering. Shame spilled through him, dark and coruscating, a bitter liquid that scoured his veins with distaste. He had behaved like an oaf, like his Viking forefathers, running roughshod over her refined sensibilities; rolling in the bed with her like a man possessed. A savage. He had not even possessed the grace to go slowly, to take his time; nay, he had barrelled into her without so much as a by your leave.

Cecily opened her eyes slowly, reluctantly, not wanting to break the spell, the magic of this enchanted time. The skin of Lachlan's chest warmed her cheek. Her hand lay flat, her fingers splayed across his ribs, the fine hairs covering his skin tickling her palm. In the candlelight, his bare chest gleamed with golden light, burnished by the flame. Her limbs felt exhausted, replete, muscles sapped of strength and yet strangely enervated, renewed. The experience had been so completely different from the time when she had been married to Peter that it was almost incomparable.

She shifted, wriggling her back against the linen sheets. The soft fabric slid magnificently against her bare skin. Hope flickered through her mind, singing with possibilities for the future. Maybe, just maybe, this marriage with Lachlan might work. How wonderful it would be to share his life, to share his bed and have his children. Was it truly possible that by committing a crime, she had unwittingly found real love? Had Fortune smiled on her, after all?

'I'm sorry.' Lachlan's voice ground out, bleak and raw. Lifting his arm from around her shoulders, he rolled away from her, across to the side of the bed.

Cecily failed to hear the chill note in his tone. 'Oh, am I squashing you?' Her laughter blossomed out, a delicate trill across the chamber. A spark jumped from the charcoal brazier, falling back down into the coals with a crackling hiss.

He stared over to the glow of red from the brazier. His heart compressed, tight with wretchedness. 'No, Cecily, you're not squashing me. Far from it.' Sitting up, Lachlan slid his bare feet down to the wooden floorboards, his back towards her. His spine bent forward; resting his elbows on his knees, he pressed his forehead into his hands. His powerful fingers dug into his hair. 'I meant that I'm sorry for what just happened... I... I lost control of myself.'

Shock rattled through her. What was he saying? That it should not have happened? She wanted to scream at him to take his apology back, to acknowledge that their lying together had been a thing of beauty, not something to be ashamed of!

'I don't understand.' Covering her naked breasts with the sheet, she edged over to him on her knees, grazing the powerful line of his shoulders lightly with her fingertips. He flinched away from her, hunkering down. Rejection sloshed over her. The jointed line of his spine faced her mutely, a rigid shield of defence. Against her.

'What have I done?' Her voice emerged, a muted note of despair. Her hand fell away from him. Desperation clawed at her. She remembered her husband, rolling away from her body with a derisory grunt, leaving her sore and shivering in the marital bed. The splatters of blood on the sheets.

'You have done nothing, Cecily. Nothing! What we did…it should not have happened. It's my fault.' His voice rolled over her, harsh, angry.

'I am as culpable as you, Lachlan,' she pointed out miserably. 'You asked me, you warned me. I had time to say "no".'

'Christ, I wish you had, Cecily. I wish you had pushed me away,' Lachlan mumbled, scrubbing violently at his face with his hands.

His voice stung. Cecily sat up, yanking the sheet up to her throat to shield her nakedness. 'Well, I am sorry you had such an awful time,' she spat back bitterly, anger rising in her chest.

He twisted around, a muscle jumping in his jaw. 'Oh, believe me, I enjoyed it.' His voice was cold. 'But it should not have happened.'

'Why not?' Her heart contracted. 'We are to be married, after all.'

'We are,' he said slowly. 'But I offered to marry you to protect you.' Standing up, he pulled on his braies. The tangled heap of his clothes on the floor, discarded in haste, mocked him, taunting him for his lack of self-control. 'I cannot offer you anything else. Our marriage will be "in name only".'

She supposed she should be thankful, yet his words tore the beauty of what they had shared; pulled it apart with icy dissection. She hated him for that. 'In name only,' she repeated quietly.

Lachlan secured the buckle on his belt. 'Aye. Marriage to me will give you protection, Cecily, but that's all I can give you. Nothing more.' He shoved his feet into his leather boots. After what had happened to his family, he could never risk loving anyone every again. The frozen lump of his heart was testament to that.

'So you used me for your own physical release.' Her voice was sour, acerbic.

His lips curled savagely as he traced the downward turn of her mouth, the dulling sparkle of her eyes. Let her think the worst of him. If she hated him, then it would be easier for him to keep his distance. Easier for him to not fall in love with her. 'Don't attach too much importance to...' his hand swept over the bed disparagingly, the rumpled sheets and bed furs '...all this. We both enjoyed it, but it means very little.'

Cecily flinched beneath his cheerless speech. He belittled the experience, making her feel like she had done something sordid, underhand. Sadness welled up, spreading out beneath her ribcage, a huge chasm of loneliness at what could never be, at what she could never have: a proper marriage with the man she could love, a marriage with Lachlan. Aye, she admitted. That was right. She could love Lachlan. Maybe she even loved him already. For a fleeting moment, it had been within her grasp, but now it was gone, shattered to a million pieces. If she married him now, then every day would be like torture, unable to touch him, unable to kiss him. She would always be thinking of what might have been, if he had been able to love her. What a shame that he could not.

Beneath the sheet, Cecily dragged her knees up, wrapping her arms around her legs. 'Then I don't want it,' she replied, her voice beginning to rise. 'I don't want your stupid marriage. I prefer to marry someone else!'

He laughed, a harsh grating sound. 'You can't marry someone like the Lord of Colcombe. He is twice your age and would use you ill.'

Her mouth twisted petulantly; she slumped back against the pillows. He was right and she knew it. 'But you're sacrificing your own life to help me, Lachlan. That's what I don't understand. Why tie yourself with me?'

Because I don't want anyone else to have you, he thought. *Because you brighten my days with your quick mind and sweet smile. Your beauty.* 'There is no one else, Cecily. No one suitable, anyway. Annoying as it may seem to you, I am your only way out of this situation.' His reasons were purely selfish: he had leapt at the chance of keeping Cecily by his side.

'There is someone, actually,' Cecily said slowly. 'I was going to discuss it with you…earlier.' Her cheeks reddened, but she ploughed onwards. 'He's a friend of mine.'

Excitement tinged her voice. This was a way
out of this untenable situation. 'It seems
pointless that you have offered to marry me
if we are both going to be miserable.' She
clutched the bed furs closer to her throat. 'I
know someone who will marry me, if the
King would agree.'

Lachlan pulled his white linen shirt over
his head. 'Who?'

'My childhood friend, William. He would
marry me.'

Jealousy, hot and unbidden, rolled through
Lachlan. He scowled, turning away to scoop
up his cloak. 'Why did you not mention him
to the King?'

Cecily spread her palm across the bed covers, brushing at a small fleck of dust. 'I'm
hardly in a position to dictate my own terms,
am I?'

Lachlan raised his fiery eyebrows. 'No, I
suppose not.'

'But you could go down now and suggest
him. You would be free, Lachlan. You've
just told me you never intended to marry, so
why do it? It would only make you sad. This
is a way out for you, if you would take it.'

But I don't want to take it, he thought roughly. Who was this William she kept gabbling on about? Possession flicked through him; he doused it quickly. This should be what he wanted. If that was so, then why did his heart feel as if it had been split in two?

'Get some sleep now, Cecily. It's late. I will go and tell the King about what you have said.' He crouched down on the floor, his fingers looping around the iron key, the errant key that had dropped from his fingers before. In another lifetime. 'I shall return in the morning with his answer.'

'Thank you,' she said. The door clicked shut behind him and she heard the heavy key turn in the lock. Then she pressed her face into the feather pillow and wept.

It was early when Lachlan walked, stripped to his shirt and braies, out into the bailey. Streaks of pink and orange streaked the sky to the east. A solitary star winked out from the luminous blue on the horizon, the moon a silver fingernail of light. His breath puffed out into the icy air, clouds of white mist. The cobbled yard was deserted, save for a few horses tied up to an iron ring in the curtain wall and a single guard at the gatehouse who raised his arm in greeting. Lachlan waved back, heading for the well in the middle of the yard.

Turning the handle on the rope, Lachlan followed the descent of the wooden bucket until it disappeared into the shadows. He heard the splash as it hit the mirrored circle far below. He stared down into the well, down at the widening ripples of water.

After leaving Cecily, he had sought out Henry in the great hall and told him of her request to marry this William instead. The King had been in a garrulous mood, florid cheeks beaming from red wine, smiling as he listened to Lachlan. He had told Lachlan that he trusted his judgement implicitly: if there was another man who would marry her whom Lachlan thought suitable, then that was fine.

Lachlan had found a place to sleep in the great hall, a wooden pallet with a thin straw mattress crammed in among other people: knights and their squires, peasants, their wives and screaming babies. Piles of chainmail had been heaped up in every available space, swords and helmets stacked on top. Stale sweat soured the air, mingling with the smell of mead, of grease. He had cared not; his mind was in turmoil, churning incessantly. Busy with the upcoming parliament, the King had effectively passed the decision of Cecily's marriage to Lachlan.

Lachlan dumped the full bucket on to the cobbles. Water sloshed over the side, wetting the leather of his boots. Cursing out loud, he seized the bucket, pouring the chill contents over his head. He gasped in shock at the cold. Water ran through his hair, over his sleep-stained face, down his neck beneath his shirt, dampening the material so that it stuck, like a glaucous skin, to his muscled chest. The gash on the back of his head throbbed and stung beneath the onslaught of water. Would he tell her what the King had said? That she could marry this… William, after all?

He shook the water from his hair, the droplets spinning out from his fiery head. The first rays of sunlight, creeping over the square-cut battlements, touched them, turned them to spinning crystals of gold. He straightened up, pushing the wet hair from his eyes, raking the short strands back.

A noise from the gatehouse made him narrow his eyes and look over in that direction. He heard the sound of the portcullis being raised, the slow clanking of metal chains. Horseshoes rang against the cobbles; the close confines of the gatehouse amplified the sound of men's voices as they rode through.

A group of knights entered the inner bailey, faces covered by steel helmets, their red and gold tunics creased and muddy. Beneath their surcoats they wore chainmail; every man carried a shield and sword. Watching them intently, Lachlan pulled off his wet shirt over his head, irritated by its clamminess next to his skin. He wadded it into a pad, using the cloth to dry the last drops of water from his neck and chest.

Was it only a few weeks ago that he had ridden in a posse of knights like that? Wielded a sword, circling the weapon around and around his head as he dug his knees into the flanks of his horse? Charged into battles without a care in the world? Because he hadn't cared, not really. He hadn't cared whether he lived or died. There was nothing to live for. Not then.

But now?

Now there was Cecily.

He took a deep unsteady breath, nodding a greeting as the knights rode past him towards the stables. He kneaded the damp shirt between his hands. He had vowed never to marry and now Henry had given him a way out. But he did not want to take it.

Chapter Fourteen

Lachlan walked slowly across the bailey. His long-legged strides covered the ground easily now, with no trace of a limp. The wound in his leg was fully healed. In the great hall, he rummaged in his leather satchel for a dry shirt, pulling his tunic over the top. Strapping his leather belt around his trim waist, he searched for his sword from habit, twisting his mouth ruefully as he remembered. With his cloak swung around his shoulders, carrying his leather satchel, he climbed the stairs to Cecily's chamber.

The young guard at the door stood aside as Lachlan rapped on the wooden planks.

The door cracked open. Cecily appeared in the gap. Beneath her gauzy chemise, he saw the sweet curve of her waist, the generous flare of her hips. His heart pinched with longing. Her face was softened with sleep, cheeks delicately flushed. Old tears tracked her skin. Guilt squirmed in his gut, jabbing deep. His cold, cruel words in the aftermath of their lovemaking. She hadn't deserved that.

'Are you ready?'

'Ready…?' she replied, her expression puzzled. 'Lachlan…it's so early!' Her beautiful hair tumbled down over her shoulders, a silken waterfall of lustrous pale brown locks. His fingers itched to touch, but he wedged his hands by his sides, forcing himself to concentrate.

'You need to get dressed,' Lachlan said. 'I have asked the maid to come up and help you. Meet me in the chapel, as soon as you can.'

'The chapel…' She stared at him, aghast. Her green eyes shimmered in the dimness of the corridor. 'You mean…'

Lachlan snared her bright eyes with his own, his expression implacable, unreadable. 'Yes, Cecily, we are to be married. You heard the King last night.'

Sweet Jesu! Was the marriage to be now? Reaching through the doorway, she placed a hand on his sleeve. 'I thought… I thought you might have spoken to him about…' Her wavering tone hollowed out, a forlorn note.

He stared down at the slender fingers, clasped around his forearm. Hands that had clung to him the night before, hands that had urged him on. He could not tell her what the King said. 'I did,' he answered slowly. 'And I am sorry, Cecily, but he said "no". He would not agree to you marrying anyone else.'

Her heart squeezed with emotion. Would she be able to bear this? She would have to learn to live alongside him, loving him from afar, and tie her true feelings close to her chest. He had made it perfectly clear how he felt about her last night. Cecily's eyes blurred with unshed tears.

He saw the tell-tale shine in her eyes. 'I know this…me…is not what you wanted.' Deep in the nub of his chest, something kindled, sparked. But it was what he wanted. Wasn't that enough?

She jerked her chin in the air. Hell's teeth, how wrong could a person be? Could he not see? 'I am in no position to "want", Lachlan. I committed a crime and I must pay for it. If the King said no, then so be it.'

Was that how she saw him? As a burden to be endured, day by day? Was his marriage to be akin to a prison sentence for her? Lachlan shifted uncomfortably, rocking from one foot to the other, acutely conscious that the guard standing at the doorway was, despite his impassive expression, drinking in every word of their conversation.

Cecily dropped her gaze. 'My life has been spared, Lachlan, and I am eternally grateful for that. And only because of you. You deserve my thanks. You could have walked away.'

Despair flickered through him. He should be walking away, right now. He should walk away now, stand aside, so that she could marry William. A wave of possessive jealousy swung through his broad frame as her bright face gleamed up at him through the doorway. Like an angel, he thought, lighting his days with her quick, vivid smile, her dainty steps at his side. He doubted he could ever walk away.

'Meet me in the chapel, when you are dressed.'

The stone chapel was deserted apart from one man: the priest. He moved about the altar on silent feet, highlighted by a flickering candle. The light bounced off the silver cross that swung over his simple dark robes, the gemstones in the larger wooden cross placed upon the altar table. A row of narrow windows, delineated by cut stone, sat high up on either side of the chapel walls. Unglazed, they allowed light and air to filter into the small space, juddering the candle flame, sending shafts of sunlight pooling on to the flagstones. Despite this, the chapel felt shadowed, crepuscular. Gloomy.

Lachlan stood beneath the wide-arched doorway, waiting for Cecily. Sadness welled up in his chest, weighing heavy against his ribcage. Marriages were not supposed to be like this. They should be full of people, music and laughter. A time of happiness and celebration.

He looked up. Cecily was walking up the narrow path towards him, her skirts brushing the blades of grass, wet with dew. At her side, the young knight who has been outside her chamber door.

'You can go,' Lachlan dismissed the house knight, as Cecily moved to stand beside him. Her skin was gossamer-clear, ethereal in the morning light. The weak morning sun kissed her face, her green eyes assessing him calmly, her mouth turning up at the corners into a slight smile. His heart flared with…what? He couldn't place the feeling, the sense of tremulous joy, new-born.

'What's the matter?' The sweet melody of her voice rang out. Tangled in his heart-strings.

What was he doing? She had been let down by so many people in her life, yet here she stood, brave, undaunted by rejection, about to marry a man who was not worthy of her. A man who had lied to her.

'You…you have no flowers,' he blurted

out, scratching about for something to say. His palms were sweating and he rubbed them surreptitiously down the front of his braies.

Cecily laughed, her smile reaching up to the corners of her sparkling eyes. 'I have no need of flowers, Lachlan,' she said. 'Besides, you would have a difficult job trying to find any at this time of year.' She reached for his hand, curled her warm fingers around his. 'Come on.'

'Wait,' he said, leaving her standing beneath the archway, and sprinted along the path, disappearing into a small copse alongside the chapel. He returned, moments later, marching decisively along the path. In his big hand he clasped a tiny bunch of hazel twigs. The stems were thin, delicate, tipped with frilly buds of deepest pink. Green catkins, unripe, hung at intervals along the pliable twigs.

'There!' he said, triumphantly, thrusting the stems into her hand.

Her face flushed with pleasure as she cradled the delicate bunch. 'Thank you, Lachlan.'

He crooked her arm beneath hers and they walked into the empty church.

'There's no one here!' Cecily whispered as they walked along the aisle, towards the priest. 'Where is the King, his knights? I thought at least they would be here to witness this. To make sure it was done!'

Lachlan cleared his throat. How could he tell her that the King didn't care enough about her to ever appear? How Henry had placed the decision of her marriage into Lachlan's hands. The tips of his fingers tingled with nervous energy.

They knelt together before the priest, knees sinking into the musty velvet cushion that sat before the altar table. The priest started to speak, his tones high and wavering. Then he coughed and his words vanished into a fit of coughing, punching harshly into the deserted silence.

Cecily squeezed Lachlan's hand. He glanced at her, at the dainty jut of her chin, at the fine tendril of hair that had escaped her veil. Chewing his bottom lip, he waited for the priest to regain his composure. With every tick of silence, guilt spread in Lachlan's chest, pressing, layer upon layer, compressing his lie, enlarging it until it filled his body with condemnation.

What was he doing? Had he truly lost his mind? How could he weld this beautiful, brave-hearted woman to his dark, troubled soul? He would surely destroy her. This needed to stop. And it needed to stop now.

Lachlan stood up abruptly, hauling Cecily up beside him. His hand grasped her elbow. 'There's been a mistake,' he said.

'My lord...?' The priest frowned at him. 'I'm not sure that...'

Lachlan turned, sweeping Cecily into his side, against him. He strode out of the chapel, ignoring the priest's astounded face.

'What is happening, Lachlan?' Cecily cried as her feet struggled to keep up with the fast pace of his stride. Her soft leather boots scuffed against the stone flagstones. 'What is going on?'

Lachlan didn't speak until they had reached the stables. The sour smell of hay, kept in storage, permeated the air. Beneath the wide lintel of the stable door, he faced her, holding her hands in his.

'I have made a mistake.' Sunlight sifted through his hair, tipping the ends to fiery gold.

Sadness, loss, plummeted through Cecily's heart. She might have guessed this would be forthcoming and yet his words still came as a shock. 'You've changed your mind,' she said carefully. 'It's understandable.' Her shoulders hunched in on themselves and she stepped back, throwing him a wan smile. 'Please don't trouble yourself, it's clear why you wouldn't want to marry me.' Rejection clogged her mind and she fought back the tears. How close she had been.

'No, listen, Cecily, you have me wrong,' Lachlan declared.

The green glimmer in her eyes read the agitation in his face, the heightened ruddy colour of his cheeks. Wrong? It seemed perfectly clear to her. She tipped her head to one side, waiting to hear his excuses.

'I lied to you.'

She folded her arms across her chest. Behind her, in one of the wooden partitions, her little grey mare whinnied in recognition of her mistress. How she wished she could fling herself on her horse's back and gallop off, away from all this heartache.

'I asked Henry about whether you could marry William...'

'I know, you told me!' Cecily toed the ground, jabbing at a loose piece of straw lying on the hard-packed earth.'

'...and he agreed that you could marry William, as long as I took you to him.'

Her head jerked up, and she clasped her hands together before her chest, into a tight knot. 'Lachlan...what? Why did you not tell me?'

Because I wanted you all to myself, he thought. *The most selfish thing in the world when I can give you nothing else but the protection of my name.*

'Because I never intended to marry,' he explained. 'And now the King has agreed to you marrying William, who you know and like...'

She thought of William, with his large brown eyes and docile manner. Half a head taller than her with an easy smile, the companion of her troubled youth. He was nothing compared to Lachlan. But beggars could not be choosers and she was bumping along the bottom at the moment. It made sense that Lachlan didn't want her, after all, given what had happened between them yester eve. His horrible words, ripping apart the beauty of their lovemaking. Well, it had been beautiful for her, anyway. Not for him, obviously.

'Why don't you just say it?' she flared at him. 'Why don't you just say that you don't want to be married to me?'

His sapphire eyes flicked over her. 'Why are you so angry? I thought... I thought you wanted to marry this childhood sweetheart of yours. He sounds infinitely preferable to me, since you seem to rate him so highly.'

'He's everything that you are not,' Cecily replied. 'Kind, good-hearted, wholesome.' There was only one problem. She didn't love him.

She tugged her long skirts around and stepped towards her horse, running her palm over the mare's soft nose. 'We had better find William then.' Her voice was sharp, bitter with regret. 'The sooner, the better.'

* * *

It was mid-afternoon by the time they reached the brow of the very last hill before they dropped down to Dornceaster, following the path of the old Roman road that led eastwards. Below them, alongside a wide, curving river, lay an abbey. White limestone quoins shone out in the angled sunlight, the sprawling buildings, barns and chapel clustered in a loose group around a central cloister on the eastern side of the River Axe. This wide flow of water, its many curving tributaries bisecting and looping across the great flat expanse of floodplain, created a mirrored net of sparkling ribbons as the river made its way out to the sea at the port town of Flete, a few miles to the south.

Half-closing her eyes, Cecily could make out tiny figures: monks, moving around the buildings. They were easily spotted by their dull white habits, woven from rough sheep wool, no doubt the same sheep that dotted the rich pastureland around the abbey. Her throat was dry, parched. Beneath her hood, her scalp was sweaty and hot, despite the cold weather. Every limb in her body ached:

her hips, the back of her thighs, her spine. Lachlan's relentless pace had taken its toll; she had managed to keep up with him, but the speed of the journey had exhausted her.

'We could go down,' suggested Cecily. 'Someone there might be able to give us directions.' She raised her eyebrows in Lachlan's direction.

Lachlan nodded. 'It is late. The monks will give us a decent meal and a bed for the night, I suppose.'

'And they might know where William is living now.' Cecily pulled the edge of her hood over her ear, stopping the wind from whistling around the back of her neck.

He shrugged his shoulders. 'Maybe.' His tone held a trace of reluctance.

'And I really need something to eat.' She smiled, her mouth curving encouragingly.

He laughed. The tension along the back of his shoulders ebbed away. 'I'm sorry, you must be tired and hungry. You've kept up with me all day. And I haven't been slow.' He searched her face and saw the bluish shadows below her magnificent eyes.

'No, you haven't,' she admitted, acknowl-

edging his quiet admiration. It had been difficult at times to keep the pace up. 'Let's go
down before the light fades.'

She twitched the reins on her horse and
began the long descent to the valley bottom. Reluctantly, Lachlan followed, his
heart clogged with despair. Every step of
this journey was taking them closer to William. Closer to the man who would take Cecily from his side. He didn't want to give her
up, yet he knew that he must. Otherwise his
dark soul would destroy her.

The stony track led alongside the field
boundary: a substantial hedge crammed
with twisted beech, stubs of glossy green
holly, red berries shining out. Powdery lichen, pale green, clung to the dark, serrated
trunks, the sharply angled twigs. Tiny stones
spun out from beneath the horses' hooves,
skittering across the track as they made their
way down to the river, crossing at a ford-
ing point. Here, the river ran wide and shallow, the water skimming over the large flat
stones set beneath the water. With Lachlan
right behind her, Cecily pushed her little

horse up the steep zig-zagging path on the other side, towards the towering walls of the abbey.

The sun hovered on the horizon and the air had grown chill when they finally reached the abbey gatehouse. Jumping down from his horse, Lachlan came round to help Cecily. Her limbs were so stiff that she had trouble even throwing her leg over the horse's neck. Lachlan reached for her waist and swung her down, his arm dropping away from her as they walked towards the iron-studded gate, firmly shut towards them.

Lachlan grabbed the bell rope, rang hard. Almost immediately a smaller door, set in the large main gate, opened inwards and an elderly monk, clad in the same simple white habit that Cecily had spotted earlier, peered out, a flaring, spitting torch lighting up his jovial features. 'Can I help you?' he asked in a quavering voice.

'Aye, we are after a bed for the night,' Lachlan explained. 'And maybe something to eat, if that is possible.'

The monk nodded. 'Yes, of course.'

'And you might be able to help us.' Lach-

Ian darted a look at Cecily, standing quietly at his side. 'We're looking for someone…a man who lives in the area. On the Duke of Montague's estates?' In the sparkling light of the monk's torch, Lachlan's eyes glowed with a metallic intensity.

The monk nodded. 'I know of it. You best come in.'

Chapter Fifteen

Cecily stared down at the contents of her bowl in dismay. Thick grease filmed the surface of the soup, great globules of fat shining out in the light of the candle set on the trestle table between herself and Lachlan. Picking up her wooden spoon, she poked tentatively at the thin liquid beneath the grease, searching for any other ingredients. A few chunks of parsnip, maybe swede, revealed themselves, almost boiled to mush, and some plumped-up grains of pearl barley.

'It tastes better than it looks.' Lachlan was eating hungrily, sending spoonful after spoonful of the hateful soup into his mouth, tearing hunks from the loaf that the monk had brought to the table. Flour dusted the sides of his mouth; he brushed the loose flecks away with his fingers. 'I thought you said you were hungry.'

'I am hungry.' A plaintive note entered her voice. She spread her palm flat on the glossy elm boards of the table, rubbed at an imaginary speck. 'But this isn't what I had in mind when the monk offered us food. I thought abbeys were supposed to be wealthy?'

'They are…but they are also frugal with their coin.'

'What does it taste like?'

'Not bad. It's better than nothing, anyway. Eat it quickly, before it grows cold. It will only taste worse if you leave it.'

Dipping her spoon in, she brought the tepid liquid to her mouth and swallowed, following each spoonful with a bite of bread. Lachlan was right, it did taste better than it looked, and she rapidly finished most of the bowl.

'Have some mead to wash it down with.' Picking up the earthenware jug, Lachlan poured some of the honeyed liquid into her pewter mug.

'Thank you,' she said.

Sitting opposite, Lachlan smiled at her. He

had removed his cloak and laid it down on the bench next to him. His arms rested either side of his empty bowl, his palms lying flat. His shirt sleeves had pulled back slightly. Corded muscle looped through his wrists, the sinew winding down into the strength of his broad hands.

She wriggled on the hard, wooden stool, looking around the high whitewashed walls of the monks' refectory. 'Is that man coming back? We must ask him about William.'

William. The name speared him like a curse.

'Eat first. You need your strength. Then we can ask questions about him.'

Cecily pushed her bowl towards him. The evening light slewed down from the high arched windows, touching sparks to his hair. 'Will you finish mine? I've had enough.'

He laughed, a muscle clenching beneath his high cheekbone, reaching out to take the bowl. 'You mean you don't want to eat any more.'

'It's horrible,' she whispered. His laugh curled around her, wrapping her like a blanket. Sweet Jesu, she had become so used to his presence, to the solid strength of his body alongside hers, his protection, it was going to be hard to give it up. A cold feeling slid through her.

'Will you stay…when I marry William?' she said suddenly.

Lachlan threw the spoon into the empty bowl with a noisy rattle. He scowled. 'I will have to. I promised Henry that I would make sure that the deed was done.'

'And then what?' she prompted.

'And then I will go back to Scotland and claim my lands.'

'What's it like…up there?' Cecily asked tentatively.

Lachlan allowed his mind to drift to those windswept lands in the north that belonged to his family, to the barren mountain tops, the rushing streams and dramatic, precipitous cliffs. He traced a knot on the wooden surface of the table. 'Wild, barren. Always windy. I have no idea what it's like now. The castle is gone. Razed to the ground. There is nothing there.' He spat the words out.

Cecily tucked her hands into her lap, wrinkling her gown. 'Then why are you going back?' she murmured.

Why was he going back? The question reverberated around his head. He had always insisted that it was to seek revenge on the clan that had slaughtered his family, but, if truth be told, the fire for that had gone out of his belly. It would make no difference to what he had done.

He raised his eyes, snared her leaf-green gaze, drawing on her quiet steadiness.

Cecily tucked her hands down into her lap, wrinkling her gown. 'I'm sorry, I should not have asked.'

His eyes pinioned her, chips of brilliant blue. He waited for the shame, the gut-wrenching guilt to tear at his belly, to eat away at his soul. The eternal punishment for a boy who had stood on a hill and done nothing. But the familiar sweep of self-hatred did not materialise. The blunt stranglehold of grief around his heart had eased. He knew the reason why. And she sat opposite him, voluminous hood pushed back to her shoulders, her hastily plaited hair gleaming, the colour of a polished hazelnut. Sweet, angelic

Cecily, the luminous oval of her face tipped to one side as she watched the emotions play across his face. The peerless beauty of her skin glowing in the candlelight.

How could he have used her so ill, rolling around on the bed with her like some barbarian of old? He was not fit to walk the ground she trod upon. By finding William, he hoped he could make amends.

Dragging his gaze from her, he pushed his empty bowl away roughly. The spoon rattled within the last gritty dregs of soup. 'Where is that monk?' His voice was suddenly sharp, dismissive; he slapped his palms on the table, then pushed back the bench with a fierce push of his legs, rising to his feet. 'He needs to show us to a bedchamber.'

The room was cramped, narrow. Entering the room first, the monk swung the flaring torch around, sparks flying over the low truckle bed, jammed up against one damp wall, made up with a thin straw mattress and threadbare blanket. An earthenware bowl and jug for washing sat on a small, spindly-legged table by the window. Taking a stub of candle from a stone niche, the brother touched the unlit wick to his torch flame and set the lighted candle back in its wooden holder.

He turned towards Lachlan and Cecily. 'There,' he said benignly, his wide smile pushing out his fat, rosy cheeks. 'Is there anything else you need?'

Lachlan ducked his head below the door lintel and peered into the room. 'A bigger chamber, perhaps?'

'Bigger…?' the brother responded faintly, his tone puzzled. 'All our chambers are the same size, my lord, I am sorry. It is either this or the dormitory, where the monks sleep.' He darted a furtive glance at Cecily, standing behind Lachlan in the corridor. 'Not suitable for a lady,' he lowered his voice with emphasis.

Bone-weary, her belly roiling with greasy soup, Cecily stared at the bed beyond the curve of Lachlan's shoulder. She didn't care that it was narrow, or cold, or that the blanket was too thin. She simply wanted to lie down and close her eyes. Taking a step forward, she nudged her fists gently against Lachlan's solid spine.

'Lachlan,' she said sharply, catching his attention. 'The room has a bed and that's all that matters. I just want to sleep, please.'

Turning from the monk, he read the fatigue in her face, the puddles of blue beneath her eyes. Christ, why was he even arguing about this chamber; the chit was almost dead on her feet!

'Never mind,' he barked, ushering the monk from the room. Cecily stepped in, her leather bag sliding to the floor where she stood. Behind her, Lachlan shut the door, the iron latch rattling into place.

The hairs on the back of her neck prickled; her skin grew hot, aware, as she sensed his attention. Silence descended, a thick, uncomfortable silence, heavy with memory. The last time they had shared a chamber and what had happened. Cecily cleared her throat, suddenly awkward, embarrassed in his presence. Her nerves rattled with anxiety, with…an unspent excitement, despite her tiredness.

She spun around. Lachlan's broad shoulders filled the door frame, his vibrant hair grazing the wooden lintel. Her heart thudded against her chest wall. 'This feels a bit strange.'

'Spending the night in a poky, uncomfortable room in an abbey.' He glanced around the dank stones walls, his mouth set in a grim line. 'Yes, I agree. It's not the best.'

'No, I don't mean that, Lachlan. I mean… I mean, you and me, sharing a chamber.'

'After what happened before, you mean,' he said bluntly.

Her cheeks burned, remembering. The slip of his polished skin against hers. Her heart fluttered; a whisper of desire stirred, deep. She hugged herself, dismayed, trying to douse the longing, praying that he would not notice. He had quite clearly shown that she was not worthy of him; why, he had even stopped their marriage!

'I can… I can sleep on the floor.' Her voice was small, hesitant. 'My cloak is quite comfortable if I roll it up.'

'Nay, Cecily, I'll sleep on the floor.'

Her heart closed around a hollow nub of sadness, aching with longing. To share a room with him, to listen to his steady even breathing, the rustle of his clothes, was sheer torture. The sooner they tracked down William, the sooner she could escape this unsettling situation and regain some sense of sanity.

In the middle of the night, she woke. Moonlight streamed through the narrow, unglazed window opening, bathing the chamber in an ethereal light. Lachlan lay stretched out on the wooden floorboards, alongside the bed; she could hear his deep, even breathing. She traced his rugged profile: the sharp, high indent of his cheekbone, his top lip finely etched; one arm flung out across the floor, his fingers relaxed, splayed out across the floor. Her heart jumped at his closeness, the intimacy of his breath, mingling with hers in this tiny space.

Cecily shivered. Beneath the thin blanket, she brought her knees up to her chest, hugging them tight. She wore all her clothes, even her cloak, yet she was so cold. She had managed to remove her leather boots; they sat at the end of the bed, near her satchel.

The chill from the window seem to target her skin, piercing her clothing, sneaking below her collar, around her stocking-covered feet. She put her hand up to adjust her cloak, to bring it closer to her neck. Nausea roiled in her belly, hung heavy. Christ, was she going to be sick?

Rolling off the bed, she stepped carefully over Lachlan's outstretched legs and staggered across the room to reach the earthenware bowl. Gripping the table for support, she hovered over the bowl, her belly heaving. And yet she was not sick. A fine sweat sprang out on her forehead, coating her neck. A boiling heat suffused her skin.

'Cecily! What's the matter?'

Lachlan was there, beside her, his arm around her shoulders, holding her up. She hadn't even noticed him get up from the floor.

'I… I felt sick…and I'm so cold,' Cecily blurted out, swaying over the bowl. The nauseous feeling receded; a violent shivering seized her slight frame. 'Go back to sleep, Lachlan. It's nothing. I can manage.'

Ignoring her flustered command, he put a

cool hand on her forehead, cursing beneath his breath. 'You're burning up. You have a fever. Come back to bed.'

'But... I might be sick.' Embarrassment coloured her tone. 'Please, leave me here.'

'I'll bring the bowl.'

He helped her back into the narrow truckle bed, tucking the threadbare blanket around her shaking limbs, settling the empty bowl on the floor. He sat on the edge of the bed, his hip nudging hers, smoothing back the loose fronds of hair on her forehead. The tendrils stuck to her clammy skin.

She shuddered. 'Your fingers are so cold, Lachlan.' Turning on to her side towards him, she hugged herself tightly. 'My skin hurts when you touch me.'

Panic slid through his chest wall, unexpected, insidious. 'We need to break this fever,' Lachlan muttered, almost to himself. Throwing off her blanket, he rolled her slight weight towards him, pulling her thick cloak away from her body.

'What are you doing?' Cecily whimpered, distraught; her head shifting uselessly on the mattress. The straw crackled beneath her head. She managed to snag the edge of her cloak, trying to haul it back again, closer against her body for warmth.

He flung it to the floor. 'Nay, Cecily, we must take this off, at least, to try and cool you down.' Frantically, he searched his memory—what was the best way to treat her? Fear churned through his brain, dragging at his thought process. What? What should he do?

He rummaged through her satchel, seizing a length of linen. He sloshed water from the jug, clumsily, into the bowl by the bed. Puddles dropped on to the wooden floorboards, staining the light oak. He plunged the flimsy cloth into the water, wringing it out with his powerful hands.

He laid the damp cloth on Cecily's forehead. She moaned, twisting her head away. 'I'm sorry,' he whispered. Again and again, he dipped the cloth into the water and pressed it against her fevered skin, against her cheeks, the back of her neck, her throat. And yet, despite this, she became more agitated, beginning to mutter incoherently, her slight body restless against the thin mattress.

She was not improving. He needed help.

Fear, apprehension, tore at him as he chucked her veil back into the bowl. An unsettling disquiet. The thought that he might lose her. Charging out into the corridor, he ran along in the darkness, blindly, thumping on doorways with his great fists. 'Help me,' Lachlan roared. 'I need some help here, please!' His voice ripped from his lungs, hoarse, cracked. She could not die! She would not die!

He reached a door at the end of the corridor and burst through it. The door slammed back in its hinges. He had a fleeting impression of a row of beds, of shorn heads rising and turning towards him in the shadows, a worried murmuring filling the air. The abbey dormitory, of course.

'What is the meaning of this intrusion?' A tall man, dressed in a grey tunic, a silver cross swinging across his chest, strode towards him. His face was creased with sleep and he carried a wan, exhausted expression. His grey hood was pushed back behind his neck, his head was shaved, his feet bare. 'I am Abbott Bertram. What is the meaning of this?'

'I need help!' Lachlan gasped, the words sticking in his throat. 'It is my…my Cecily! She is ill.'

Abbott Bertram grabbed Lachlan's flailing hands. 'Calm down, young man, and take me to her.'

They crowded into the narrow chamber, Lachlan, the Abbott and two monks who had accompanied them, all peering at Cecily. She lay on her back, her skin blotched with red patches, her head wrenching pitifully on the mattress. Her lips were dry and Lachlan seized the wet cloth once again and pressed it to her face. 'She is worse,' he muttered.

'She is very ill,' the Abbott agreed, 'but we cannot treat her here…'

'What? What do you mean?' Lachlan roared, his heart splintering. 'What do you mean, you cannot treat her? Don't you have a hospital? Brothers who have studied medicine?' A huge sense of loss tore through him, a rickety vulnerability. The thought of Cecily, not being at his side.

'Let me finish, my lord.' The older man laid a comforting hand upon Lachlan's forearm. 'You are too hasty with your speech.'

'What is it?' Lachlan demanded. 'Speak, man.'

Shock crossed the Abbott's face. He was not usually addressed in such a violent manner. 'The nuns can treat her. They live in the priory next door; they have a hospital. The sisters will be able to tend to her. John, Francis—' he flicked his gaze to the brothers waiting by the door '—please carry this good lady to the priory gate…and careful how you go.'

'I will carry her,' Lachlan growled possessively. Dipping down by the bed, he slid his arms beneath Cecily's slight weight, hoisting her up easily. Her head lolled against his chest, one arm trailing down limply. The heat from her body seared through his tunic; his heart lurched, staggered with despair.

'Cover her with her cloak,' the Abbott instructed one of the monks. 'We will be out in the cold.' His hazel eyes met Lachlan's. 'Follow me and do not worry.'

The gateway to the priory was a wide

arched door set into the thick wall surrounding the abbey. An iron bell, crudely made, hung outside and, grabbing the rope that hung from it, the Abbott proceeded to ring it, violently, for a long time. At first there was nothing, no noise from the other side of the door, and then, thank God, Lachlan heard footsteps approaching.

The door opened, a fierce squeak to its hinges. A woman's face peered through the crack, a face completely encased in a tight white wimple. 'Abbott Bertram,' she exclaimed. 'What is it?'

'Sister Agnes, forgive this intrusion so late at night. This lady is ill and must be treated,' the Abbott explained calmly. 'She is running a high fever.'

The nun stared at Cecily, lying against Lachlan's chest. She lifted her eyes towards him. 'Bring her in, my lord. The first chamber on the right.'

With slow, infinite care, Lachlan laid Cecily down on to the bed in the chamber indicated by the nun. She slumped across the mattress, drawing her knees up, mumbling incoherently. Kneeling on the floor, he pushed her damp hair back away from her forehead. Perspiration coated her neck, a rapid pulse beating in the silky dip of her throat.

Her eyes flicked open, observing him blearily, the brilliant green of her irises dulled by the fever. Her small hand drifted upwards, almost in wonderment, catching at his sleeve. 'William?' she whispered. 'Is that you?'

His heart split, ripped apart by her words. He rocked back on his heels, misery crashing over him. Christ, if he needed any proof that she wanted to be with someone else, then he had it now.

'My lord.' Standing behind him, the nun cleared her throat. 'You must leave now. Your lady is delirious and we must treat her.'

Cecily's eyes had closed again, yet she still muttered incoherently. Lachlan rose to his feet, frowning. 'Nay, I would stay.' He towered over the diminutive nun.

The sister folded her arms across her pristine white habit and took a step closer to him, lines etched deep into her forehead. 'Men are not allowed in here. You must leave.' Her voice was gentle, but firm. 'We will take good care of her, my lord. Please be assured of that. If there is any danger, we will send a message immediately.'

If there is any danger...

'You mean if she's going to die.'

The thought stabbed him, gouged his heart. Defeated, he stumbled backwards. His breath roared in his ears; a wild vulnerability seared his heart. He could not lose her, yet he could do nothing to protect her against this.

'If you do not leave now, my lord,' the nun continued, 'then I'm afraid I will have to fetch someone to help you leave.'

A nun, threatening him?

'I am leaving.' Lachlan struggled to find his voice. 'But hear me, Sister. I will only be on the other side of that wall.' He jabbed the air in the direction of the gate. 'Please, you must let me know the moment anything changes. Anything, you hear me?'

The nun nodded. 'I hear you, my lord. Rest assured that we will do everything in our power to make her better.'

Bending down over the bed, Lachlan

placed his hand on her forehead. Her skin burned against his palm. 'I will fetch William for you, Cecily.' A churning desolation swept through him. 'You need to fight this, Cecily, so that you will see him again.'

Lachlan turned away, his heart breaking into a thousand glittering pieces.

Chapter Sixteen

Cecily scrubbed at her eyes, her vision blurred as she dragged them open. She lay on her back in a bed, but it was not the same bed, not even the same chamber, that she had gone to sleep in the night before. Narrow oak rafters formed the ceiling above her head. Mottled with greenish mould, the roughly plastered walls were bare, except for a single niche containing an unlit candle and a silver cross. Cecily swept her gaze around the chamber. Where was Lachlan? There was no evidence of him ever having been this room at all: no cloak slung in a heap, no sword or belt.

A vague disquiet scraped the lining of her chest. Trawling her sluggish brain, she searched for fragments of memory. Nausea roiling in her stomach; a fleeting impression of being carried within powerful arms and a deep voice, Lachlan's, in her ear, reassuring. Her flesh ached, her muscles felt weak, useless, beneath the coarse sheet. As if she had fallen from a horse, thumping the hard ground heavily, or had been run over by a cart wheel. She remembered the heat suffusing her body, the clamouring thirst—she had been ill, that was it.

But where was she? And where had Lachlan gone? Pointing her toes to stretch her legs, she realised her legs were bare. The rest of her clothes had been removed for she wore only her chemise and under-garments. Searching the small space, she spotted her gowns and cloak folded neatly on a stool in the corner.

A glorious scent filled the chamber: a sumptuous beeswax mixed with the aromatic herb, rosemary. And lavender, too— she caught the faintest whiff, reminding her of summer. Bundles of dry herbs lay by the door; had someone treated her illness with them? But who that someone was she had not the faintest memory.

Throwing back the sheet, Cecily swung

her feet to the floor. The chamber spun and she fought the swirling dizziness in her head, trying to regain a sense of balance before she rose to her feet. This was ridiculous! Her body was normally so strong; there had been no time for her to become this exhausted. Shoving her feet into her mud-stained boots, she resolved to go and find someone who could tell her where she was and what had happened. And if that person was Lachlan, then so much the better.

Cecily struggled to open the chamber door; the wooden planks seemed unusually heavy. Her white nightgown billowed out around her and she shivered. The dim corridor was empty, hushed. Was it too early for anyone to be awake? From outside she heard the first stirrings of dawn, the burbling twitter of small birds. She began to walk, resting her hand against the dank plaster wall for support.

'Hey!' she called out. 'Hello? Is anyone there?' Her voice sounded unusually hoarse, stuck in her throat. She moved forward purposefully. Sweat coated her limbs beneath her gown; her breath emerged in short little pants, as if she had run up a hill, not walked along a corridor.

A round, diminutive nun crossed the corridor at the end, then stopped, her eyes falling immediately on Cecily. 'Oh, thank the Lord, you are awake!' She bustled along the corridor, towards her. 'But you should not be out of bed, my lady.' She smoothed her hands down her white habit. A wooden cross swung down from the thin leather belt that circled her substantial waist.

'I woke up and had no idea where I was, or what had happened to me.'

'You have been gravely ill, my lady, with a very high fever. Your husband carried you over from the abbey.'

Her cheeks flushed heavily. Of course, the little nun would naturally assume that Lachlan was her husband, for what else would she be, a single lady, travelling alone with a man? 'So…are we next door to the abbey?'

'Yes. This is the nuns' priory. We are of the same Cistercian order as the monks. We share their provisions, but no man is allowed in here…unless they are ill or wounded.'

'Lachlan…he is at the abbey still?'

'I believe so, my lady. He was waiting outside the gate for ages, waiting for any news about you. But the Abbott had to order him back inside to take some food and sleep.'

She imagined him pacing the corridors of the abbey, impatient, itching to continue with his journey. The sooner he could hand her over to William, the sooner he could continue up to his estates in Scotland. Cecily was merely an encumbrance. 'How long have I been here?'

'More than three days.' The little nun bustled forward and put a hand on Cecily's shoulder. 'How do you feel, my lady? I'm not sure you should even be out of bed yet. You still look a little peaky.'

'Three days!' Cecily fell back against the wall. 'I must... I must go to Lachlan.'

Sister Magdalena laughed. 'I think you might need to put some clothes on before you go back into the abbey, my lady.'

She helped Cecily into her garments, sliding the lilac underdress with its tight-fitting sleeves over Cecily's head, followed by the sleeveless tunic of dark purple wool. Cecily's fingers fumbled over the rows of tiny buttons, until Sister Magdalena finished the job for her, closing the fabric over Cecily's bare arms. Dividing her shining hair into two loose bunches, Cecily plaited the glossy tendrils, securing the ends with short leather laces that she found in her bag. Winding her linen headscarf around her head, she tucked her silver circlet back into her bag, not wanting to wear it in such austere surroundings.

'You had best wear your cloak, my lady.' Sister Magdalena lifted the one remaining garment from the oak coffer and swung it around Cecily's shoulders. 'It's bright outside, but there is a cold wind.'

Linking her arm in Cecily's, Sister Magdalena led her along the corridors of the priory, out, out into the brilliant sunshine. They walked towards the arched gateway set into the thick stone wall that divided the abbey from the nuns' priory. Slanting sunlight lit the bare, frilling branches of an oak tree standing alongside the path, striking the nubbled bark at an oblique angle. Through the few remaining leaves, sparrows darted about in a flurry of wings, sudden streaks of white. Further to their left, down on the river floodplain, across that flat grassland studded with sheep, starlings swooped and turned in the quiet afternoon chill, a wave of swirling black dots.

Sister Magdalena lifted her hand, grabbing the bell rope that hung to one side. Cecily held her breath; her heart picked up a beat, beginning to race. The gate creaked open and a monk peered through, his skin creased, tanned, from a lifetime spent outdoors. A fraying rope gathered his rough habit around his portly waist.

'Where is Lord Lachlan?' Sister Magdalena asked. 'I would take Lady Cecily to see him.'

The sound of Lachlan's name, spoken on the nun's lips, rolled through her. Cecily's nerves tightened with anticipation. Quickened.

'Oh…he is in the stables,' the monk replied. 'But you cannot come in here, Sister. You know the rules.'

'Step aside, young man.' Sister Magdalena's voice rose, strengthened with protest. 'This is not a time to be handing out orders. Stand aside, I beg you.' Dipping his head in acquiescence, the monk did as he was told and the two women swept through into the grounds of the abbey.

'Do you know the way?' Cecily asked, as the little nun steered her down a grassy slope, in the direction of the river.

'I do,' Sister Magdalena replied, giggling. 'It's my secret; tell no one. We will go through the abbey gardens.'

Cecily lifted her chin, tipping her face up to the weak, winter sunshine. The tepid heat kissed her skin. She turned to Sister Magdalena and smiled at her. 'It's so good to be out in the fresh air,' she said. 'I feel as though I have been cooped up for ages.' The stiff breeze, racing up the river valley from the sea, whipped at their skirts, sending their hems flying upwards as they walked along the narrow path through the neat gardens of the abbey.

They followed a corner around the bottom of the slope and proceeded along a path bordered by a trellis. A climbing rose had been carefully trained and tied along its length, vigorous thorns poking out at intervals from the green arching branches. A rosebud, petals brown and folded into a solid clump, clung tenaciously to a stalk.

'These are the stables.' Sister Magdalena stopped at an open gateway in a stone wall. Inside was a cobbled yard, surrounded on three sides by low, open-fronted buildings. A pile of horse manure, mixed with straw, steamed slowly in the middle of the yard. 'Can you see him?'

In the dimness of the stables, Cecily spotted the familiar flick of brindled hair. Her heart jolted.

'Yes.' What, in heaven's name, was she going to say to him? Her brain seemed washed blank from the illness.

Sister Magdalena frowned at Cecily's pale, washed-out features. 'Do you want me to come in with you? You're still a little unsteady on your feet.'

'No, no, you go back. Thank you, Sister.' Cecily grabbed the nun's hands. 'Thank you for looking after me.'

'It was my pleasure.' Sister Magdalena smiled. 'Now go to your husband.'

Shame flicked through her at the lie. She sighed. At what might have been.

* * *

Lachlan was grooming the stallion that he had borrowed from King Henry. His sinewy fingers curled around the brush, moving over the animal in long, sweeping movements. The horse's pelt gleamed, shining in the bright sunlight.

As Cecily walked slowly towards him, her heart thudding, she watched the strong ripple of his shoulder muscles beneath the snug-fitting tunic. She remembered the sleekness of his limbs against hers, the sheer ecstasy of their lovemaking. She would never know such closeness again. Her relationship with William wouldn't even come close to what she had shared with Lachlan. There, she had said it. She had admitted it to herself, at least. She wanted Lachlan and no one else.

At the sound of her light step, Lachlan turned, brush suspended in the air. The bristles shone in the dipping light as it slipped from his fingers, plopping down on to the straw-strewn cobbles. 'Oh, my God… Cecily,' he said, striding towards her. 'You're… here!' He lifted her freezing hands, big thumbs playing over her knuckles. Her face was vivid, cheeks slapped bright with the cold air. 'And...you are well again? How do you feel?'

'I feel...fine,' Cecily said. Smiling, she traced the lean angles in his face, the generous curve of his mouth. Her heart twisted with love for him.

Squeezing her fingers tight, Lachlan shook his head. 'I was so worried about you, Cecily. My God, when you were in that bedchamber, tossing and turning, feverish... I thought...' his blue eyes darkened '... I thought I would lose you.'

Cecily frowned at the possessiveness of his words; wondering at it. Her head spun and she swayed before him. Why would it even have mattered much to him? He was going to leave her, anyway.

'Come, sit down here,' Lachlan muttered, leading her to a wooden seat outside the stables, pushing her down gently on to it. He studied her face, the shadowed hollows beneath her cheeks, the daubs of blue beneath her eyes, then sat down on the bench next to her, stretching out his long legs over the cobbles. 'You gave me quite a shock.'

Her chest squeezed beneath the soft atten-
tiveness of his voice. 'Really, I'm fine now,
Lachlan. I have recovered from it now.'

'It was that wretched soup,' he growled.
'That horrible greasy soup.'

She tipped her face towards him, laughing. 'But, Lachlan, you ate most of it and you
weren't ill at all!' His face was very, very
close. Her eyes grazed the hard contour of
his jaw, the edge of his mouth. The lips that
had claimed her own.

'I have the constitution of an ox, Cecily,
so my mother used to tell me!'

His words echoed out into the sifting air.
Rang out. There was a pause, a long silent
beat. Cecily studied her hands, pillowed in
her lap. 'Your mother,' she said tentatively.
'You have never spoken of her before.'

Because I couldn't, Lachlan thought. *Because I was not able.* His brilliant eyes
roamed Cecily's delicate features, drawing
in the perfect bloom of her cheeks, the delicate tip-tilt of her nose. *You have helped me
to speak of her again*, he thought. *You have
done this.*

Cecily bit her lip, hesitating. Should she

risk his anger, his coldness, if she asked about his mother? She took a deep breath, gaining confidence from the soft look in Lachlan's eyes. 'What was she like?'

His gaze followed the white curve of the scarf that framed Cecily's face. He thought of her misplaced bravery, her efforts to protect her family, her resilience in the face of despair.

'She was very like you,' Lachlan said. 'Brave. Beautiful.'

Cecily flushed. 'I'm neither of those things.'

'You underestimate yourself, Cecily. Do you have no idea of your own worth?'

No, she thought. She shifted uncomfortably on the bench, stretching out her legs beneath her skirts, feeling the cramped muscles in her legs relish in the movement after being stuck in bed. 'I just did what had to be done.'

'Because there was no one to help you,' Lachlan said softly. 'No one to look out for you or share some of the burden.'

Cecily's head whipped around, snagged his eyes, translucent blue, shimmering in the afternoon light. 'Exactly. That's exactly how it was.'

'And will William look out for you? Will he care for you and be a good husband?'

The name doused through her like cold water. Her chest caved in with sadness. 'Yes, William will look after me,' Cecily replied dully.

'The monks know where he lives. They have given me directions. Only a few miles from here, in fact. That's why I'm saddling the horse; I was going to fetch him for you.'

Please. Don't go, her mind screamed at him. But Lachlan didn't want her. Despite the fact that he thought she was brave and beautiful, he still didn't want her and, practically, she needed a husband to protect her from the King. William would have to do.

Cecily closed her eyes, leant her shoulders back against the stable wall. 'How long will you be?' she murmured.

'A few hours, at most,' Lachlan said. He traced the delicate line of her jaw, sinking his gaze into her creamy, alabaster skin, the faint flush of her cheek. The fragile skin of her eyelids, like petals over the brilliance of her eyes. A few hours, and the light would go out of his life. 'I will bring William back to you.'

Cecily sat, her eyes closed, alone in the sunshine, for a long time. She heard the click and slide of hooves on the cobbles as Lachlan rode away. Sadness sunk through her, a heavy, grating despair. How could she let him ride away from her like this, how could she give him up, so easily, after all they had shared together? Her hands splayed out across her skirts. Lachlan had told her how beautiful she was, how brave, yet she was just sitting here, feeling dejection wash over her like physical pain. Where was that bravery, that courage, now?

She needed to fight for him.

Cecily jumped up, swaying slightly. The silver embroidery around the hem of her purple gown winked, sparkling in the sunlight. There was no time to saddle her horse. She strode, fast-paced, through the abbey gates, following the track on which she and Lachlan had approached the abbey, all those days ago. Weakness sapped the customary strength in her legs, her leather boots stumbling over the loose stones, and she pursed her lips, hating the frailty caused by her illness.

The track led her through an area of flat pasture, cropped grassland that would cover with water when the river was in flood. Below her, the river broke into several tributaries, casting a shining net of water across the floodplain before heading out to sea. Lines of willow followed these curving streams, branches a burnt orange colour, rising straight and tall, vivid against the washed blue sky. A few sheep grazed idly, their white woollen coats dotting the sparse green landscape. They eyed her warily as she walked past, following the flap and snap of her cloak as the breeze tugged out her hem behind her.

Her gaze tore over the landscape, searching for him. Then, in the distance, she spotted the glossy rump of Lachlan's horse, shining out against the dull grasslands. He was not that far ahead, almost level with a clump of willows that bordered the main channel of the river.

'Lachlan!' she shouted, her breath catching in her lungs. Holding her skirts high, she sped down the track, her feet slipping, skittering over the stones, the sticky patches of mud. Her heart pounded, struggling with the effort of running. Her head spun. But she had to reach him, stop him. She had to fight for him. For right now, she had nothing to lose.

Her step slowed as she ran through a soggy patch of ground. Horrible, stinking mud clung to her boots, splattered her skirts as she staggered on, her eyes pinned to the flash of his hair, the flowing lines of his cloak. In dismay, she watched him steer his horse into the river, plumes of water splashing up as he rode through the shallows. Had he not heard her calling?

Cecily reached the water's edge, boots crunching on the shingle beach. His horse had slowed, thank God, as he steered the animal into deeper water.

'Lachlan!' Cecily shouted, cupping her hands around her mouth. Above her head, seagulls wheeled and screeched, and she shouted again, her cries fighting through their high-pitched calls, 'Come back! I need to talk to you!' The force of her voice scoured her throat, but she cared not.

Lachlan turned his head in astonishment, his eyes immediately pinpointing the lone figure on the shore. The violet gown, wool mud-spattered and wet, clinging to the delicious indent of her waist. The white veil blowing across the beautiful oval of her face. The liquid green of her eyes, pinning him to the spot. What in hell's name was she doing?

His heart melted, coalescing with love at the sight of her. Christ, how he loved her. The words burst into his brain, searing into the back of his skull. *Yes*, he thought, *I do love her.* With a scowl he dashed his foolish thoughts away. She didn't want him, she wanted to marry William.

He flung his arm towards her. 'Cecily, don't be an idiot, go back!' he growled. Christ, why was she out here, on her own? Her face was pale, wan, and she hugged her arms around her middle as she wavered on the riverbank.

'I'm not leaving here until you come back and talk to me!' Her words carried across the swirling water towards him, cutting through the feral screech of seabirds, the clack of rooks as they squawked past.

Had he heard her aright?

'Oh, for God's sake, Lachlan! Come back!' Lifting her skirts impatiently, she took a step forward, almost running into the water in an effort to reach him. Incredulous, he stared at her for a moment, before realising her intention.

'Cecily, stop! I'm coming,' he bellowed, squeezing his knees into his horse's flank to turn the animal, pushing the animal at full speed into the water. Plumes of water fanned upwards, frothing white as he reined the animal in, sharply, beside her. 'What are you doing, you foolish woman?' he yelled down at her. 'You're just out of your sickbed, do you want to be ill again?'

'Why did you lie to me about what Henry said?' She stood, legs planted wide beneath her skirts as if to give her some stability on the stony bank. 'Why did you lie?' She rested one hand on his horse's neck as he brought the animal alongside her. Her cheeks were flushed, the ends of her linen headscarf trailing limply across her bodice.

Because I wanted you for myself, he thought. His heart quivered, split in two. He couldn't do this. Loss knifed through him like a physical pain.

'Tell me, Lachlan.' Her eyes flashed, limpid green fire, searing straight to the very core of him.

'You're making no sense, Cecily.' He avoided answering her questions. 'Why have you come after me? I thought you wanted me to fetch William. You asked for him, Cecily.'

'I did not!' she shouted up at him, dancing from one foot to another to keep the chill from claiming her body. 'When in heaven's name did I do that?'

He sighed. 'You said his name when you were ill, Cecily. You thought I was William.'

Cecily slapped her forehead with her palm, mouth tightening as she stared off downstream for a moment. Her eyes shimmered with unspent tears. 'Oh, my God, Lachlan, how could you be so stupid? I was delirious, I had a fever! I was probably saying all sorts of things.' A great shiver seized her body and she swayed in the breeze.

'You should not be out in this cold wind,' Lachlan said. Something, deep inside him, shifted. He kicked his boot from the stirrup. 'Come up before me.' Hoisting her leg up with difficult, Cecily stuck her toes into the stirrup. With one arm, Lachlan reached right down from the saddle, grabbing Cecily around the waist and hoisting her up in front of him, bundling her skirts before her. Reaching his arms around her, he kicked his heels into the horse's flank, heading back for the abbey.

'I think we need to talk.'

Cecily waited outside the stables while Lachlan secured his horse. He strode out and her heart leapt at the sight of his tall, strong figure, the silky fall of his fiery hair across his forehead. He pushed the vigorous strands back with one hand.

He wound his arm into hers, tucked her close into his side. 'Let's walk in the gardens,' he suggested. 'Do you think you'll be warm enough?'

I will be with you next to me. 'Yes,' she said.

'If you close up your cloak, you will be.' He sought her gaze with twinkling eyes, reaching around to secure the loose ties on her cloak. His knuckles brushed her chin. A pang of longing seared through her chest; her eyelashes dipped, fluttering down.

They walked through the arched gateway in the wall and into the sheltered abbey gardens. The late afternoon sun skirted the top of the wall to the south, filling the space with a semblance of warmth. A solitary robin perched in the bare, gnarled branches of an apple tree; the bird's trills of song filled the air.

'What is all this about?' Lachlan said softly, as they walked slowly, arm in arm, along the cobbled paths. 'You risked your health coming after me like that, running about in the cold air.'

Cecily cleared her throat. 'I know you want me to marry William...' she said. Her voice cracked with hopelessness.

'I don't.'

'What...?' She rounded on him, her skirts swirling. 'What do you mean, you don't?

You were the one who suggested it!' Her bright, luminous features snared his.

'Because I didn't think you should marry me. I am not good enough for you.' He snared her fingers.

'Why on earth not?' she rapped out.

The sun touched his skin, highlighting the lean angles of his face. 'Because I was so set on avenging my family, so set on riding north.' His fingers drifted up to her face, touched her chin. The coarse skin on his fingertips rasped against her soft skin. 'My heart was hard, numb, devoid of feeling. I didn't want to subject you to that. A marriage so bleak that it would destroy you.'

'Was...' she breathed. Her head spun with a wave of dizziness, heart teetering with uncertainty, as if she walked over a crust of thick mud, every step beset with danger. She clung to his fingers, as if they were a lifeline. 'I... I'm not sure I understand what you are saying.'

'You were right, Cecily. You have been so right all along. You asked me why I would go back to Scotland, when there was nothing there for me, only horrible memories.

I had a lot of time to think while you were sick.' His hand slid around to cup her jawline. 'I am not going back there, Cecily. You have made me realise how worthless such an action would be. I have so much to live for down here.'

The resonant pitch of his voice sank slowly down into the tumultuous chaos of her brain. Hope flared in her chest. 'You're…not going back?' She wanted him to repeat the words, to make sure.

His blue eyes flared over her, irises ringed with black. 'Aye, that's right, Cecily. And I don't want you to marry William, either.'

She turned her face into his palm, sighing. 'I know, Lachlan. But the King has said I have to marry as payment for my crime, so if I am not going to marry William, who should it be?'

'Me, Cecily. You should marry me.' He stepped back from her slightly, holding her hands lightly. 'That is, if you'll have me.' His powerful words shimmered in the hush of air. 'I would not blame you if you did not. I have treated you so badly.'

'You have done nothing to me, Lachlan,

that I did not want you to do.' Cecily lifted her hand to his face, caressing the raw, angled slant of his jaw. She lifted her fingers to his hair. 'I wanted it all. I didn't want to marry anyone else.'

He laughed, easing the tension between them. 'Nay, you didn't want to marry at all! But the choice was taken from you with the King's pronouncement.'

She paused. Should she risk the truth? 'But, Lachlan, don't you see? I was in love with you before you offered to marry me.'

'God in Heaven, did I just hear you right?'

'Aye, Lachlan, you did. I love you, you silly man.'

His arms swept around her and he pulled her close, up, into him. 'My God! I've been such a blockhead, a stupid, ignorant fool!'

'Oh, well, I wouldn't…'

'Don't you dare tell me anything different, Cecily. I know what I have done and I am not proud of it! From the moment I first saw you, trying to navigate that flooded river, I have fought my feelings for you. I thought that after my family were killed, and my courage failed me on that fateful day, that I could never love again. But you have shown me how wrong I was.'

'You mean…?'

'Aye, Cecily, you have it right. I love you, my sweet, darling Cecily. I love you with all my heart and no one can take that away.' Lachlan wound his great arms around her slender frame and pulled her close, lowering his mouth to cover hers in a kiss that would seal them together, for ever.

Epilogue

Outside the great hall at Okeforde snow was falling. Great fat flakes brushed down past the high-arched open windows, huge whispering feathers, blowing in occasionally on a breath of icy breeze. A row of torches were slung into brackets along the stone walls; the flames wavering, flickering, casting great shadows up to the dark-raftered ceiling. The glorious scent of winter sweet filled the air: long ropes of shiny green leaves twisted around the steps leading up to the high dais, the tiny white flowers sending out their powerful scent. A magnificent fire crackled in the hearth, warming the crowds of people on this cold winter night. Musicians, perspiring heavily, fuelled with a vat of local cider, played merry dance tunes from the corner of the hall. The tables in the main area of the hall had been pushed back; couples danced and laughed, joining hands to form great weaving chains across the stone floor.

'I never thought I would ever see this place again.' Cecily turned to Lachlan, her heart brimming with love for the tall, flame-haired man sitting next to her. Her wedding gown, fashioned from a lustrous cream silk, glimmered in the candlelight. Hundreds of tiny pearls decorated the neckline, swirled around the wide hem. Beneath her wedding veil, gossamer silk, her hair had been plaited and coiled into intricate loops, secured with diamond-tipped hairpins. 'Thank you for talking to Lord Simon.' Her eyes flicked to the thin, brown-eyed man dancing in the main hall.

Lachlan smiled at her. 'He hasn't quite for-given you, yet. It will take time. But he had no wish to deny the fact that your mother and sister wanted to see you again. He knew it was important to you.'

'Lord Simon has punished her roundly for what she did. Making her work here, as his servant. Last night, when I visited her in her chamber, she asked for my forgiveness.'

'As she should,' Lachlan murmured. 'She did you a great wrong. But your sister has fared better.'

Cecily nodded, her eyes faintly bemused as she watched Isabella catch Lord Simon's hand across the dance floor. 'It seems they do well together. And he has taken in her child as his own. I am so glad, Lachlan, that Isabella has not suffered. She deserves this happiness.'

Cecily splayed her hand out across the pristine tablecloth, waggling her fingers this way and that, watching the light catch the brilliant gold band around her finger.

Following her scrutiny, Lachlan laughed. 'The ring is real, you know.' His arm stretched out along her back; now, he tugged her shoulder into the muscled hardness of his chest. He swept his hand around the crowded hall. 'All of this is real.' His vivid blue eyes roamed over her, intense, possessive.

'When I left here, I had no idea what my future had in store for me,' she whispered. 'I could never have imagined such happiness. This wedding day has been like a delicious dream. A wonderful dream.'

'Then we must be having the same dream,' he murmured, squeezing her fingers. Small bone buttons secured his shirt sleeves to his wrists; his wedding tunic was of dark green wool, fitted to his large frame, a dark leather belt pulling the fabric into his slim torso. The bright filaments of his hair were wayward, tousled.

My husband, she thought. Tilting her chin up, she grazed her lips to his mouth, a brief, fleeting touch. His pupils widened, a knowing blackness flooding the iridescent blue, the promise of the night to come captured in a single kiss. A roar rose from the bobbing crowds, smiles casting up towards the couple. Cecily flushed beneath the attention.

Lachlan's chin rested on top of her head. He glanced along the table, across the shining faces of the knights and ladies who had gathered here to celebrate their wedding, over the magnificent outfits, the sparkling jewels in swords and circlets. His heart swelled with happiness, with hope, for the life he would share with the woman he loved most in the whole world: Cecily, his darling wife, whom he would cherish for a lifetime.

* * * * *

LET'S TALK

Romance

For exclusive extracts, competitions
and special offers, find us online:

f facebook.com/millsandboon

◎ @millsandboonuk

𝕏 @millsandboon

Or get in touch on 0844 844 1351*

For all the latest titles coming soon,
visit millsandboon.co.uk/nextmonth

*Calls cost 7p per minute plus your phone company's price per
minute access charge